30 Nights
WITH THE
BILLIONAIRE

BY:JM SNAP

I write for the adventures I want to get lost in and the dreams I want to make a reality. Through the tests, struggles, and the battles of good versus evil — in my world, true love prevails. To all the dreamers out there ... this book is for you.

Chapter 1

Jean closed her eyes as she tried to get comfortable on the plane. She had spent the last few weeks filling in as a secretary for another firm while they were short-handed. It was chaotic and exhausting, but she was finally headed home for a much-deserved break.

She felt the seat move next to her, and she opened her eyes to see a man sitting down. He was on his phone, and he moved his fingers deftly as he texted someone. She closed her eyes again, not wanting to stare at the gorgeous specimen. He had thick, dark locks of hair that seemed perfectly set in place. His eyes were such a warm brown that they looked golden.

He was probably texting his girlfriend, letting her know that he was on his way home. Lucky woman. It must be nice. She had many flings in high school and had been out on plenty of dates as an adult, but with no one who caught her interest. Lately, she was so busy with work that she didn't have time for a relationship. It was something she wanted, though. To have a family again.

She swallowed the lump down that formed in her throat as she thought about her parents. It had been fourteen years since the accident. She was ten years old at the time, but it still haunted her. She could still hear the sounds of tires screeching and glass shattering. She vividly remembered seeing their lifeless bodies while she screamed in the back seat of the car. They had both been killed instantly. Her life had completely changed after that. She moved in with her Gran Gran, who didn't have much but showered her with all the love she could. She lost her two years ago and was now all alone in this world.

What she wouldn't give to hear their voices one more time. She opened her eyes and swatted away the tears that threatened to escape.

"Afraid of flying?" a rich baritone voice asked.

She turned her head to meet with the amber-brown eyes of the man next to her. His brows were knitted together as he looked at her with concern.

"No. It's just been a long few weeks. I'm happy to be going home." She watched as he nodded his head curtly and returned to his phone. Guess he wasn't much of a talker.

They heard a few trills, and then a voice came over the speakers. "Attention all passengers. This is your captain speaking. Due to the nearby cluster of storms, all flights have been canceled for the next two days." The rippling sounds of disappointed groans filled the air as people began to make their way off the plane.

Jean sighed as she reached above her to get her carry-on luggage. Luckily, it was all she had, but she found herself struggling to undo the compartment latch. The man next to her stood up and flipped it open with ease. Grabbing her bag, she turned to thank him, but he was gone. She could just barely see the top of his head before he faded from her sight.

She made her way off the plane and opened her cell phone to call nearby hotels for a room. She went down the list and began to feel desperate. They had all filled up due to the canceled flights.

"Towering Heights Hotel, can I help you?"

"I need a room," Jean said, holding her breath.

"We do have one room available—"

"I'll take it. My name is Regina Newman, and I'll pay with a credit card."

"But I need to tell you, it is the—"

"Doesn't matter. Please book the room for me. I'm on my way there now."

Lucky! She managed to get the last room at the final hotel on the list. She didn't care if it was smoking or non-smoking. It was a room, and she needed one. It wasn't like she had anything or anyone to rush home to. She had a few weeks off before returning to work, so she would take the next couple of days to relax. Reminding herself of her good fortune, she hopped on the shuttle and headed to the hotel. It wasn't long before she arrived and was making her way up to the counter.

"Hi, Regina Newman, I made a reservation just a little bit ago." The receptionist punched away at the keyboard and then nodded his head.

"Yes, Miss Newman, I have you right here. That will be $5550.00 a night. How would you like to pay?"

Jean almost choked on air as her eyes bulged out. It had to be a mistake. "I'm sorry, how much?"

"For the presidential suite, it is $5550 a night. It comes with two rooms, a mini refrigerator, a small home theater, a luxury spa and—" The man continued to ramble and she started to feel sick to her stomach. She needed a room to sleep, but at that price, she simply couldn't afford it.

"I don't care about the price. Just give me any room available." A familiar tone sounded next to her.

"I'm sorry, Mr. Cross, but we do not have any rooms available. I am checking across our system and I am not seeing any rooms anywhere," the receptionist said apologetically.

"Perfect." The man from the plane let out a frustrated groan.

Jean chewed on her inner lip for a moment as she thought about the situation. Even splitting the room would be expensive, but it would be better than full price. And there were two rooms in the presidential suite. Would it be really weird to ask him if he wanted to split the room with her? And was she asking for trouble, sleeping in the same room as a man that looked like he came out of a magazine? She thought about the price of the room again and went for it.

"Uhm, excuse me," Jean whispered as she turned to look at Mr. Cross. His golden eyes met with hers and she offered him a weak smile. "I have the presidential suite. It has two rooms. If you want to split the cost with me," she started to say, as she scrunched up her nose and shrugged. "Honestly, it's too expensive for me alone, but I can manage if we split it. I was told there are two rooms, so if you'd like—" she trailed off as the man stared at her. It looked like he was studying her, looking for an ulterior motive. She wondered what was going through his mind. Maybe she shouldn't have said anything and lived off of dirt for the next year. She was about to say never mind when he looked over at the receptionist and pulled out his gold card.

"Put it on my card. I will pay for it in full."

"You don't have to do that—" Jean interjected, but the man raised his hand, shaking his head.

"It's done. Thank you, I appreciate your kindness—"

"Regina, but you can call me Jean," she said, extending her hand.

"Benjamin, but you can call me Ben," he said, as his lips twitched up in a smile.

"If you two will follow me, I'll take your luggage to your room," the bellhop said, as he led them down the hall.

"Thank you," Jean said quietly as they stepped into the elevator. Ben looked up from his phone at her. "For paying for the room. That would have set me back a lot." He nodded his head and returned his gaze to his screen. Okay, it felt a bit awkward. He seemed very disinterested in talking with her. Well, with his lack of interest, at least sleeping in the same suite wouldn't be weird.

They arrived at the top floor, where there was only one door in the hallway.

"Where are all the other rooms?" Jean asked as the bellhop turned to smile at her.

"The presidential suite is the entire floor of this wing. You are the only ones up here." The man's eyes wandered over her as she stepped past him. He was admiring her beauty openly until the man next to him cleared his throat.

"Careful," was all Ben said. The man fidgeted, fumbling with the card key in his hand before opening the door.

Jean remained oblivious and walked in, looking around in awe. This was something she had only ever dreamed of—a luxurious and spacious living area greeted her with open arms. A well-equipped kitchen stood off to the side, beckoning her with its promise of delicious meals to come. In the center of the room, a massive television rested against the wall in front of a plush, brown leather couch, inviting her to sink into its comfort. The ceiling was adorned with sparkling crystal lights that cast a warm glow over the space, while large bay windows offered a stunning view of the city below. It wasn't just a hotel room; it was more like an elegant and sophisticated apartment, more glamorous than anything she had ever imagined. The sound of the door shutting brought her attention back to her companion for the next two days.

"Which room do you want?" Ben asked as he grabbed her luggage.

"I don't have a preference. Any place with a bed is fine for me." She watched as the man sighed before heading off to the far right.

"This room has a walk-in jacuzzi tub attached to the bathroom. Women tend to like those sorts of things, so you can have this room."

Women ... she wondered if this was going to be a difficult situation to explain to someone. "I'm sorry if this arrangement causes any problems for you with anyone." Ben stopped and turned to look at her. Amusement flickered in his eyes as his lips curled up into a smile.

"Is this your way of asking if I'm single?" he asked, his voice full of mirth. He watched as her face turned crimson red, her mouth gaping open.

"I'm sorry. I didn't even think about how that would sound. I didn't even realize it. You'll have to forgive my lack of eloquence."

"Not at all. Your words are honest, and it's something I appreciate." He smiled at her for a moment before leading the rest of the way into the room. "No, this situation isn't going to bother anyone. I'm unattached. I don't really have time for dating. You?" he asked casually, resting his golden-brown eyes on her.

She shook her head as she ogled over her luxurious surroundings. "No. One day, maybe. I mean, I want a family, but I've been so busy that I haven't made time for dating. I've been on blind dates that were set up by my friends, but they were bad. They mean well, but I wish they'd let me do my own boyfriend shopping." Just then, her stomach grumbled loudly, reminding her that she was close to starvation. She rushed to the plane without dinner and had planned to snack during the flight. She glanced up at Ben who chuckled lightly.

"I'll order us something to eat."

"You paid for the room. I can—"

He picked up his phone and walked away, not allowing for any objection. He turned to look at her as he stepped into the doorway. "Why don't you get freshened up? Dinner should be here within the hour. Are you allergic to anything? Anything you don't like to eat?"

"Not that I can think of," she answered as he closed the door. What an interesting guy. She grabbed her clothes and walked over toward the bathroom. He seemed to be familiar with the layout of the room. Perhaps he stayed here before. She wondered what he must do for a living, since he didn't even bat an eye at the cost of the room. The price for staying in this room for two nights would cover her apartment rent for almost the whole year.

With a flick of her wrist, the room suddenly illuminated, and a plethora of light revealed the shiny new fixtures within. An impressive, beveled-glass shower filled the far corner of the bathroom, and in front of that was a large walk-in jacuzzi tub with sparkling jets. In its presence, she could almost feel the warmth and comfort of a long day's bath. She would never see an expensive room like this again in her lifetime, so she might as well make the most of it.

Even if Ben didn't have time to date, she was surprised he was un-attached. He seemed kind, financially secure, and devastatingly handsome. Through his shirt she had noticed his well-toned physique. She wondered what the bellhop thought as he escorted them to the room. He probably wondered what a guy like that was doing with someone like her. Though, she wasn't exactly ugly. In fact, she considered herself attractive even despite being a harsh critic of her appearance. At first, she wondered what skeletons Ben had in his closet to be single, but on second thought, it wasn't fair to think like that. Maybe he actually was really busy and didn't want to settle for just anyone.

After she soaked herself longer than she should have, she finished with a quick shower. She put on a camisole and shorts, since she didn't really have clothes for company besides her work outfits. She left her room and was greeted with the heavenly aroma of food. Gosh, she really was starving. Her gaze shifted toward the kitchen where Ben had just finished placing their food on the table. She was relieved to see he was wearing a pair of shorts and a black tank top, though this gave her a much better view of the chiseled muscles that decorated his body. It was as if he had been sculpted to perfection. She realized then that she had been openly staring at him.

He glanced up and she put on a smile, making her way to the table. "The food smells delicious."

"I ordered Italian. I figured that was a safe bet. There's salad, garlic rolls, fettuccini alfredo, and tiramisu for dessert," Ben said as he took a seat.

"Perfect, I love Italian. It's my favorite." She looked at the food as she excitedly took her place at the table.

"Mine too," he murmured quietly as he began to eat.

"So ... what do you do for a living?" she asked bluntly as she twirled her noodles.

"I'm a businessman," he said simply, not wanting to elaborate more than that. "You?"

"I'm a secretary for a law firm. I was helping out a sister firm for a few weeks while they launched."

"They couldn't just hire someone for that?"

"No, they're using the same system, and it's complicated. They needed someone to go and train the new secretary as well as work. I was the lucky one who was voluntold to go." She laughed, letting out a sigh. The other secretaries had families and she didn't. She was the obvious choice to be sent away. At least she was getting several weeks off with pay to compensate her. They quietly ate their food for a few moments. He seemed perfectly content to not talk. She decided to try to start up a conversation again. "Do you travel a lot?"

"Sometimes. It just depends on the circumstances." He listened as she giggled and he glanced up at her, raising his brows questioningly.

"Sorry." She pursed her lips together with a smile. "It's just that you never elaborate. As if you're part of a secret organization and can't let your secrets slip." She watched as his lips curled up into a smile.

"Maybe I am." He chuckled as he lifted his head to look at her fully. "I'm sorry. I'm not always the best company. My mind is often racing over things that need done."

"I'm sorry," she said, waving her hands. "I didn't mean to make you feel that way. Please, don't take it personally."

"I'm not. It was a reminder that I need to decompress at times too. I often don't even realize I'm doing it. It causes me … problems." His voice grew quiet, and she decided not to pry further.

"I'll clean up the mess here since you bought dinner."

"You don't have to clean up. Housekeeping will do that."

"Well, I can make their job a little easier, then. Just because someone will clean up the mess doesn't mean we have to be pigs about it." She winked and stuck her tongue out at him.

A warm chuckle reverberated in his chest as he began to help her pick up. "Don't you think you're being a bit feisty with a stranger you barely know? No one has ever stuck their tongue out at me before."

"I'm sure they have, just not to your face."

"Perhaps, but most wouldn't dare."

"Okay, Godfather," she teased, placing the garbage next to the door and brushing her hands together. "Thank you for dinner. Tomorrow, I'll take care of our food." She lifted her fingers to cover her mouth as she let out a yawn. "I hate to eat and go straight to sleep, but I am exhausted."

"Have a good rest."

"Are you going to bed?" she asked as she walked toward her room.

"I need to get some work done first. Good night."

"Nighty night."

She shut the door and ran to her bed, plopping on it like a child. It felt as if she were lying on a cloud. Her body felt completely weightless as she hugged a pillow tightly. She closed her eyes and began to think about her roommate. He was not at all how she expected him to be. He was mentally preoccupied, but he wasn't stuffy like she imagined a wealthy man would be. He seemed really nice, but he looked tired. Even looking tired, she could get lost in his eyes. Why couldn't she find a man like that?

"Jean? Jean, wake up."

She sat up quickly, her fists gripping the blanket as she panted heavily. She blinked several times as she tried to gather her senses. Ben was next to her, his eyes full of concern.

"Jean, are you okay? You were having a nightmare."

Only it wasn't a nightmare. Jean reached up to brush the damp tears from her face. "I wish it was a nightmare. Sometimes reality is worse." She shook her head and then offered him an apologetic smile. "Sorry, that was a bit dark and deep for a stranger." She glanced over at the clock to see it was four in the morning. "I'm sorry, did I wake you?"

"No, I was out in the main room doing work. I couldn't sleep, so I thought I might as well get things done." He opened his mouth for a moment as if he was deciding what he wanted to say. "Let's see what's on TV. I could use the company."

It wasn't like she could go right to sleep after that. She knew her Gran Gran used to come to her at night, but she never knew she yelled in her sleep. It must have really startled Ben, because he was looking at her like she was about to break.

"Yeah, that sounds good."

A few moments later, they were both sitting on the couch. He was flipping through the channels as he glanced over at her. "Do you want to talk about it?"

Her gray eyes darted over at him as she quietly thought it over. "There isn't anything to talk about. It was just a memory of when my parents were killed. It's been fourteen years, but sometimes the memories still haunt me. I can't help but wonder, why didn't I die with them? Why was I the one left alive?" She gave him a weak shrug.

"There are no answers to those questions." He watched her nod her head as she stared back at the television. That was his cue to drop the topic. "Anything in particular that you want to watch?"

"Something light-hearted and funny. Cartoons would be great." She watched as he opened an app on his phone and cast his screen to the television. Soon, a big Looney Toons emblem popped up on the screen. "Perfect!" She smiled as she settled into the back cushion of the couch.

She was warm, as if she was wrapped up in a cocoon. She nestled her head into ... something warm but breathing! Her eyes popped open. She was lying against Ben's chest. He was lying at a slight angle on the couch. His well-defined arm was wrapped around her protectively, holding her captive. She could see his head leaning back on the couch awkwardly. He had to be very uncomfortable. She lifted her head to see his eyes flutter open, confusion apparent on his face.

"I am so sorry. You must be so uncomfortable." She straightened up as his arm slid away from her. His warmth was comforting, and she instantly missed it. It was wrong to have those thoughts, since he wasn't hers. What happened was just an accident. She turned to look up at the clock. It was almost noon! She had fallen asleep and didn't wake up once, which was unusual for her. She never slept that soundly. She watched as Ben stretched out his arm and rubbed his neck. He had to be sore from the position he was in. He reached for his phone, eyes widening as his mouth parted slightly.

"Noon?!" he breathed out, as he blinked at his screen as if it wasn't correct.

"I didn't mean to fall asleep on you. I'm sorry. I toss when I sleep, and I must have rolled onto you."

He shook his head. "You fell asleep and began to slide down, so I let you lay on me. I don't know how I fell asleep, though. I have never slept like that."

"I'm sure sleeping on the couch is unusual for you." She imagined he usually slept on beds like the one in her room.

"Sleeping anywhere is unusual for me," he said quietly. "I can't remember the last time I slept so well. Even with my pills, I barely sleep." His golden eyes gazed at her curiously. "I suffer from insomnia and don't sleep. I didn't have my pills with me last night, so I knew it was pointless to even try to sleep."

"I must be a sleep charm," she teased, but his serious gaze made her wave her hands and shake her head. "I'm just joking." Still, he quietly looked at her, making her feel excited and hot inside.

"Would it be okay if we tested this again?" His eyes were locked onto her with so much hope that she didn't have the heart to turn him down. However, it was one thing to accidentally fall asleep together. It was another to plan to. It felt a bit awkward, and her thoughts of him weren't entirely pure. Which wasn't his fault, it was hers. With a sigh, she gave him a small shrug.

"I guess. I mean, it can't hurt anything, except maybe a blood-deprived arm from my head laying on it." She laughed as she studied his perplexed face. "I'm sure you were just beyond exhausted. Or maybe you just need someone with you to sleep—"

"I've been with people before, at night. It didn't change anything. I've been beyond exhausted before too." Of course he had slept with people before. It wasn't like she didn't think he had. She was just trying to find a logical answer for him. Whatever, they had another night at the hotel anyway. What could it hurt?

Chapter 2

"Where are you going?" Ben asked, as he watched Jean begin to gather her things.

"I need to get some things from the store. I'm cooking dinner tonight."

"Is that right?"

She watched as he sat his papers down and moved to his feet. A sexy half smile reached his lips as Jean's heart began to beat faster. What the hell was wrong with her? She watched as he slid his shoes on and grabbed his phone.

"Where are you going?" she asked. A chuckle rumbled through his chest.

"With you. Isn't it obvious?" He flashed her a million-dollar smile as he moved to the door. "I'll carry the groceries for you. Unless you don't want the company?"

Jean shook her head swiftly. "No, that isn't it at all. I'd love the company. It's just ... I'm sure you're really busy."

"Even businessmen have to eat." He winked at her and opened the door to the hall, letting her go through first.

As she moved past him, she brushed against his chest, making impure thoughts immediately invade her mind. Why was she suddenly this sex-starved woman who couldn't control herself? Yes, this man was attractive, but she worked with attractive men all the time. What was so different about him? Was it pure chemistry? Or was it because they were sleeping in the same hotel suite together? That had to be it. *Okay, Jean, knock it off and quit dragging him into your sick thoughts.*

Ben followed her closely in the supermarket. He looked around the store with almost child-like wonder. He even seemed interested in the whole process as she paid for the groceries and as they were placed in bags. He immediately took them, not allowing Jean to carry even one.

As they walked back to the hotel, she gave him a quick side glance. "Do you get your groceries from a high-class grocery store? You seemed a bit lost."

"I've never gone grocery shopping." His voice was quiet. Suddenly he reached out and pulled her to his side, the bag in his hand swinging violently with his movements. Just as he did, a kid on a bike rushed past her. "What are they doing riding their bike on the sidewalk?" he growled, keeping her firmly locked to his side. "You need to be more alert." He shook his head.

"Sorry. Thank you." She went to step away, but he kept his arm around her. "I'm okay now."

"It's safer next to me. I'll pay attention for you," he snorted, seeming almost angry. She had inconvenienced him, and he must be annoyed with her. He kept his firm grip around her even in the hotel. It wasn't until they reached the elevator that Jean finally was able to step away from him.

"I'm sorry for all the trouble."

He looked at her blankly before directing his attention back to the opening elevator doors. "It wasn't your fault. That kid had no business riding that fast or on the sidewalk. Someone could have been seriously injured."

Jean followed behind him quietly back to their room. She could understand his concern. Had the kid hit him, it would have slowed down his work. Time is money, or so she had heard.

She began setting all the items she needed on the counter. Ben was watching her thoughtfully and she smiled at him. "Plan to watch the whole process?"

"So, these are all the ingredients for chimichangas." He smiled at her before walking away. "Thanks for cooking dinner. I'll try to get a few things done while I wait."

She wasn't sure why, but she wanted to impress him with her cooking. She had always been a decent cook, and this was one of the dishes she was always complimented on. She went to work dicing up the food and carefully wrapping the ingredients up. She eased the tortillas into the oil and then glanced up at Ben. He had unbuttoned the first several buttons of his shirt, revealing his sexy chest hair. It made her want to run her fingers through it and entangle it between her fingers. She wondered how he would feel underneath her, with her hands sprawled over his chest ...

"Is something burning?" He glanced up as she looked away, embarrassed. Did he catch her ogling him? Uh oh. Shit! She forgot about the chimichangas that were cooking and scorched one side of them.

"I'm sorry. I wasn't paying attention." She moved them to another plate as her shoulders sank. So much for showing off her cooking. "We can order out."

Ben walked over and put two of the chimichangas on a plate. "I like my food well cooked." He winked at her before moving to the table.

"Seriously, it's okay. You don't have to eat that. I'm usually a decent cook. I was just ... daydreaming. Thinking of things I need to do when I get home." She lied. But she could hardly tell him the truth. Without a word, he began to eat her food. He ate it so enthusiastically that he convinced her that it wasn't that bad. That was, until she took a bite herself. How was he eating that? It was horrible.

"You cooked, so I'll do the dishes."

"Do you want me to explain to you how the dishwasher works?" she teased as he shot her a wide grin. He walked up to her, making her breathing stop as he leaned forward. His lips brushed against her ear as his hot breath pelted against her skin.

"You smell good," he whispered sensually. "You should probably wash this smell off or I'm liable to have more to eat ... later tonight. Men can do crazy things while they sleep." He chuckled, moving back to the sink, leaving her confused and excited at the same time. "Seriously, I've got this. You can go ahead and get a shower. Remember, you're sleeping with me tonight."

"I still think it's silly. The idea that you can fall asleep just because I'm next to you. I mean, you know that's ridiculous." She listened as he let out a little hum, turning on the sink.

"I guess we'll find out, right?"

She smiled, shaking her head as she walked to her room to get a shower. It was just a coincidence that he was able to fall asleep. It didn't mean he was able to sleep because she was next to him. He would see after tonight that it was just a fluke.

She turned on the shower as she remembered the slight touch of his lips on her ear. Was he flirting? She shook her head. No, he was just teasing her. It was his way of getting back at her for her little joke. It was just her wanting it to mean something. She suddenly paused. Did she want it to mean something? No ... no, she just watched too many romance movies. Her mind was tricking her. After tonight, she would probably never see this man again.

After she finished drying her hair, she headed back out to the main area. Ben was already sitting on the couch and had the news on the television. She suddenly felt a bit anxious as she shuffled her way toward him.

"So, uhm, should I just sit here?" she asked, pointing at the far end of the couch. He raised his brow at her and tilted his head.

"I got a quick shower too, so I don't stink. Unless—you're really afraid I might eat you." The way his lips curled up had her body tensing in response.

"Quit teasing me. I've never done this before and wasn't sure what I should do."

"And I have done this before?" He chuckled, watching her face turn red.

"That's not what I meant," she answered nervously as he laughed.

"I think, in order to really test this out, we should recreate what we did last night." He patted the seat next to him. "I'll only bite if you want me to."

Her heart hummed like a hummingbird's wings as she took her seat next to him. She glanced up at the screen, watching the stock numbers roll across the bottom. Knowing she was supposed to fall asleep next to him somehow felt exciting. Sure, it didn't mean anything, but there was something intriguing about all of it. Not to mention the fact that the man was gorgeous.

"Do you want me to put cartoons on?" he asked quietly.

"No, this is fine." She grabbed a blanket, pulling it up to her neck. She didn't think she would ever fall asleep, but watching the scrolling numbers had a hypnotic effect. And before she knew it, her eyelids had closed.

Ben felt her body begin to slide in his direction and he moved his arm around her. He stared at her blonde head resting on his side. The woman was a stranger, but oddly he felt very comfortable with her. She intrigued him, and not many people did. She was beautiful and incredibly kind. And she blushed easily, which he thought was adorable. Was she really the reason he was able to fall asleep last night? Was it because of her calm aura?

He sighed and then moved slowly, gently lifting her in his arms. One thing was for certain. They would both get a better night's sleep if they were laying on a mattress. He gingerly laid her in bed and slid in next to her, pulling the covers up over both of them. She immediately rolled, resting her head on him. A small smile reached his lips as he embraced her in his arms. If she really could help him fall asleep, then he had to keep her. If he was able to fall asleep again tonight, then he would need to think of a way to keep her by his side. At least enough that he could get a good night's sleep every once in a while. An irrational idea crept into his mind, imagining a life where she stayed by his side forever. It would be nice to have a woman like her to live his life with. Though that was something he still wasn't sure he was ready for. Not after what he had been through.

He nuzzled his nose into her hair, inhaling the scent of her freshly shampooed locks. Even if he couldn't fall asleep, he was content just being close to her. In that moment, he cherished her presence and closed his eyes, eventually drifting off to sleep without even intending to do so.

The next morning, she found herself waking up next to his sleeping body. Her head was resting on his shoulder, and she gazed at his sleeping face, which was dangerously close to hers. She was cradled in his arms again and could smell his heady scent. That was when she realized they were lying down, and not on the couch, but in bed.

"How did I get in here?" She sat up, breaking herself free as Ben groaned, slightly annoyed.

"I moved us in here after you fell asleep. I figured this would be more comfortable for both of us." He opened his eyes lazily, moving his gaze to the clock. "Ten hours of sleep this time. No meds. Just you next to me." He leaned up on his elbow and stared at her with intrigue. His lips tugged up in a crooked smile.

She wet her lips nervously and shrugged. "Maybe it's the room?" He raised his brows at her as he shook his head.

"I don't know why, but it is you. Something about you relaxes me and helps me sleep. I've been thinking—I'm going to propose something crazy, but please, consider it. Would you be my sleeping companion? There are times I really need to sleep. I can only go so long on an hour here and there before I collapse. It wouldn't be all the time. Just every few days."

She stared at him in disbelief. "You want me to be your human pillow?" She let out a nervous laugh, unsure how to answer. "This is like a Pretty Woman offer, only I'm your sleep prostitute without the benefits."

"Do you want the benefits?" His lips twitched up as he chuckled, seeing her shocked expression. "I'm teasing. I need a non-complicated relationship. A human pillow. Just when I need to get some sleep, badly. I'll pay you."

"Eeewww, that really does make me sound like a sleep hooker." She shook her head. "I don't want your money."

"Then consider it paying me back for half your share of the room." A devilish grin spread over his lips. Damn, he had her there. She already felt guilty about him paying for the room. Now this would be her way of paying him back.

"For how long?" She chewed on her inner lip as she watched him look up at the ceiling.

"At least thirty nights of sleep would be fair. And we can go from there if it works out well."

"I think this was just a fluke, so I wouldn't get your hopes up."

"I guess we'll see about that."

"Of course, if either of us starts dating, this situation will be problematic." She watched as something dark and unreadable flashed in his eyes.

"You agree to at least thirty nights, regardless."

There was something almost possessive in his tone. However, it might have just been his desperation to sleep. "Yes, I do."

"Okay, good. We can figure it out after that," he said, as he reached for her phone. "Call me anytime you want. Let me know if you ever need anything from me." He sat her phone down and then promptly rolled out of bed. "We better gather our things and get ready. We have a plane to catch."

Jean stood there in disbelief as she realized what she had just agreed to. She had just agreed to sleep next to a man she found incredibly attractive. Though, it seemed it was a bit one-sided. He never once made a move on her. To him, she was just a pillow, a living, breathing pillow. She inwardly winced. *What have I gotten myself into?*

Chapter 3

The plane ride was quiet as Jean dwelled on her thoughts. Ben was busy typing up a document for most of the flight. It wasn't until they began to descend that he turned to talk to her.

"Is someone picking you up?"

She turned to look into his amber eyes, shaking her head. "No, I'm just going to get a taxi." She watched as his lips pulled down in a frown.

"No one can bother to come and see you after you've been away?"

A small laugh escaped her lips as she smiled at him. "I don't have any family alive. It's hardly a friend's duty to come and pick me up.

Not that I'm that close with any of them anyway. Who's coming to pick you up?" she asked, changing the topic to him.

"My mother," he said with a sigh. "She worries when I'm away, since I don't sleep. She'll be there to inspect me." He chuckled. "She likes to worry about me."

"That sounds nice," she said, her voice heavy with restrained emotion. He locked his gaze onto her face as he tried to decipher her hidden feelings. She remained silent, her mouth a tight line of control, until his lips slowly curved in a knowing smile.

"I'll worry about you from now on."

"No, no, no. Honestly, I'm—"

"My pillow needs to be looked after properly, don't you think?" His charming smirk sent her heart racing as a wave of heat rushed through her body. She glanced away in embarrassment, but the burning sensation on her cheeks was unmistakable. She was struggling to put up a wall between them, but the more she fought it, the stronger her attraction grew. He was like forbidden fruit, tantalizingly out of reach yet irresistible, daring her to take a bite and damn the consequences. She could feel the burn of desire in her chest, a wildfire consuming her every thought until there was nothing left but him. He wanted a non-complicated relationship. Just a human pillow. What the hell was she doing? What was wrong with her?

"Don't worry. Your pillow has been looking after herself just fine." She felt the plane come to a stop and she unbuckled her seatbelt.

"That was before you became mine. I take care of what belongs to me." There was a territorial rumble in his chest that made her toes curl.

"For thirty nights," she reminded him as she stood up. "It's more like I've been rented out, so I'm not yours." A quirky smile rested on her lips as his eyes flashed to her.

He stood up in one smooth motion, towering over her. His broad shoulders and toned arms filled her with an inexplicable hunger. He was like a predator stalking his prey, and she couldn't help but feel like the target of his gaze. She was both excited and terrified, unsure of what would happen next. But then, to her disappointment, he looked away. He chuckled, reaching up to grab her carry-on bag.

"Is something amusing to you?" she asked, as he carried her luggage down the aisle. Was he laughing at her? Her reactions to him must be simple to read. He probably thought it was funny how easily he could get a rise out of her.

"Nothing. Just thinking. I don't rent anything, but I do test them out first." He continued walking away as she mulled over what he said. Test them out? So, what happens if he likes what he tests out? Surely he didn't mean it the way it sounded. Just something else to get a reaction out of her most likely.

His long legs moved at a pace she couldn't keep up with without trotting, which she refused to do. He had her luggage, but she wasn't about to race up to him. She looked to the side, seeing all the people being greeted by their loved ones. It was only a few seconds, but when she looked forward again, he was right in front of her, waiting.

"Sorry about that. I'm not used to waiting for someone else."

"That's okay. Thank you for handling my luggage, but I can take it from here." She reached out, placing her hand on the handle next to his. She glanced up at him waiting for him to release his grip.

"Let me take you home."

"You have family waiting for you. I'll be okay."

"BENJI!" a sweet, angelic voice called out. Jean watched as Ben turned toward a beautiful woman. She had shiny chestnut hair, with eyes that sparkled like sapphires.

"Mom, I told you that you didn't need to come," he said as he hugged the woman.

"Nonsense. I needed to see my baby boy." She stepped back, looking up at his face. "Well, I must say ... you look well. Better than you have in a while. I insist on more breaks from work."

"I was able to sleep the last two nights. It's done wonders for me."

"Thank goodness. Well, make sure you repeat what you need to in order to sleep like that again."

"I plan on it," Ben said, throwing a side glance over at Jean. "Mom, I'd like to introduce you to a new friend of mine." He shifted to the side and the woman's blue eyes landed on Jean. "Jean, this is my mother, Rebecca."

"It's very nice to meet you—" she began to say as his mother came up to her to shake her hand.

"You are lovely. Simply lovely. How serious is the relationship? We've been wanting Benji to settle down now for a while. You are a beauty. You'll make beautiful children."

Jean felt the dreaded scarlet heat creep up her neck. She stuttered, trying to come up with a response, but the words caught in her throat. She had not expected such a direct question, especially not from his mother.

"Mom." Ben stepped next to Jean, wrapping his arm around her shoulder protectively. "Jean and I are just getting to know each other. Let's not put any pressure on things. But if there are any nights I'm not at home, then you'll know who I'm with." Jean felt her throat constrict with what he was insinuating. Yes, what he said was true, but his mother was getting the wrong idea about it.

Rebecca clapped her hands together as she flashed Jean a big white smile. "Are you coming back to our house? You'll have to go out with me sometime. We can have a girl's day."

Jean smiled awkwardly, still not sure how to respond. She glanced up at Ben, silently pleading for him to rescue her from the uncomfortable situation. He must have sensed her distress because he tightened his grip on her shoulder, pulling her closer to him.

"Mom—"

"I know, I know. I'm not pushing for anything, just hoping. In either case, my offer still stands, Jean. Let's do lunch sometime."

"Lunch sounds lovely." Jean smiled at how genuine Ben's mother seemed. She was not like the mothers in the dramas she watched. The wicked wealthy mother who must approve of any friends her son has. Of course, in those movies, they were multibillionaires who owned big family corporations.

"Regina!"

Jean turned her head to see a waving hand and a relieved face heading toward her. His blonde hair bounced as he ate up the distance easily. It was Scott, one of the baby-faced attorneys at the office. He was attractive, but she never understood the hysterics behind him. He was an up-and-coming hot shot, so why was he here?

"Mr. Rhitt?" she said, turning to greet him. She felt Ben's hand slowly slip from her arm as she stepped away. "What are you doing here?"

"It's Scott. I told you to quit calling me Mr. Rhitt," he snorted as he looked at her. "Mr. Hamen asked me to come and get you. We need you to come to the office immediately. All the ladies are out with the flu, and there's no one who knows how to work the software." Scott's green eyes were pleading with her as her shoulders dropped with a sigh. She was promised a break from work.

"Competition," Rebecca muttered as they turned to look at her. Her eyes widened and she waved her hand laughing. "Oh, don't mind me, I was just thinking out loud."

"So ... Mr. Hamen has demoted you to being a gopher? You know you could have called," Jean said as his lips twitched up to the side.

"I thought I'd go for desperation, and I figured it would be harder to say no to my face."

"Dirty. So, I'm to head straight to the office now?" She glanced down at what she was wearing. It wasn't exactly office attire.

"Don't worry about how you're dressed. We just need your skills. I'll take you out to dinner afterwards to show my appreciation."

"She's having dinner with me tonight." Ben's voice was low and controlled, his gaze fixed intently on Scott. Jean could feel the tension in the air, a palpable energy that made her heart race. She didn't know what was going on between the two men, but she could sense a rivalry of some kind brewing, a challenge that had been issued and accepted. And since when was she having dinner with Ben? They hadn't discussed anything about when they would meet again.

"Is that so?" Scott's voice was casual, but there was a hint of amusement in his eyes. He chuckled lightly. "Well, I guess I'll have to take a rain check then. There are other nights." A small smile, almost a smirk, rested on his face as he looked at Ben. "I'm Scott Rhitt, an attorney at the firm she works for." The man looked very familiar, but he couldn't be who he thought he was.

"Ben."

"Hmm, Ben. I don't think I've ever heard you mention a Ben at work before." Scott moved his gaze to Jean, who shifted on her tiny feet. He even had the same first name as the Cross Industries CEO. In either case, it was a chance meeting, and he was certain there was nothing between them.

"To be fair, Scott, I don't really talk about my personal life with you." A strange look fell across his face for a moment. Maybe disappointment? But he quickly covered it up with his charming smile.

"I guess we haven't gotten to chat for a while. Well, we can catch up on the drive to the office. Shall we, then?" He gestured to Jean with his head toward the exit. "We don't want to keep Mr. Hamen waiting."

She nodded, still uncertain about what was going on. "I guess it can't be helped," she muttered disappointedly. After the flight, she wanted to go home and relax. Instead, she was being put to work.

"You don't have to, Jean." Ben placed his hand on her shoulder as his amber eyes studied her. "You don't have to go in. You must be tired after the flight."

"Are you going to work today?" She raised her brow at him knowingly and listened as his mother laughed. "You must be just as tired as I am. It's alright. I don't mind helping out." She then turned to look at Scott. "But this day doesn't count as my time off."

"Not at all." He chuckled. "I'll take your bag."

She looked at Ben, not sure what to say. This wasn't exactly a handshake and see-you-later relationship. How was she supposed to part from him? He basically alluded to his mother that they were a couple, though she supposed there was a reason behind that. If she thought he was dating her, it would make sense when he stayed at her house. It was simpler than explaining the human pillow thing, which she already knew was weird, so how would others perceive it?

Ben's hand landed on her shoulder, spinning her into him. He stared into her eyes as if he needed to memorize them. "We just had Italian, so what do you want tonight?"

"Well, you ate my burned chimichangas yesterday without any complaint, so I guess it's your turn to pick." She laughed as his fingers rubbed over her arm sensually.

"I want to know what you want," he demanded gently.

"You mean as far as dinner is concerned?" she teased coquettishly as his lips curled up.

"As far as anything is concerned."

He was back to teasing her again for a reaction, only this time she wasn't going to give it to him.

"I want you ..." she said seductively, as his fingers tightened on her, "to pick the restaurant." She grinned as he let out a low chuckle.

Ben leaned in until his breath tickled her ear. "How about seafood?" he asked in a low, sensual growl that made a shiver race through her body. Okay, she was horrible at playing games, especially when she was the only one who was being affected.

Scott coughed discreetly, interrupting their moment. Ben shot daggers at the man, whose lips curled up in a haughty grin. "We really need to get going."

"Seafood sounds great," Jean said, as Ben looked back at her. His eyes lingered on her, and then slowly he moved his head closer. His long, black lashes covered his eyes as his lips landed on her forehead.

"Seafood it is, then. Text me when you're close to being done. I'll come and get you."

"I can get a taxi and meet you—"

"I'll pick you up," he said, leaving no room for objection. "You'll be at Hamen and Young Firm?"

She opened her mouth, slightly surprised, and then nodded. Of course, he heard Scott mention Mr. Hamen, so he just put it together and figured out where she worked. "I'll see you this evening," she said, turning to leave with Scott.

Ben watched as Jean walked away with that young, smug man whose eyes wandered over Jean far too much. Jean was beautiful but was oblivious to how others looked at her. Even the bellhop couldn't stop staring at her. He felt a sense of possessiveness as he watched her disappear from his sight. He wanted to keep her by his side and away from the greedy eyes of other men.

"You really like her, don't you?" his mother asked, stepping next to him. For a moment, he was quiet. He had only known her for a few days, but something about her set his mind at ease. She was real. She didn't put on an act around him. She wasn't trying to impress him. She was just Jean. He knew he wanted to see her again even before being able to fall asleep. That was just the perfect excuse, the perfect opportunity to be able to continue to get to know her.

He had never felt like this before. With just a glance from her, he felt his heart beat faster. The moment he saw her adorable blush, he wanted her. He purposely tried to recreate the delicious red stain on her cheeks over and over again. She didn't even seem to realize the effect she had on him. At this rate, thirty nights wouldn't be enough. He was going to need all of her nights.

"That Scott fellow is definitely interested in her." His mom's voice sounded annoyed.

He looked down at his mother and smiled. "He won't be the one sleeping with her tonight."

"Don't be overconfident. She isn't yours."

"Yet." He smiled as he looked down at his mom.

"Does this mean you're serious about her?" She watched him as he remained quiet, deep in thought. "She's beautiful, but out of curiosity, why her? You've never taken an interest in any of the other women who have been interested in you."

"She's special. There's something about her that just makes everything inside of me feel calm." He looked down at his mom. "She's the reason I was able to sleep. I felt comforted in her presence." His mother smiled and nodded her head.

"Your father is special to me, too. I didn't think I would ever find a love like I did with him. Sometimes someone is just your person. However, that doesn't mean you automatically get them. If she's the one for you, then never let her go. Fight for her with every breath you have, so she knows how important she is to you."

Ben chuckled, "Like I said, mom, we're still getting to know each other."

"That's what you say." She shrugged. "But the way you tensed up watching her walk away with another man says otherwise."

"My life is complicated. You know this, mom. We don't exactly live normal lives."

"What's normal anyway?" she teased, but then saw the slight crease in his forehead. "You're borrowing trouble from tomorrow. If you find the right person for you, then you'll work through the complications." She gave his hand a reassuring squeeze as she watched his shoulders slump in resignation.

"I guess time will tell." Reluctantly, he turned away from where Jean had disappeared into the crowd. "Come on, let's go home." Feeling a strange weight in his pocket, Ben reached his hand in and pulled out a phone. He forgot that he grabbed it off her seat right before they got off the plane. He planned to play a prank on her but had forgotten.

"Mom, you head home without me. I need to drop this off to Jean first."

Chapter 4

She could still feel the sensation on her forehead where he'd kissed her. He kissed her! Not on the lips, but still ... it was something. Okay, if she was being honest with herself, it really wasn't anything. A casual peck on the forehead. So why was her heart still racing from it?

"Jean?"

She turned her head to look at Scott, who had glanced at her while he was driving.

"You back on earth? You spaced out there for a bit." A white, toothy grin rested on his face as she looked down in embarrassment.

"Sorry. I'm still jet-lagged."

"How long have you been dating that guy?" Was it just her, or was there some agitation in his voice? She looked over at him, but his face revealed nothing.

"Oh, well, we're still getting to know each other." This situation with Ben was becoming more and more complicated. They were going to need to discuss this over dinner. If they were going to be seen together, people were going to think they were dating. Is this what Ben was going for? Logically, it would make sense for her to be seen with the man she was dating. When she agreed to this, she wasn't thinking about others seeing them together and the questions they would ask.

"Hmmm," Scott hummed with an interesting tone. "It's still casual?"

Too many questions, and she wasn't ready to answer anything without talking to Ben. Time to abort this topic. "You're awfully curious about my life today." She giggled as his eyes flashed over at her.

"I've been really busy with the new cases I was given. We haven't had time to really talk. I'd like to get to know you better."

Her gray eyes studied him before she looked ahead at the road and shrugged. "There isn't much about me to get to know. Most things are the same—"

"Except having a boyfriend is different," he said pointedly. He was starting to feel agitated. If that was really Benjamin Cross of Cross Industries, why was she dating him? Why was he dating her? He was starting to feel territorial over the woman sitting next to him.

And he was back to talking about the boyfriend thing. "How are those cases coming along?" She watched as a wry grin spread over his face.

"Are you purposely avoiding conversation about your new guy?"

Damn it, she forgot he was a perceptive lawyer. He was one of the best up-and-coming attorneys in the firm and had a talent for spotting deception.

"With all due respect, I don't feel comfortable discussing my personal love life with you. When it comes down to it, you are one of my bosses. It's rumored you'll be making partner soon. I think it would be inappropriate to have a close relationship with one of my employers."

"It isn't a problem if you no longer work there."

She looked at him, wide-eyed. "What do you mean?"

He chuckled. "I was just thinking that you could even marry one of the partners if you wanted and just not work there. You wouldn't even have to work."

She laughed. "Except they're all old and married."

"Except me."

"Not if Alicia has anything to do with it." She giggled and then noticed his serious expression. Alicia was one of the clerks at the office. She had been dating Scott casually for the past few months.

"We broke up."

"Oh, I'm sorry."

"It's alright. I stopped by her apartment to surprise her. I ended up being the one surprised. She was tangled in the sheets with the new security guard." He reached up from the wheel and rubbed the back of his neck. "The man has an eight pack and muscles that could crack boulders. I can't compete with that. Sure, financially, it's no contest, but I guess she wanted more of a man than me."

"Don't say something like that. Don't judge yourself based on someone else's choices. Their decisions don't define who you are. You don't know their reasoning or what they're going through. Trust me, there are plenty of ladies that would be overjoyed if you even looked their way."

"Would you?"

She turned her head, her eyes moving over his face. What exactly was he asking here? "Are you asking if I think you're attractive? Of course you are," she answered politely. He turned his head to look at her and raised his brows, as if saying that wasn't what he meant.

"If you weren't with Ben, would you be interested in me?"

Shit, he said it. The look in his eyes said he was serious. No way did she want to dip her feet in those shark-infested waters. Alicia was scorned by all the women in the office for dating Scott. She couldn't not answer him, though. He was hurt by Alicia and was looking for a comforting response, probably thinking she was a sure thing to make him feel better. The thing is, she wasn't interested in Scott, but she couldn't tell him that. It wasn't like he asked her that because he really wanted her, though. He just wanted to feel better. She had to handle this tactfully.

"Hmm ... well, I'm not like most women. My choices are different. For me, it's important to be with a family man. I want someone who will love me like my father loved my mother. Having children and having a fun family is something I dream about. That's what's most important to me."

"Is that what Ben wants?" There was a sharpness in his tone that she didn't misinterpret.

"You don't like him, do you?" She watched as his forehead wrinkled.

"It isn't that I don't like him. I don't know him. I just don't like him with you," he said bluntly, clearing his throat. "I mean, I don't know if he's the man you're looking for."

"Don't worry. I'm not the type to settle." The conversation had taken a strange turn, and if she didn't know any better, she would say he was jealous.

They finally arrived at the law firm, taking the elevators to the office. It was a quiet ride to the top, and Jean tried to stand as far away from Scott as possible. The moment the doors opened, they saw a stout, round man with a well-groomed mustache waiting. It was Mr. Hamen.

"Miss Newman, finally! You're here! We have quite a mess. Cases are piling up and need to be filed. There is no set time for you to be here. You can leave once the files are in the system. Scott, can I have a word?"

"Certainly." Scott watched Jean as she walked over to the front desk. His eyes lingered on her before he turned to talk to his boss.

Jean sat down and turned her computer on. She began to open their catalog program, Wink, expecting there to be a queue of about five, maybe ten case files that needed to be entered into the system, at the most. Her eyes bulged and her mouth gaped open. There were three hundred files pending. This couldn't be right. It seemed like hardly any work was done while she was gone.

"Uhm, excuse me, Mr. Hamen," she said in a slightly shaky voice. His eyes flickered over to her in slight annoyance. "How long have the other secretaries been absent?"

"It's been two days," he said tersely.

"Mr. Hamen, there are over three hundred case files that need to be logged into the system." He stared at her blankly. These numbers meant nothing to him. "We don't get this many files in a day. This is weeks of work not done. It isn't possible for me to complete this today."

"Well, take all the time you need to get it done."

She clenched her jaw and took in a brave breath. "Mr. Hamen, might I remind you that I am on break. I came in to help, but this is too much work for one person to do. This will take me a week to complete.

I don't think any cases were filed while I was gone." She watched as the stout man waddled toward her. Scott trailed behind him slowly, but there was a look of fear in his eyes.

"Miss Newman, might I remind you that you work for me. It isn't your job to manage the other secretaries. I need these cases filed and I need you to do it. You can take your break after."

She wasn't sure what came over her, but she felt her eyebrow twitch angrily at his total disregard for what she was saying. "Okay, say I work this week getting the files caught up. Then I take my break. What then? I'll come back to three hundred more cases that haven't been filed?"

She watched as his face began to turn a dark shade of red and return to its natural color quickly. A cruel smirk spread across his face. "Why, you're right, Miss Newman. What was I thinking? I can't give you those few weeks off. I need you here in the office working. I'll expect you to report to work as normal, without the break." He watched her open her mouth to fire back and he curled his lips back angrily. "That's the end of it. I'm retracting your break, and I need you to get these case files into the system. Welcome back," he said smugly before walking away. "Scott?"

Scott stood there silently, his eyes heavy with sympathy that seemed to echo every emotion she was feeling. She felt her hands tremble uncontrollably as she clung to the last shreds of her composure. He silently mouthed his apology as he slowly walked away, leaving her alone in a state of shock. She felt her world crumble around her until finally she collapsed in a heap on the chair, unable to do anything but stare blankly at the computer screen. Tears streamed down her face as she processed what had just happened.

She was in such a daze that she didn't even hear the elevator door open.

"Jean?" She looked up in shock to see Ben staring at her. He studied her face as he came around the desk, kneeling in front of her. "What happened?"

"Ben." She quickly swatted the evidence from her face. "What are you doing here?"

"I have your phone." He handed it to her, capturing her hand in his own. "Jean?"

"I'm okay," she said, trying to sound brave, but the tremble in her voice gave her away.

His hand reached up to cup her cheek. Her silver, watery eyes looked down at the ground as she tried to gather herself together.

"Talk to me."

"I don't think I'm going to be able to do dinner tonight." She turned to look back at her computer screen. "I don't think they did any work while I was away. They left it all for me to do." Her voice faded to a quiet breath. "I told Mr. Hamen, and he didn't care. Worse, he took away my time off and expects me to complete all these cases." His thumb gently brushed away her tears as his lips formed a thin line.

"Is he still here?" Ben's expression darkened as she nodded her head.

"Yes, he's in his office, down the hall."

"Okay, pack up your things, Jean. You aren't working for a place like this," Ben said matter-of-factly.

"Ben, I need this job."

"No, you don't need THIS job. You can work for me, and if you don't want to work for me, I'll find you another job. You are not going to be mistreated like this. Let this place collapse without you." Ben growled as his hands settled on her shoulders. He stood up, lifting her with him. He wrapped his arms around her, resting his head on hers. "I'm going to take care of you, Jean. Don't worry."

Just then, Mr. Hamen waddled down the hall with one of the secretaries on his arm, one of the ladies who was supposed to be sick with the flu.

"Miss Newman, you aren't to have guests—" Mr. Hamen stopped as he stared at Ben. "Mr. Cross? I wasn't expecting you to visit our office today. What can I do for you?" Scott came around the corner, as well as a couple of other attorneys who worked in the building.

"I came here to see my girlfriend. I believe you know Regina Newman," he said, holding her tight against his side.

"Your g-g-girlfriend?" Mr. Hamen stuttered as Jean regarded his new demeanor. He knew Ben and, for some reason, was afraid of him.

"Imagine my surprise when I heard that she was going to cancel our dinner date that I was looking forward to. And then she canceled our planned time off together. All because she was told she had to work, since your other secretaries were lazy and didn't do any of their work while she was gone." Jean's heart was racing as she listened to the words Ben was saying. Her eyes darted over to her boss as she waited to hear his response.

Mr. Hamen began backpedaling and stuttering. "W-w-well... I-I-I didn't know she had plans. Why, this is all just a big misunderstanding. Yes, it was a misunderstanding." A misunderstanding? She didn't misunderstand anything. She looked up at Ben curiously. Just who was this mysterious man that was sticking up for her?

"I see ... a misunderstanding. Well, that's good. I don't have to remind you of how dangerous it would be to upset me, right?" Ben's voice rumbled with barely-contained fury, the air pulsing with menace. His gaze was a lancing flame that reduced the pudgy man to cinders. His eyes cut through the air with an icy glare, narrowing dangerously as his lips curled up in disdain. "As it is, I don't feel comfortable with my girlfriend working here. You see, she's my sleeping beauty, my princess. She isn't your Cinderella. I won't allow anyone to mistreat her."

She felt the thudding of her heart as she listened to his words. It was as if she was watching a scene from a movie, unable to believe that this was happening in real life. Ben's words were cold and calculated, his voice barely above a whisper, but it was enough to send shivers down her spine. It was obvious that Ben was not a man to be trifled with by Mr. Hamen's reaction to him.

"L-l-like I said, Mr. Cross, it was a misunderstanding. A mistake."

"Yes, it was a mistake. Yours." Ben then turned to Jean and brushed the back of his hand tenderly over her cheek. "Gather whatever is yours. You're leaving here and not coming back."

"Mr. Cross, she is our best secretary. We are in a real bind here. You can't—"

"I can't what?" His lethal glare attacked the man. "Go ahead. I'd love to hear what I can't do." His lips twitched into a smirk as he challenged the man. Silence filled the room, and Ben chuckled. "That's what I thought."

Jean felt her breath catch in her throat as she looked at Ben in awe. He was like a force of nature, commanding and powerful, and she couldn't help but be drawn to him. He glanced at her with a smile, and she nodded quietly. She turned and began to gather her things from the table. She felt like she was in a daze and couldn't believe what she was doing. The environment at the firm was toxic, and she finally had her blinders removed. She wasn't sent to the other office because she was single. She was sent because no one else wanted to go. This whole time, she was always the one doing the extra work and doing the jobs no one wanted.

The notion of walking away from her job was inconceivable at the beginning of the day. She would have scoffed at the mere suggestion.

But now, her emotions were swirling in a violent vortex, and she could feel the flames of rage flickering inside her. It burned, consuming her thoughts and fueling a sense of betrayal. How dare they take advantage of her, the only one who had tirelessly worked while they all grew fat off her efforts!

She looked at her empty desk, making sure she didn't forget anything. When she first started working here, she was so excited. The job was close to home and had decent pay and benefits. Like watching a playback reel, she saw her memories clearly. Piecing things together, she saw just how much she had been used. She had no pleasant memories to look back on, only foolishness on her part.

Ben's arm wrapped around her protectively, like a shield. With his other hand, he grabbed her luggage. They walked past the others without sparing them a glance and headed straight to the elevator.

"Regina," Scott said softly as he stepped next to her at the elevator. "I'm sorry. I should have said something. I should have—"

"'Should have' is easy to say after the fact, isn't it? Don't worry, I took care of it. I did what you should have." Ben's words were filled with a mixture of anger and disappointment as he turned to Jean. "Let's go. We have better things to do than waste our time here."

Jean stepped into the elevator next to Ben. She looked at Scott as the elevator doors slowly shut. With it, a chapter of her life had also closed. So much was racing through her mind. What now? She needed a job. Was Ben serious about offering her one? And the one plaguing her the most, who exactly was Ben Cross?

Chapter 5

B en kept his arm around her, burning her with the heat of his body. She could smell his cologne and feel the rise and fall of his chest. Even after the elevator doors opened, he kept his arm around her.

"Stay," he commanded softly when she tried to step away from him. At first, her heart began to skip, thinking he wanted to be close to her. "They could be watching us from the window." Idiot. She had to stop reading into this as much as she was. Why was her heart betraying the logic of her mind? It was like they were at war, and she wasn't sure which one would win.

They approached a black SUV and a tall man stepped out from it, opening the back door. The man had blonde hair and sky-blue eyes, his face blank as he stared at them.

"Mr. Cross." The man nodded, and Jean felt pressure on her back as she was ushered into the vehicle. The door shut and Ben quietly talked to the man before walking around to get in on the other side. The man placed her luggage in the front before getting into the driver's seat.

Ben sat next to Jean, his eyes moving over her as he tried to decide what to say. "Do you want to come back with me?"

"No, I think I need to go home. I—" She stopped as the reality of what happened slammed into her. She didn't have a job. There was no one to fall back on. Maybe she shouldn't have quit until she had a backup job. Ben might have been serious about working for him, but that seemed problematic.

"Hey," he cooed to her as he interlaced his fingers with hers. "It's okay." She turned her head to look out the window, staring at her old place of work for a few moments.

"I never realized just how much I was being taken advantage of. I tend to put blinders up, but now—I can remember so many things. I shouldn't have quit like that, though. I have bills. I should have just quietly looked for a new job."

"Jean, you don't need to worry. I'll take care of you."

She sighed and turned to look at him. "I'm a stranger you barely know. You aren't responsible for taking care of me."

"I'm the one who quit your job for you. That makes me responsible. You didn't quit on your own. That was me." He gave her hand a gentle squeeze.

"I appreciate your offer, Ben," she said softly, her eyes meeting his. "But I can't just let you take care of me like that. It's not fair to you, and I don't want to be a burden on anyone. Plus, I think it gives the wrong impression about us. Our relationship is confusing. I don't know what to call us when someone asks."

"Sure you do. I already said it. You're my girlfriend, so naturally that makes me your boyfriend." His lips curled up in a grin as he locked eyes with hers.

"Won't that be problematic? Don't you think it might get confusing?" She watched as his eyes flickered with amusement. He lifted her hand toward his lips, softly touching her skin.

"What's confusing about it?"

"Ben, quit teasing me," she said, pulling her hand away from him.

He sighed and arched a brow at her. "What are you afraid of, Jean? I'm not a bad guy. I'm not going to take advantage of you, so I don't understand what the problem is. Do you not want anyone to think you're dating me? Is there someone you like? Is that why it's problematic?" Inwardly, he felt a storm brewing at the idea of her wanting someone else. Was it that Scott guy? He would have him shipped to another country and buried under a stack of paperwork. Would it be horrible to get to know each other better? He could see himself falling for her, but maybe she didn't want to be with him.

Her heart raced as his words echoed in the air. She wanted to scream that she was afraid of developing feelings for him, and she couldn't handle falling in love with someone so unattainable. To develop feelings for someone she could never have. Why would she risk that pain? However, saying that seemed too absurd to even vocalize. How could she anticipate the emotions that would arise from such a short meeting? But deep down she knew it was already too late. He'd already cast an invisible spell over her. She feared that the more she was around him, the harder it would be to let him go, and that by pretending to be a couple, she might be the one fooled.

She didn't know who he was, but it was obvious that he was from a prominent family, or else Mr. Hamen wouldn't have acted the way he did. Someone like that could never be with someone like her. They could be friends, but they could never be a real couple. If people thought he was dating a nobody ... wouldn't this be a problem for him?

"Ben, I have no one who would care about who I was dating. There isn't anyone that I would be worried about." She paused as he nodded his head, wanting her to continue. "I have a feeling that the people in your world would have a problem if you were dating someone like me, right?" She listened as he chuckled and nodded his head.

"I'm sure some would have a problem with it, especially the gold diggers who have been trying to snag me as their own. I'm not worried about it, so you shouldn't be either. Besides, my mother already thinks we're dating. She expects to meet you for lunch sometime. I'd hate to disappoint her." He grinned and then reached for her hand again. "That's settled. Now, about the job thing—"

"I have to find a job. When I go home, I'm going to start searching for one."

"You don't want to work at my office?"

"Ben, I think we both know that having your *girlfriend* work for you would be a problem." She listened as he chuckled.

"Okay, well, I have other connections too."

"I'm skilled with computers and can learn programs quickly. I've been working as a legal secretary, so I'm used to those procedures. Honestly, I'm not overly picky. I just want a decent job that I can take care of myself with."

"I like that about you."

She looked at him curiously.

"That you want to work and earn things on your own. It's admirable. I'll check around and find you a good job. Please don't object. It's the least I can do," he quickly added, seeing her lips curl in protest. "I'm still going to give you some money. I don't care what you say. You're mine, remember? My pillow. I need to make sure you're relaxed so that I can relax when I'm with you. It doesn't matter how much you object. So, give Clint your address so we can be on our way." He then leaned into her ear and whispered in a husky voice. "Besides, I want to see where I'm sleeping tonight."

They pulled up to her apartment complex, and soon she was leading Ben to her place.

"It's nothing luxurious like what you're used to, but it's home," she said as she opened the door. She watched him with interest as he stepped inside. He looked around the place curiously and then began searching.

"Our room?" he asked as he pushed a door open.

It wasn't a king-size bed like at the hotel. Nor did the room have the wonderful bathroom suite. She was certain that, after tonight, he would find out that she wasn't the reason he was able to sleep.

"When you find out that I'm not the reason you were able to sleep, will you still help me with that job?" she asked. He turned his head, his eyes lingering over her, making her heart begin to race again. He slowly moved toward her, reaching out and playing with her strands of hair.

"And when we determine that you are the reason I can sleep—" He lifted her blonde hair to his mouth, kissing it lightly. "It will be your duty to stay with me forever, don't you think?" With a wink, he turned back to look at the room. "It looks cozy. I can see the charm here."

She felt her cheeks flush with heat as a shiver ran down her spine. Her heart was racing, and she was beyond in trouble. She was setting herself up to get hurt. She knew it, but at the same time, she wanted to enjoy it. Her season with him may soon end, just like an autumn breeze carrying on its way, but the memories would be something special she could keep. She just had to remind herself that this was just temporary, and he wasn't serious. However, she was going to have to do a better job playing this flirtatious game. It seemed he was unaffected by her, but everything he did made her stomach clench in excitement.

"Yeah, it is pretty comfy here," she said as she sauntered over to the bed, sprawling out on it. "Do you want to test it out?" Her heart was threatening to beat out of her chest. She couldn't believe she just said what she did. She was trying to think of a way to get to him and ended up sabotaging herself. She watched his hawk eyes land on her. As if the predator had its prey in its sights and wasn't about to lose it.

Gray and amber held their gaze, neither wavering. "I think that's a wonderful idea," he murmured, his voice low and husky. He smirked, slowly making his way toward the bed. She could feel the tension between them, thick and heavy, almost suffocating.

Just as he reached the bed, his phone began to ring. He breathed out a silent curse as he reluctantly lifted his gaze from hers.

"Hello." His gruff tone sounded slightly irritated as his eyes landed back on Jean. "He did what?" He groaned as he pinched his brows together. "The timing of this couldn't have been worse. Yes, I get that. Oh no, she isn't? Ugh." He sighed in exasperation. "Where's Steph at? Of course. Yeah." He hung up the phone, a scowl resting on his lips.

She sat up on the bed and stood up. "I'm sorry, you have work to do today. This stuff with me has offset things for you."

He moved closer to her until he stood right in front of her. He leaned in, and she could feel his breath fanning her lips. His hand landed on her waist, pulling her closer to him. She closed her eyes, anticipating his kiss. But it didn't come. "I'm afraid I'm going to miss dinner tonight," he murmured, his voice low and husky. He then pulled away and she opened her eyes. She wondered if the disappointment was evident on her face.

"That's okay. I'm sure you have a lot of work to do," she whispered, as she tried to put on a blank face.

"It isn't okay, but don't worry." A devilish grin spread over his lips as his finger traced over her neck. "I'll make it up to you."

"You are such a flirt." She giggled as his amber eyes looked at her, full of mirth.

"I'm not flirting. That's a promise." He gave her one last, lingering look before heading toward the door. "I'll see you tonight." She heard the door click shut and let out a breath she didn't know she had been holding. The butterflies in her stomach were rampant as she tried to get herself under control.

It was hard to keep up with him, but she was determined to play his game. She got up and walked over to the dresser, studying her reflection in the mirror. She was wearing a simple purple shirt and blue jeans that accentuated her curves perfectly. She ran her fingers through her hair, touching the strands that had been kissed by him moments before.

She had things she needed to do, but it was hard to concentrate. All she could think about was him. The way his gaze lingered on her, the way he touched her, the way he made her feel. She knew it was dangerous, but she couldn't help herself. She would just keep telling herself that it wouldn't last. No matter what, this was only temporary.

Maybe she could fool herself later, so it wouldn't hurt as bad when he left for good.

Her phone erupted into a cacophony of shrill ringing. She instinctively reached for it, her heart racing with anticipation. Was it Ben? But as she glanced at the caller ID, disappointment crashed over her in waves. It wasn't Ben's name that flashed on the screen, but Tilly's, her once-close friend who had drifted away since getting a boyfriend.

"Hello?" She could hear the light sobbing sound on the phone.

"Gina, Brad is cheating on me. Can you meet me for dinner, my treat?"

"What time?"

"I'll pick you up in a couple of hours. Wear a nice dress."

Jean hung up the phone and headed toward her closet. She knew Tilly's taste. She came from money and would be taking them somewhere way too expensive.

Jean never liked Brad. She always felt like he was using Tilly for her money. It seemed she might have been right.

She rummaged through her closet, throwing garments in a wild frenzy until she found the perfect piece to complete her transformation. She pulled out the all-black dress that Tilly had bought her for a Christmas party last year. It had a plunging neckline and a form-fitting silhouette that clung to her curves like a glove. She grabbed her matching black heels and headed toward the shower. Sometimes it was fun to play dress-up and imagine she led a different life. Tonight, she wasn't Jean, the unemployed woman who was a pillow for a man she barely knew. She was a mysterious temptress in control of her own destiny. With one last glance in the mirror, she smiled, daring herself to take the challenge.

As she stepped out of the shower, Jean felt invigorated and alive. She slipped on her black dress, admiring how it molded to her body.

She decided to let her hair dry naturally, hoping for a casual yet sexy look. She applied a light layer of makeup, focusing on highlighting her eyes and lips, and sprayed a hint of perfume on her neck and wrists. She slipped on her black heels and grabbed the matching clutch.

She was completely transformed into another person, almost not recognizing herself. As if by shedding her skin, she pushed away her problems. None of that existed tonight. Finally, the doorbell rang, and Jean took a deep breath before heading to answer it.

She opened the door to Tilly, who was wearing a hot red short dress that pushed her cleavage up to an eye-catching level. She was fairly certain they were bigger than they used to be.

Tilly's eyes widened as she took in Jean's appearance. "Wow, Jean. You look stunning." Tilly complimented her and clapped her hands together. "I'm so glad you got the memo. Tonight, we're cruising for new men, and you're my wing-woman. You're my sexy bait to help reel them in, and then I'll hook them. I think I want Italian."

"That's fine with me. You know I love Italian food."

Tilly giggled. "No, my sexy bitch. I mean, we're fishing for Italian men." She grabbed Jean's hand and they walked to her expensive sports car. For some reason, Jean kept thinking about Ben and wondered what he would think about this. Why was she thinking that? It wasn't like they were really dating. And she wasn't really going to pick up men. This was just for Tilly. For reasons she couldn't explain, she felt guilty. *No! No, Jean, don't do this. You're unattached, and you're playing pretend. Let loose and have fun for once, woman!*

Chapter 6

"Dad, I wish you wouldn't have done this," Ben said, pinching the bridge of his nose.

"Liam, you really put your foot in it," his mother scolded his father, who looked like this mortally wounded him.

"I'm sorry. I thought you and Melissa liked each other. I didn't mean any harm," his father Liam said, as he gave his wife puppy-dog eyes. "Don't be mad at me. It's just one dinner, and it was a favor to her father."

"Keep your butt home and out of the office. Had you stayed by my side, none of this would have happened." Rebecca pouted, folding her arms across her chest. "I really like Jean, so this better not mess anything up."

"Don't be mad at me," Liam cooed, wrapping his arms around his wife. "Ben will handle it."

"I understand why you did it, dad, but next time, text me first." Ben groaned as he turned his head away in frustration. His father had agreed for him to have dinner with the daughter of a very prominent family for dinner. Only this wasn't just anyone. It was Ben's ex-girl-friend, who he wanted to avoid as much as possible.

"I don't know why you and Melissa stopped talking anyway. You two were on fire at one point," his father said, as a loud snort was heard from the doorway.

"That was until Ben found out that Melissa wasn't a one-man type but preferred a sample platter."

Ben looked up to see his sister Stephanie setting her shopping bags down. She grabbed her sunglasses off her face and tossed her brown hair behind her shoulders. "Oh dad, how could you not have known? Now poor Benny has to have dinner with that nasty skank."

"It's alright, Steph. Dad didn't know. Mom has already scolded him well. It's just dinner. I'll survive." He groaned.

"So, what is this I hear about you having a woman you're interested in?" She wiggled her brows at her brother, who chuckled.

"She isn't his yet!" His mother snorted as she pointed a scolding finger at him. "He can still lose her."

"When are you going to bring her here?" his father asked as Ben laughed, shaking his head.

"Sometime after I tell her who I am. I don't want to scare her off."

"Scare her off? Isn't being the CEO of a multibillion-dollar cor-poration a selling point?" Stephanie laughed as her brother shook his head.

"Not with her it isn't. She isn't like that. Because of me, she doesn't have a job right now, and she is refusing to take my money. Not that I'll give her a choice. I'm going to take care of her. She insists on working, though. Speaking of that, who do we know that will hire her? She's good with computers and was a legal secretary. It needs to be someone who won't mistreat her, because I'll kill them."

"Yep, he has it bad." Stephanie giggled as she clapped her hands together. "Oh, I know, isn't Lincoln looking for a personal assistant?" She listened to Ben groan in annoyance. "Link would treat her well regardless of your feelings for him. I'll text him and let him know I found him the perfect person."

"I don't want her being too busy." Ben pouted.

"Link won't overwork her. He keeps normal business hours for his employees. Now hush. It's perfect." His sister scolded him as a cruel smile spread over her face. "Don't you need to get ready for your date?"

"Don't call it that," he snapped as he turned to glare at his father. Damn, it had to be Melissa. He was quite smitten with her several years ago. When he found out she had been playing him, he was furious. She was even sleeping with his close friend at the time. There was still a scar there. And it made him feel completely out of control. It was around this time that the insomnia got worse, as if it triggered it out of control.

Whatever, it was just one dinner. He could force his way through it and then never see her on a personal level again.

Ben walked in and went straight to his reserved seat. Melissa was already there, and she looked up at him excitedly. Her bright red hair was curled and put up in a clip. She stood up, revealing a dress that left little to the imagination. At one time, this would have turned Ben on. This time, it left him disgusted.

"Ben, darling!" she beamed, wrapping her thin arms around his neck. "How have you been?"

He reached up, pulling her arms off him as he glared at her. "Listen, I'm here because my father asked me to come. I don't want to be here."

"Aww, Ben, don't hurt my feelings," she said, batting her lashes at him. "Our daddies like the idea of us together."

"Let's get this dinner over with," he said, sitting down.

"I've missed you, Benny." He felt her foot slide up his leg slowly, a smile resting on her face.

"You miss the idea of me. I was a game to you." Ben grit his teeth as he shifted his leg away from her. "I mean it, Melissa. I'm not interested in you at all."

"Not even in staying with me tonight?"

"Especially not that. I have plans with a real woman tonight." He listened as she slammed her glass down. Her green eyes were menacing as she tried to control herself.

"Well, the night is still young." Her voice was strained as she hissed through clenched teeth.

She had already attracted attention from her minor tantrum. He cast his gaze over the people seated near them and stopped when he met with a pair of familiar gray eyes. Jean was staring right at him. Her eyes looked momentarily wounded before she turned her head away.

She looked amazing. Her stunning beauty was like a magnet, drawing his gaze and causing his hand to unconsciously tighten its hold on the table. She was sitting with another woman, probably a friend of hers. He couldn't take his eyes off her. He had to stop himself from going straight to her and capturing those beautiful lips with his own. He wanted her to know this was just business. She was bound to misinterpret the situation. Maybe he could just tell her really quickly. The moment he decided to get up, two men went and sat next to her. He watched as she laughed up at one of them.

He clenched his jaw so hard that he thought it might break as he watched the scene unfold in front of him. His eyes narrowed to slits, fixating on one of the men who had his lecherous eyes on Jean. Burning fire spread across his chest when he saw that same man place a hand on the small of her back while whispering words in her ear. The jealousy surged through every vein in his body, taking control of his will like a savage beast. It was an alien feeling, something he had never experienced before, something so fierce that it made him want to possess her for himself and keep away anyone who attempted to come close. He couldn't tear his eyes away from them. He had to see what was happening. If that man dared to make one wrong move, he wouldn't be able to control himself.

"Ben!" Melissa hissed. "Stop staring at other women. It's rude."

"I don't give a damn, Melissa. You think I care about being rude to you? What do you call sleeping around on me? This doesn't even begin to make us even. So, deal with it or leave," he growled, taking her by surprise. Ben had never spoken to her that way, not even when she cheated on him. She directed her poisonous gaze over at the women Ben was staring at. Finally, she stomped her foot and stood up.

"I was going to give you another chance, but to hell with you!" she screamed furiously, her footsteps pounding against the ground as she stormed off.

Jean gulped down her fruity alcoholic drink and sat her glass down. She couldn't believe it. He had canceled their dinner plans and gone out with another woman. They weren't really dating. It was just pretend, but she couldn't help feeling betrayed.

"Would you like another, madam?" the waiter asked, motioning to her empty glass.

"Yes, please." She watched the man next to her smile as he leaned his head on his hand.

"Looking to have fun tonight?" he asked.

"That's why we're here," Tilly answered as Jean gulped another glass down. Whatever, tonight she wasn't his pillow. And if he didn't care, then she shouldn't either.

She couldn't remember how many drinks she'd had, but her head was starting to spin slightly. "Do you want to dance, beautiful?" the man asked as he ran his greedy hand over her side.

"Ssssure, letssss dance." She felt the man pull her up and escort her to the side room. She was buzzed and couldn't even remember his name. The man spun her into him as he gripped her close, swaying to the music. They were only out there for a few minutes when she heard a familiar voice.

"You're going to have to find yourself another dance partner. This one is mine," Ben growled.

"Drop dead." The man chuckled as Ben grabbed onto his arm.

"You touch my woman again and you will be."

The man stared at Ben and then looked back at Jean. "Do you know him?"

"Surrre, we sssleep together." Her voice slurred slightly as she pointed at Ben. "But you were naughty. Bad Ben." He caught her fingers in his hands, pulling her safely into his arms. He looked up at the man with a challenge.

"What a waste. She was liquored up to perfection," the man snorted as he stomped away.

"He's dead," Ben snarled as Jean began to dance to a rhythm different than the music. She swayed her hips erratically as she pressed into him. "Jean..."

"I'm having fun tonight. I'm not Jean but an enchantressss," she purred as her fingers trailed up his chest.

"Jean, I'm calling a cab and going home with Marco," Tilly said as she glanced at the stranger. "Do you want me to call a cab for you?"

"I'll take care of her," Ben said, but Tilly ignored him.

"Gina?"

"I'm his pillow, just a pillow."

"Gina, do you know this man?" Tilly asked, not wanting to leave her friend with this stranger.

"Yessss, he's my sleeping buddy." Jean waved her hand clumsily. "I'm his pillow and he likes—"

"Okay, Gina," Tilly said frantically, not wanting her friend to start spilling intimate details. "I'll leave her to you, then." She nodded her head politely to Ben with a tight smile before leaving.

Ben could feel the heat in his face. Jean was completely unaware of the subtle implications and unintentional impressions she was creating with her words and actions.

"There it isss." Jean reached up to cup his cheeks. His amber eyes looked down at her curiously. "I can do it too. Turn your face into a delicious red apple." She giggled as her fingers traced over his lips. "Do you taste like an apple?"

She grabbed Ben's head and crashed his lips into hers and, without warning, passed the threshold and thrust her tongue deep into his mouth. With a savage hunger, she attacked his tongue, letting out a soft moan.

He kneaded her shoulders fervently as he felt her soft lips against his own. Her lips felt like heaven upon his, and he wanted nothing more than to continue. But not like this, not with her judgment impaired. He made a rough sound in his throat before he tore away from her, holding her in place to stop her advances. His shoulders heaved as he panted. He had to grip her arms tightly as she tried to grab his face again.

"You don't want to kiss me, Ben?" she whimpered as her shoulders sagged. "I'm not as pretty as your date was. Sheee was pretty."

"Jean ..." Ben cooed softly as he pulled her tight against his chest. He leaned his head on hers and inhaled her scent. "She wasn't my date. I know you won't remember this, so I'll tell you again tomorrow." He pressed his lips against her head. "You can have all of my kisses, Jean, when you're ready for them." His voice was low and husky as he lowered his gaze to her. "Let's go home."

It was like wrestling a wild cat, getting her buckled into her seat, and then again struggling to get her into the apartment.

"Ben Ben Bo Ben Banana Nana Fo Fen Be My Moe Men Ben!" Jean sang loudly as she sauntered to the bedroom.

He chuckled, shaking his head as he looked through her drawers for night clothes. "You're not to ever drink without me." He turned around and dropped the nightshirt he had in his hands. Jean was standing there with only her panties on.

"Look Ben, these are like pillows too. Do you want to sleep on them?" She lifted her breasts up, moving them around as she grinned at him.

A throaty growl reverberated from his chest as she threw her arms around him, pressing her chest against him.

"You're making this hard, Jean." His voice was hoarse as he fought to not lose control. Her hand slid down his front, gripping his burgeoning cock.

"You're right. It is hard!"

With a control he didn't know he had, he stepped away from her. The nightshirt he found of hers wasn't long enough to cover her. He unbuttoned his shirt and then took his white undershirt off. In one swift motion, he pulled it over her head. Now at least she was covered.

He inhaled sharply as he felt her tongue trailing over his chest. "Jean …" he growled as he lifted her head away from him. "You're being such a temptress tonight."

She stuck her bottom lip out and folded her arms over her chest. "I'm not a good one, though, am I? You won't even let me taste you."

"Jean, if you want to taste me tomorrow, you can, as much as you want." As he went to brush her hair behind her ear, she reached out and grabbed his finger. Her hot mouth sucked on his finger, moving in slow motion as she hummed.

"Mmmm..."

With a shuddering breath, he pulled his hand away from her. A small pout formed on her lips. He was so close to giving in. It took every ounce of his self-control. He watched as she lifted her fingers out to touch his chest. Her fingers danced on his skin, tracing over his muscles. The soft touch sent shivers down his spine. All too soon, her fingers retreated, curling away from him. He watched as she flopped on the bed, curling up on her side.

"I'm lonely, Ben." She pulled a blanket up and tucked her chin to her chest. "I'm alone in this world." Her voice was only a quiet hum, but he heard her.

"You aren't alone. You have me."

"Not forever. You won't always be here, will you? In the end, I'll be alone." Her voice sounded pained as he moved to the bed. "It's okay, though. I understand. I know you can't stay with me."

"I'm not leaving, Jean. I want you to stay by my side, always." Silence. He listened as her breathing evened out and looked at her face. A wet streak stained the side of her cheek where tears had fallen. He dried them with the back of his hand and pushed her golden strands behind her ear as he sat there, admiring her. Did she not know how beautiful she was? It took all of his willpower to refuse her tonight. She was drunk, but he wondered what she meant about being lonely. Did she really feel like this, or was it the alcohol talking? "My sweet Jean," he whispered.

He turned and headed for her bathroom to take a cold shower. She had him beyond worked up, and there was no way he could lay beside her right now. Tomorrow, when she was sober, he was going to make her pay. He would pay her back for every touch, and for embarrassing him in public. He would taste her lips tomorrow and begin to work on making her his, forever.

Chapter 7

A blanket of warmth surrounded her as her mind tried to piece everything together. She remembered going out with Tilly, and Tilly picking out two men to come and join them. She swallowed hard as she remembered seeing Ben there with a beautiful red-headed woman. But after that, everything was fuzzy. She had images of dancing and then some flashes of her in her bedroom. Oh no.

Her eyes opened and she blinked, trying to focus. Someone was holding her. Inwardly, she winced. *Please say I didn't bring a stranger home*. She glanced up at Ben's resting face. At first, she relaxed. But then she noticed his sculpted bare chest and, upon further inspection, the man's shirt she was wearing. What did she do? She didn't have a bra on, just underwear on the bottom. *Think, Jean, think*. She couldn't remember. She had to try to escape. She tried to move, but his arms tightened around her.

"No," he mumbled. "Still sleepy."

"You were able to sleep again?" Her voice, soft and tender, pierced the silence and his lips responded with a gentle curl into a smile. With slow, deliberate movements, his eyes opened to reveal a mesmerizing golden hue that seemed to radiate warmth and comfort. They found hers effortlessly, like two lost puzzle pieces finally reunited. The sight of him filled her heart with joy and contentment, like a warm embrace on a cold day.

"Indeed, even after everything you put me through, I was able to sleep. I decided that, after last night, you owe me way more than thirty nights." He shifted comfortably in the bed, holding her hostage.

"What happened last night? What about your date?" She listened as he snorted.

"First, that was not a date. That was a business favor my father set up without asking. She ended up leaving almost immediately."

Inwardly, she sighed with relief hearing it wasn't a date, though she was curious as to why the woman left so soon. "Why?"

"Because I couldn't take my eyes off of you." He grinned as a red stain seized her cheeks. "I've also decided you are NEVER allowed to drink unless I'm around."

"What did I do?" Her gaze fixated on the arc of his lips curving upward, a hint of amusement dancing in his eyes. Her heart fluttered like a trapped bird, its wings beating rapidly against her chest. Her fingers traced over the solid muscles of his chest, igniting a spark of desire within her. Uncensored thoughts flooded her mind, creating a whirlwind of temptation and longing.

"Well, after I chased the man away who tried to dance with you, you declared to your friend that we're sleeping buddies."

She gasped as she looked down at the shirt she was wearing. "How did—"

"I'll get to it," he said in a satisfied tone as his fingers played with her hair. "You forcefully stole a kiss from me—" his grin widened, seeing her mortified face, "and I had to fight you to buckle your seat belt.

"Oh my gosh—"

"Oh, we aren't done. After we got back to the apartment, you took your clothes off and invited me to sleep on your breasts, since they were like pillows. You even bounced them around for me."

"I didn't!" she cried as she bit her lip anxiously.

"You threw yourself on me naked and you licked my chest. Not to mention you grabbed my manhood. Then you sucked on my finger." He clicked his tongue as he pretended to act offended. "I demand you take responsibility for me, now that you've spoiled my virtue."

"I'm so sorry." She shook her head, chewing on her lip.

"Any other man would have taken you up on what you were offering last night. You put my willpower to the test. And for that, you must be punished." He then shifted his body on top of hers. He looked at her cherry red cheeks and pressed his nose against them. "A stolen kiss ... for a stolen kiss," he whispered sensually before his mouth closed on hers.

Her lips softened and parted easily under the prodding of his tongue. He made a pleased groan in his throat as his hand rested behind her neck, allowing him deeper access. She moaned softly under his touch, her body coming alive as his lips explored hers. Her hands found their way to his back, pulling him closer as she felt heat emanating from deep within her.

His kiss was a force to be reckoned with, stirring up a storm of emotions within her. It was both demanding and commanding, yet somehow tender in its intensity. She responded eagerly, her body arching up to meet his as their lips melded together in a fiery embrace. Every touch, every caress, every possessive hold ignited a deep hunger within her that she couldn't deny.

Lost in the moment, she surrendered herself completely to his touch. His hand roamed down her trembling body, tracing the curves and dips of her hips and thighs with expert ease. She moaned into his mouth, her breaths coming in quick gasps as he continued to explore her with his skilled fingers.

As he reached her slightly exposed stomach, a shiver ran through her. She arched toward him, desperate for more of his touch, more of his possession. In that moment, nothing else mattered but the intense connection between them and the insatiable need driving them both forward.

Tension hung thick in the air, suffocating and all-consuming as their lips crashed together. The kiss ignited a wildfire of passion, consuming them both with an insatiable hunger. His hands roamed over her body with desperate urgency, demanding more from her with every touch. Their bodies pressed against each other with unbridled longing, sending electric shocks of desire through every inch of her skin. She could feel his heat radiating off of him, searing into her and leaving her breathless and powerless to resist. With a deep growl, he bit down on her lower lip before pulling it into his own mouth to suck on it greedily.

Suddenly, he pulled away from her, leaving her gasping for breath. He smiled at her, a wicked gleam in his eye. "You've been a very naughty girl," he said, his voice low and husky. He moved his head to nibble on her ear, pleased with the way her body was responding to him. "I think I've punished you enough for now." He softly kissed the tip of her nose and shifted away from her. As he did, her phone began to ring.

She felt completely flustered as she blinked at him. In a confused daze, she rolled to get her phone. She stood up and saw that it was Tilly calling.

"Hello?" she answered, as she watched Ben begin to type on his phone. As if he hadn't just gotten her all worked up.

"Gina, I felt so guilty leaving you like that, but it seemed like you were in good hands. I just wanted to call and make sure you did make it home okay."

"Yes, I did—"

"So ... A sleep buddy? You're going to have to tell me all about that deliciousness later. Anyway, Marco is still here, but I wanted to check on you real quick. Have fun!" Her chatterbox friend Tilly instantly hung up the phone without letting her get another word in. She reached her hand up to her head. It felt like it was drumming. She closed her eyes as she waited for the worst of it to subside. Warm hands cupped her cheeks. Her eyes fluttered open to see two concerned golden orbs studying her face.

"Let's get you some aspirin." His thumb caressed her skin as a small smile rested on his lips. He thought about last night and some of the things her intoxicated mind had said. He wondered if she really did feel lonely. "We'll call last night a hiccup for the both of us. I won't be dating other women. I'll just be with you, and I want you to do the same. After all, it is hard to sell our relationship if we're seeing others, right?"

"I wasn't there to go on a date with anyone," she admitted quietly. "I went with my friend. She liked the one man, and since he wasn't alone—" She shrugged. "I wasn't interested."

"You're lucky I was there. That man would have taken full advantage of you last night."

"I wouldn't have drunk so much if you weren't—" She clamped her mouth shut. Idiot! What was she confessing to him? "I mean, I usually don't drink like that."

His eyes settled on her, the small corners of his lips revealing a hidden smile. "I insist that you only drink with me from now on. Too many animals out there who would love to take a bite out of you." He watched as the color flooded into her adorable cheeks. He would love to take a bite out of her himself. And he planned to ... in time. He wanted to continue to explore this interesting connection with her and not scare her off.

He lazily looked her over, his eyes landing on her exposed thigh, then traveling slowly upward. "I've already told you that I would take care of you, but if you insist on working ..." He watched as she nodded her head, looking at him curiously. He leaned in close to her so that his lips touched her earlobe.

His hot breath sent shivers down her spine as his hand landed softly on her waist. She had no problem chastising men if their advances were unwanted, but she didn't have the urge to stop him at all. His touch wasn't just wanted ... it was craved. She didn't want to explore why, only relish in the soft tingles he sent through her.

"I found a job for you," his low seductive voice whispered as he pulled away to look at her face. "It would be as a personal assistant to a *family friend*, if you're interested?"

He said "family friend" with the hint of a negative undertone. However, she was too thrilled to ask more about that. "Really? Yes, I'd love to! I'm excited about the change from legal secretary, too. Thank you!" Her eyes widened happily and the throb in her forehead began to pound again. She winced and reached up to touch her head. When she did, her shirt also rose up, revealing the lacey underwear she was wearing.

"I used up all my willpower last night. I'm going to step out so you can get changed. Unless you want to throw yourself at me naked now? It's a different story when you're sober. Go ahead, ask me if I want to sleep on those two pillows of yours." His lips curled up, watching the delicious color on her cheeks spread over her neck and ears. He chuckled and winked at her. "Maybe another time, when you're ready."

He walked to the doorway and then turned to look at her. "I have to head into the office today. How about you meet me for lunch, and then I'll take you to meet your new employer?" He watched as she nodded her head. "Get dressed and then come out. I need to talk to you about something before I leave."

The door closed softly, and she stood there in mild bewilderment. It felt like their relationship had entered this new, dangerous flirting game, only now he seduced her with his kisses. Though the term "game" needed to be remembered. He was just playing with her, punishing her for last night. She didn't even want to think about what she did. Waves of embarrassment washed over her as she headed to her dresser.

She groaned and slapped her hand on her forehead. She really flopped her breasts around and asked him if he wanted to sleep on them? She didn't know many men who would deny themselves sexual gratification, especially when it was presented to them on a platter. She put her light purple blouse on and then paused. Was it really willpower? Or was he just not interested in someone like her? She remembered how posh and beautiful the red-headed woman looked last night. That memory was clear. That was the type of woman he was used to dating.

Of course, he enjoyed making her flustered and seeing her get embarrassed. It was a game to him. That's what this morning was. For a moment, she foolishly believed it could be more. She could almost curse her body for how it reacted to him. On the other hand, she had nothing to be embarrassed about. She was an adult woman with no attachments, so why not play his game? There was no going too far, as long as she could handle it when it ended.

She heard a knock at the door, and she quickly stomped into her shorts. Stepping out of her room, she saw the man who had picked them up earlier, Clint. Ben was buttoning up his shirt and talking swiftly to him.

"No, move that meeting off my schedule. I want my afternoon freed up."

"Yes, sir." Clint typed on his tablet, quickly glancing up at Jean. "I'll wait for you in the car."

"Wait," Ben said, turning and holding his hand out to Jean. She curiously walked up to him. Once she was within reach, he curled his arm around her, bringing her next to him. "Jean, I want to formally introduce you to Clint, my right-hand man. You will see a lot of him, so I want you to be comfortable around him. Of course, not too comfortable. I'm the only one you are to sleep with."

He was trying to provoke a reaction out of her again. Instead, she decided to go along with it. "I guess I'm not allowed to get drunk in front of him and offer my pillows?" This time she was rewarded with Ben's ears turning a dark, candy apple red. She knew the memory was now flashing into his mind, and there was a moment of sweet satisfaction. No wonder he enjoyed making her blush.

"I will be receiving any offers you may have in the future. Anyone else who tries will become a strange smell in the woods." His fingers curled into her more, his voice unmistakably possessive. "Remember that, Clint. This one here is my person." He cleared his throat and lifted his gaze to his assistant. "So, look out for her for me."

"I'll make sure to keep others away."

She blinked as she searched their faces. They looked completely serious. There was no hint of it being a joke. They had superb poker faces.

"Clint is going to come and pick you up for lunch." Ben then glanced up at the man. "Wait for me in the car."

He waited until Clint left and then spun her so that he could look at her fully. "I need to tell you something. This doesn't change anything between us, but there is something you should know about me." Normally this would be something that would excite a woman, but he had a feeling it would do the opposite for Jean. "I work at Cross Industries." He watched as her expression changed, her mouth opening as she raised her hand.

"You are *THE* Mr. Cross of Cross Industries. That is your company." She tried to pull rational thoughts together as she realized who Ben was. Cross Industries was a multibillion-dollar company, one of the largest in the world. Mr. Hamen had been trying to land their account for years. Now it all made sense. However, she felt sick to her stomach. She was certain now that he could never be in a relationship with her. Men like him would have a business marriage.

Jean could be used to keep unwanted women away. By having a *girlfriend*, he wouldn't feel pressured into having to take out the daughters of business partners. Yeah, this news didn't change anything for her. This was what he needed ... a non-complicated relationship. Someone who would be by his side until he was ready to settle down with the woman he chose, which could never be her.

No wonder he suffered from not sleeping. If she was the CEO of a company like that, she doubted she could sleep either. All those jobs you were liable for, so many people depending on your business.

"It must be very stressful on you," she murmured, stammering up at him.

A tired smile reached his lips as he nodded. "It can be. Especially when you can't sleep. It's hard to make important decisions like that. I feel rejuvenated now, though. As if I can really attack things head on, and I have you to thank for that." He enclosed her in his embrace, bringing his head to rest on top of hers. "You are the calm to my storm."

A storm was right. He was her storm. He would come and go as the wind took him, but he could never stay with her. She did enjoy a good storm when it came. They relaxed her. She loved listening to the rumbles and seeing the flashes of light. She would enjoy his touches and company until the wind took him away.

"Now that you really know that I can afford to take care of you, are you sure you want to work?"

"I want to work and support myself."

"You are refreshing, Jean. I always dreamed that I would marry someone who would work by my side. You might have been made for me."

"I was at least made to be your pillow." She listened as he hummed.

"Maybe not just that." He stepped back, grabbing his suit jacket. "I'll see you in a few hours. Think about what you want for lunch." He went to reach for the door but stopped. He spun around and quickly pecked her on the cheek. "See you soon, my genie."

She stared at the closed door, chewing on her inner lip. Turning her head, she caught a glimpse of herself in the mirror. This simply wouldn't do, not if she was going to match him at the game he was playing. She flung her blouse off and quickly jumped in the shower. Afterwards, she headed for her closet to grab a cute, floral sundress. It cut down to a low V-neck, exposing the flesh of the top of her breasts. She put her hair up in a clip and applied a light layer of make-up.

It was bizarre to think about who Ben was. He didn't act like a billionaire. Though she had never met one before, she imagined they acted way more uppity. They would not have been okay sleeping in her apartment. He acted like a normal person who probably lived a life she had never even dreamt about.

Maybe ... had he just been Ben and not Mr. Cross Industries, things could have been different. She could envision a life with him. Waking up in his arms, her making dinner while he played with their children in the living room. It was the first time she was able to picture a future with someone, and it was someone she couldn't have one with.

She shrugged slightly as she looked at herself in the mirror. This was about as good as she would get. She glanced back at the clock to see she still had some time. Heading back to the kitchen, she decided to prepare them lunch. It would help the time pass faster. She started feeling excited and nervous about seeing him again. She was also a little intimidated to be meeting him at his company. *Please, don't let me do anything to embarrass myself.*

Chapter 8

C lint arrived to pick her up, and she rode in the seat next to him. He had opened the back door for her, but she immediately objected to it. She didn't want to feel like she was being chauffeured around.

"So, how long have you been working for Ben?" she casually asked, glancing over at the man. His brows furrowed a bit as he kept his eyes on the road.

"For about four years now, but I've known Ben longer than that. He's a really good guy. He gave me this job after I lost my dad, when he walked out on my mom. I had just graduated from college and my dad left us with nothing. He took his wallet and moved in with a younger woman. He hasn't reached out to me once. Sorry, I can be talkative. It's better that I don't get started because then I ramble and ramble—like I'm doing now."

Jean giggled as she flashed him a smile. Clint instantly made her feel comfortable. "Please, talk. I enjoy conversations. How has it been, working for Ben?"

Clint chuckled as he gave her a quick side glance. "If you're looking for me to say something negative about Ben, it will never happen. I might be his personal assistant, but we have a good relationship. I help him, especially when he struggles due to lack of sleep. I'd do anything for him. Anything," he repeated quietly.

"I'm not looking for any juicy gossip or anything like that." Jean laughed lightly. "I'm just curious. I haven't known him long, and I'm curious about the person driving me around."

"Fair enough." He grinned. "That smells amazing, by the way. Did you pack him a lunch?"

"Mmhmm. I don't have many talents, but cooking is one of them. I made us turkey wraps with glazed bacon. They're simple to make and great for packing. However, I'm feeling a bit insecure about it since I don't know what he likes. I'm sure he's used to much grander things," she said, clutching the bag in her hand.

"He'll love it, especially because you made it for him." A peculiar smile rested on his face, but he wasn't looking at her anymore. "I hear you're going to be working for Lincoln Summers."

"Is that his name? He didn't mention the name, just that I would be working for a family friend." She listened as Clint snickered.

"Link is good friends with Ben's sister Stephanie, but Ben only tolerates him. Barely that. Those two always end up bickering and being passive aggressive. You'll see. It's actually quite funny. For him to let you work with Link must mean he really cares about you, especially knowing he'll be running into Link more."

"Not really. He just owes me a job since he quit the last one for me." She laughed but Clint gave her a sideways look.

"No. Ben wouldn't tolerate Link for just anyone. His sister is the exception, and it looks like you are now, too. Just between us, though, Ben pretends to hate Link more than he does." There was a weird look in his eyes as he stared at the road.

She pondered over what he said but there was no other explanation. He agreed to find her a job, and he did. He probably didn't worry about it since they weren't really a couple. In the future, she could continue to work there, and he wouldn't have to see Link.

"This is it," Clint said as he nodded his head to the side. Jean looked at the window and felt as if the wind was knocked out of her. She held the bag closer as she looked back at him. "Go in through those main doors there and let them know you're there to see Ben."

"You aren't coming with me?" she asked and listened to his gentle, rumbling laugh.

"You aren't that attached to me already, are ya? Naw, I get it. You're intimidated. Don't be. Ben's got ya taken care of. I have another errand I have to run." He looked at her nervous face, giving her a soft smile. "If you need me to, I can walk you in."

"No, you have work to do. The building is so big, but I'm sure I can manage. Thank you for the ride," she said politely as she stepped out of the car. He rolled the window down and she turned to look at him.

"Don't worry, you've got this," he said with an air fist pump before driving away.

She inwardly laughed in exasperation as she looked at the towering gray stone building. A large silver crisscross with a circle around it protruded at the top of the building. An emblem of their company. *Alright Jean, in we go.* With a deep breath, she bravely walked forward.

She entered the building and her heels clicked on the shiny black tile. There was a waiting area off to the side with several chairs and couches. There was even a television playing. In front of her was a large, white marble desk with three women sitting behind it. They were busy typing on their computers and answering phones. Behind them was another hallway with several elevators.

She headed for the receptionists and waited to be acknowledged. One of the women lifted her eyes above her glasses, giving her a once-over, before she pressed her lips together forming a tight smile.

"Can I help you ma'am?"

There was clear annoyance in her voice, but Jean ignored it. She wasn't there to cause trouble. "Yes, I'm here to see Ben Cross." The woman's brows knitted together before she spun her chair to the side.

"Anita," she said in a dull tone. "She's here to see Ben Cross."

"Another one? What does she want? Mr. Cross already donates to charity, miss. He is very busy, and he has scheduled dates for these sorts of things."

"I'm not here for charity." Jean felt slightly offended, but she supposed these things had happened before. "I have a lunch appointment with Ben." She raised her lunch bag as if to prove her point.

"Oh. My. Gosh." Anita clicked her tongue. "A stalker. We haven't had one of those in a while."

"No, I'm not a stalker. Look, please just let Ben know that Jean is here to see him."

"Don't embarrass yourself, Jean. Just turn around and leave before you're escorted out by security. As if Mr. Cross would have dinner with you, and of all things, a packed lunch." The other woman snickered.

This was about how Jean pictured Ben's world would be. She was just shocked at how accurate she was. They took one look at her and knew she wasn't the same as him. More proof that she didn't belong in his world. Sadly, it looked like people faked having an appointment to see Ben. So, while their rudeness was unnecessary, they were right to be wary.

"I appreciate that you're just doing your job. It's okay. I'll let Ben know I'm here." She reached for her phone and opened her contact list. She almost choked when she saw the name he had entered. Jean's Sleep Buddy. When did he enter this?! She pressed her finger on the name and within one ring he picked up.

"Jean."

"Sleep buddy, really?" She listened as he chuckled.

"We can switch it to lover if you want. Are you here? Come on up."

"Yeah, about that. They won't let me." She could have sworn she heard him curse lightly.

"One minute. I'll take care of it," he said before hanging up.

She turned to look at the secretaries as she waited for him to call them. A minute went by, and she could hear the secretaries snickering behind their desk.

"How embarrassing," one of them said, making sure it was loud enough for her to hear.

There is a difference between doing your job and being plain rude. Ben must have gotten another call, so it was taking him longer. She would just bear with it for a few more moments. The elevator dinged and she looked up in shock to see him step out. He headed right toward her, his gaze never leaving her eyes.

"Ben, I—" she started to say as he stepped into her. He wrapped his arm tightly around her waist and swooped her up, pinning her to his chest and devouring her lips with an all-consuming hunger. Waves of pleasure surged through her body as the world around them faded away, leaving nothing but them in that moment. She felt the people around them gasp in surprise, but Ben remained undeterred by it all until he reluctantly parted from her lips, giving her one last gentle peck.

"I'm sorry you had to wait. That won't ever happen again," he said as he lifted a threatening glare to the secretaries. The women looked shocked and terrified at the same time. They were no longer laughing and making snide comments, but instead just sat there with their mouths agape.

"Ben," she said softly, bringing his gentle amber eyes back to her. "I hope you don't mind, but I made us lunch." She watched as his ears began to turn red, and he looked a bit flushed.

"You made me lunch," he whispered in awe as his eyes traveled to the bag and then back to her. "I've always wanted to have a girlfriend who would make me a lunch." He grinned at her as he snatched the bag. "I might be a little too excited for this. Come on, let's go find a place to eat." He grabbed her hand like a schoolboy and tugged her behind him. "Do you want to eat outside? Or in my office?"

"Outside sounds nice." *Boy, he really likes putting on a show*, she thought wryly to herself.

"Did you make a big heart with ketchup? Or cut out heart-shaped apples?" he asked as he sat down under a tree. She laughed as she took her place next to him.

"Maybe next time. I made turkey bacon wraps. I hope you like them, but it's okay if you don't." She watched as he lifted it up to his mouth, not hesitating to bite into it.

"Oh wow. This is amazing. Jean, you should be a chef."

"Quit teasing me, Ben."

"Who's teasing? Don't work as a personal assistant. Work for me. Cook for me and sleep with me."

"You really like it?" Her eyes lit up as she watched him eagerly devour it.

"I love it," he mumbled with his mouth full.

"Slow down Ben, you'll choke."

"Second best way to die."

"Second? What's the first?" she asked as his eyes flickered over her.

"Dying in your arms."

She rolled her eyes and shook her head. "Are you sure you should have done that earlier?"

"Done what?"

"Kissed me," she said as she chewed on her inner lip. She did this a lot when she was anxious or in deep thought.

"You're my girlfriend, right? Now everyone knows it."

So it was a stunt to spread the news faster. She guessed it made sense, though it lit a fire inside of her. She could easily get lost in his touch and kisses. It was a reminder that she was completely affected by him, and it wasn't reciprocated.

"Don't you dare make your new boss any of your food." Ben pursed his lips together with a small pout. "I'd still rather you work for me."

"So, about my new boss—" She listened as Ben groaned, turning his head to the sky.

"His name is Lincoln. Link is what we call him. He's an artist, I guess."

Jean giggled. "I can see he's not your favorite person." He gave her a wry grin and laid down, his head landing on her lap.

"We're just different. He isn't a bad guy, but he annoys the hell out of me. I know he'll be a good boss, though. I wouldn't let you work for anyone who wouldn't be." He closed his eyes as he thought about

Link. They actually used to be good friends, but things changed. He felt her fingers move through his hair slowly.

"Oh, sorry," she muttered, retracting her fingers.

"Please, don't stop."

She moved her fingers through his dark, silky hair and watched his relaxed face. "I could get used to this." He hummed, turning his head to the side. "You look incredible by the way." Her lips parted in shock as he opened one eye to look at her. "But I think you should wear turtlenecks when you go out in public."

"It's hot out!" She laughed as she looked at his serious expression.

"I don't like others looking at you."

"No one is looking at me." She practically snorted. No one spared her a glance, except a mocking one, like in his building.

"At least they know better now," he said in a satisfied tone. "I still need to make sure Link knows his place." He then moved to stand to his feet. "I guess I need to take you to meet your new boss." As he reached his hand down to help her up, a sleek snake slithered next to her. She shrieked and jumped, grabbing Ben's shirt. "Don't worry, it isn't going to hurt you." He chuckled as he felt her death grip on him.

"It startled me," she defended herself as she released her grip. A mortified look came over her face. "I'm so sorry, Ben. I tore some of the buttons off of your shirt."

He glanced down and shrugged. "It's alright. I have spare shirts in my office."

He felt her arm tug on him as she hissed, "Ben, you can't go in there."

"Why ever can't I?" He laughed.

"Look at yourself, Ben! They're going to think—" She trailed off as she took in his appearance. With his tousled hair and half-open shirt, it looked like they just got done making love. She watched as he put it together and a wicked glint shined in his eyes.

"This is even more perfect."

"Ben! Think of the things they'll say—"

He turned to her, with a dark expression. "They know better than to breathe out anything that could get back to me." His eyes drifted from her face and down to her pillows. The soft part of her exposed skin had been driving him wild. When he first saw her, his breath caught. She was beautiful. But when he saw what she was wearing, he had to taste her. He was just going to come down and scold the receptionists, but his plan soon changed. He needed to feel her lips against his. This woman was so oblivious to the way other men looked at her. She probably had no idea how badly she affected him. Her touch sent shivers through his body and drove him crazy.

He needed to satisfy himself with her electric lips again. He stepped into her, grabbing her hand and placing it on his bare chest. "Jean, look what you did." He leaned down to whisper against her ear. "You need punished."

With a sharp intake of breath, her chest rose and fell rapidly as his skilled hands slid up her sides. She could feel the heat of his body against hers, the small nibbles on her neck sending shivers down her spine. But it wasn't just her neck he was focused on. Soon his lips were on hers, tasting, teasing, and igniting a fire within her that threatened to consume them both. In a desperate need for more, she wrapped her arms around his neck, pulling him closer until their bodies were pressed against each other in an intimate embrace. As their lips moved in sync, the line between who initiated the kiss blurred and became irrelevant. All that mattered was the hunger being satisfied between them as his tongue dominated hers. His hands roamed over her body with purpose, tracing every curve and dip with precision and leaving a trail of goosebumps in its wake. A low growl rumbled from deep within his chest as his hand tightened around her perky ass, pressing her firmly against his hardening cock.

Someone coughed and then cleared their throat loudly. "Mr. Cross." This time the snarl he made was not one from arousal. He turned his body to the man, exposing his bare chest and disheveled hair. Inwardly, Jean winced. She could just hear the talk now. The CEO took her in the park next to the company building.

"I'm sorry sir. You left your cellphone, and your father has been trying to reach you."

She watched as his eyes changed hearing his father's name. He then hooked his arm around Jean and began to walk toward his company. He made sure he kept her tight against him as they entered the building. No one dared to make direct eye contact with him. He led her to the express elevator that shot up at a speed she wasn't ready for. Had Ben not been holding onto her, she would have fallen.

He tugged her along to his office and shut the door. She stared at the floor the whole time because she was too embarrassed to lift her head. Ben left her side and quickly dialed on his phone. While he was talking, she found a mirror in the corner of the room. She went and looked at herself. Her lipstick was smudged around her lips and her hair was displaced. Her dress looked more wrinkled, and there were leaves on the bottom where she had been sitting. *Well, that's it. I'm the office whore now.* Good thing she wasn't working here. She already had a reputation, and no one knew her. She knew how these things spread. She'd heard the malicious gossip at the office where she used to work.

"Jean." She turned her head to look at the lazy grin he was giving her.

"Is everything okay?"

Ben snorted angrily. "Yes. He wants me to pick up my mother's gift on the way home. Something like that is a dire emergency to my dad. My mother is his world. I've never seen a love like theirs."

"That's sweet." Jean smiled as Ben nodded.

"I want what they have." His eyes then drifted over her. "And I intend to have it."

His eyes looked over her possessively as if his statement was addressed to her. Under his predatory gaze, her heart began to race again. She couldn't take her eyes off of him, even after he turned away to grab an extra shirt. It wasn't until a smirk rose across his face from catching her staring that she turned away.

"It's yours, whenever you want it. You don't need to ask, just take."

Her face was instantly hot, and she refused to look at him again. She heard his soft chuckle as he stepped in front of her. He tilted her head up to him and brushed his thumb around her lips. "There, all straightened up. Come on, let's go meet Link."

Chapter 9

Jean was securely tucked into Ben's side as they stepped out of the elevators. He wasn't leaving a gap between them. "I think I might have to start insisting that you visit me every day. It's nice not getting bothered when I try to leave." He laughed as she gave him a pointed look.

She glanced up and saw Clint heading toward them. "I see you survived," he teased, arching a brow when he saw her face.

"You have no idea what happened."

"This little minx practically ripped my shirt off," Ben teased, making her hiss up at him quickly.

"Ben!" She glanced around, mortified at who was eavesdropping on their conversation. A few people swiftly looked down, which told her they had overheard.

"Incoming at your 3 o'clock," Clint said tersely. Jean's eyes moved in the direction to see a man around the same age as Ben heading in their direction. He looked to be in his mid-twenties with dark brown hair and brown eyes that were pinned on Ben.

"Benjamin," the man said as he stood in front of them, blocking their path. "We had a meeting."

"Lewis, that meeting was rescheduled." Ben glanced over at Clint, who nodded his head. "I'll meet with you tomorrow."

"I need answers, Ben!"

"I have other plans today. This isn't a brush-off. I told you I would meet with you, and I will." Ben could feel the agitation from the man. Lewis was technically his cousin. He was the son of his mother's stepsister, who they never associated with. She was a daughter from a previous marriage, and after her mother married his grandfather, she made his mother's life hell. His mother didn't say much about her, just that she wasn't a nice person. They didn't blame Lewis for his mother's wrongs, but it was still a complicated relationship.

"Is this your other plan?" Lewis' voice was less than pleasant. Ben instantly felt his blood begin to boil. "Whose daughter are you? What favor is Ben doing today?"

Jean felt completely taken aback by his words. Ben was the first to respond, not giving her a chance to. "I'm doing myself the favor, and she is giving me the privilege of joining me." Lewis seemed unconvinced as he pried again.

"What do your parents do?"

"My parents are dead." She watched as his brows knitted together.

"So, you run their company now?"

"Lew, my girlfriend is not your concern." Ben could see how Lewis' face changed and as he looked Jean over. Then a wicked smile spread over his face.

"Oh, I get it. Girlfriend." Lewis winked at Ben and then chuckled. "Someone to pass the time with and keep your bed warm until you have to take a bride. I can see the attraction. She is pretty enough. She must really give you a ride—"

Ben pulled back to punch Lewis, but Clint beat him to it. Clint's fist collided with Lewis' cheek, making him stagger back in shock. He grimaced and spit blood out on the floor.

"Who the hell do you think you are?! I expect this to be handled accordingly, Ben. You don't want bad publicity," Lewis growled as he took a step back in fear, looking at Clint's eyes.

Jean watched as the man quickly scurried away. Almost instantly, Ben led her outside, with Clint at her side. It wasn't until they got into the car that Ben finally spoke.

"Damn it, Clint, why—"

"I couldn't let you do it, Ben. They're just looking for a reason to get your money. It's better for me to do it and you fire me. Had you hit him, well, you know the mess you would have been in."

"Wait, fire you?" Jean asked, as Ben sighed into his hand.

"He has to, Jean. He has to respond accordingly. Lewis is from a decent family, and they won't accept anything less. It's alright." Clint turned to look back at them.

"At least until things cool down, you won't be able to be with me." Ben looked up at Clint and gave him a sad smile. "Thank you. You really saved me."

"Well, at least I got the gratification of slamming my fist into his face. The man's a creep. I've never liked him."

"I'm not a fan either." Ben sighed and then his eyes lit up. "I know. For now, you'll be Jean's driver. I want you to stay with her and keep her safe. Especially at work."

Clint chuckled, reading between the lines. He wanted him to make sure no other man moved in on Jean. But there was still a problem. "They'll check if I'm on your payroll."

"You won't be. You'll be on Lincoln's payroll, and I'll be paying Link for an unknown service." Ben smirked as he relaxed back in his chair. He reached over, intertwining his fingers with Jean's. "Sorry about that, Jean. Lewis is … well, the relationship is complicated. His family is wired differently than mine. In the future, I'm going to make sure the line is very clear. If he dares to say something after that, I'll go after his parents' company without mercy. Family ties be damned."

"You don't have to do that. It's fine. I sort of figured this was how the business world worked. I'm sure it's a shock for you to be with someone who doesn't have anything to offer—"

"Don't say such things. That's how some work, but not me. You're everything. You're amazing just the way you are. Don't ever say you don't have anything to offer. Next time, you'll be punished." He arched his brows, a crooked smile spreading over his lips. "Of course, I don't mind disciplining you, so by all means." Her cheeks began to turn colors again and he gave her hand a soft squeeze. "It's all settled. Clint, you'll be taking care of my Jean for a while. Now, let's head to Lincoln's place and get it over with. And Clint," Ben looked up at him and smiled. "Thank you."

"Don't go trying to make me blush. I don't want you taking a bite out of me," Clint teased, beaming his white teeth at Ben.

"Turn your ass around and drive," Ben snorted, listening as Clint laughed at him. His gaze shifted to Jean sitting beside him, her lips barely bearing a trace of lipstick. He remembered her kisses and the way they made him feel … like he was being consumed by an inferno of passion. His entire body throbbed with desire for more. She had ignited something within him that no one else ever had—a maddening possessiveness, a powerful need to protect her, and an uncontrollable urge to be with her. He didn't want to scare her off. He knew these feelings were too intense for the short time they had known each other. So, he would wait, stealing touches and kisses when he could. He hoped she would soon begin to crave him as well. He hoped that soon she would desire him like he did her.

If at any moment she had pulled away or given him the impression that she didn't like it, he would have stopped immediately. But she never did. She actually responded to him vigorously. And she was the one to close the gap between their lips. If they hadn't been interrupted, who knows how far things would have progressed. He felt like his plan was working. He just needed to give it enough time so she wouldn't think it was weird. How much time would it take?

"So, Ben, you have a sister? What is she like?" Jean asked, trying to stop her mind from racing and thinking irrational thoughts. He was still holding her hand. Her heart fluttered nervously, trying to convince her that his actions meant that he liked her. But her mind, rational and logical, told her it was just a simple oversight, a meaning-less gesture. She could feel the tug of war between her emotions and her thoughts, each vying for control of her reactions to the situation. Her heart longed for affection while her brain tried to protect her from disappointment. It was a familiar battle, one she had fought many times before. But in that moment, with him sitting beside her, she couldn't help the hopeful flutter in her chest despite the logical doubts lingering in her mind.

"Yeah, I do. Her name is Stephanie. We get along like typical sib-lings. We fight sometimes, but we always have each other's backs. I

want to introduce you to her soon. My dad wants to meet you too."
He watched her eyes widen as her hand tensed in his. "They'll love
you. I promise. My family are not the demons you have in mind. Be
prepared, though. They'll fall for you and instantly start planning our
wedding." He winked at her, scooting closer to her side.

Her beautiful eyes stared up at him anxiously as she wetted her lips.
His eyes drifted to her soft pink lips that were all but inviting him
to taste them again. He moved his head slowly, his nose touching her
forehead. Then the car began to slow down, and they pulled over to
the curb.

"We're here," Clint said, and Ben could have killed the man. *Read
the room!* He was so close, so close to tasting her again, but now she
had turned her head away to look out the window.

"Oh wow. Is this it?" Jean gasped, staring at the luxurious building surrounded by glass windows. She began to feel anxious as she
watched the fancy clothes of the people walking in and out through
the doors. She was so fixated that she didn't notice Ben had left the seat
next to her. It wasn't until her door opened that she jumped, startled.

Ben chuckled as he reached for her hand. He grabbed her fingers
and pulled her into him. He quickly pecked her lips with a softness
that left her body tingling for more. "Don't worry. I'll protect you."
His arm curled around her, escorting her inside.

"Ben ..." She glanced around nervously. "Are you sure he wants
someone like me to—" Ben spun her around, capturing her chin with
his thumb, tilting it up to him.

"I told you the next time you said something like that, I would
punish you." His lips curled up wryly. "Maybe that's what you want?"

Jean's whole body slightly trembled in anticipation as he leaned
closer to her. She felt his hot breath fan her lips.

"It's Fender Bender!" a rich male voice said, causing Ben to growl lowly.

His hand moved away, his gaze promising her that this wasn't over, before turning toward the voice. "Stinkin' Lincoln. How ... nice to see you again."

The man walked up to Ben and offered him a cordial handshake. He was tall and lean, flashing a million-dollar smile. He had two dimples that dipped into his cheeks and seemed to enhance his charm. He ran his hand through his dark mahogany hair that looked silky and soft. A moment later, his bright green eyes shifted to Jean. "So, is this my new assistant? I'm Link." He looked her over as he reached his hand out to her. "And your name is?"

There was something strangely familiar about him, but she couldn't place it. As if she knew him, but how could she? She realized that, like a putz, she was in a daze, staring at the almost-sparkling man. "Regina, but please call me Jean." She felt his fingers squeeze hers lightly, lifting them to his lips and pressing a soft kiss upon her skin. She could feel her cheeks beginning to heat up as he held his position.

"Alright, that's enough." Ben grabbed her hand from him and pulled her to his side. "No lips. No overly touchy. I don't want your scent getting on her." She watched as an almost Cheshire Cat grin grew over Link's face.

"Ben, I've never seen you like this before." His green eyes looked at Jean. "He must really like you. Don't give in to him. Make him work for it," he said with a wink. "Although he needs a good romp. Maybe it will help him relax some—"

"That mouth of yours." Ben shook his head in agitation. "Did you ever think that's the reason you can't keep a woman by your side? Try not talking. You'll do better."

"I'm waiting for the right person."

"Is that what you call it? I thought this is what a chicken looks like, because they are afraid to tell the person they really like." Ben gave him a knowing look. Link had always had a thing for his sister, but he hadn't moved on his feelings. Unlike his family, Link came from poverty. He worked hard to get where he was. Even Ben couldn't deny that of him. He thought that was the reason Link never told Stephanie his feelings.

"What do you know?" Link scoffed and then started to walk in the other direction. "Well ... come on."

Jean felt Ben's fingers curl around her waist softly as he gently nudged her to walk next to him. Link and Ben didn't act like people who didn't like each other to her, but rather really good friends who teased each other. If Ben really didn't like this man, she doubted he would converse with him. Or he would be a stiff level of polite, like you would with a stranger.

"What's that look for?" Ben asked, glancing down at her.

"Mmm, nothing," she said as she smiled up at him. He arched his brows as she let out a quiet giggle. "I think you two are actually good friends."

"We are." Link waved his hand in the air dismissively, not turning around. "Don't let him tell you any different. Ben has some trust issues—" He quickly stopped, not wanting to air his friend's dirty laundry. "But the fact that he brought you to me shows how much he trusts me, whether he wants to admit it or not."

She glanced up at Ben curiously, but his terse face revealed nothing. The remainder of their journey was accompanied by silence, broken only by the sound of their shoes clicking on the polished marble floor.

"This is my personal space," Link said, holding a hand out toward the open door. Jean stepped through first, her eyes darting around the room. When she had heard Link was an artist, it brought to her mind images of paint-splattered canvases and clay-covered hands. But as she stepped into his personal space, she was met with rows upon rows of clothing instead. It was like walking into a department store, the walls lined with shelves of fabric in every color and texture imaginable. Mannequins stood tall, displaying garments in various stages of completion—some fully clothed, while others only had parts of their outfits in place. The overwhelming array of fabrics, patterns, and designs made it seem almost magical. It was a surreal sight, unlike anything she had ever experienced. A pair of ten-dollar flats was an exciting find for her. She couldn't imagine the cost of everything in this room.

In the front, there was a rack of clothes that seemed to be finished. They had handwritten tags attached to each of them as if they were personal orders. That was when her eyes found it. Minno. Minno was a famous personal designer. She had only heard of him through Tilly, who raved about his stuff. She felt the lump form in her throat, feeling slightly dizzy. She felt like she should move. Everything was more valuable than she could possibly ever afford. If she accidentally broke or ripped something, she could never pay him back.

"Is everything okay?" Link asked, stepping in front of her.

"Are you sure you want someone like me working here?" She heard Ben clear his throat loudly, coming up next to her. His head leaned down next to her ear, his teeth nibbling on her ear lobe as he talked.

"That's double the punishment for you later." His voice sent a shiver down her back as she tried to maintain her focus. Damn, why was she so affected by him? With just his breath, she became flustered and had a hard time thinking.

"I mean, I don't have any experience handling clothing or art—"

"You're perfect." Link gave her a reassuring smile. "I need someone I can trust. Ben vouched for you, so I know you're trustworthy. I've had my share of assistants steal things from me."

"You don't have to worry about that." Jean chuckled and Link raised a brow, waiting for her to elaborate. She quickly realized that what she said could be taken as an insult. "I mean," she motioned over the clothes she was wearing. "I live a simple life. Your designs are exquisite, but there isn't an event that I would go to that would require such elegance."

"I wouldn't bank on that." Link's lips twitched up, revealing his double dimples. "In either case, if Ben trusts you, then I trust you." He looked her over and his eyes lightened up. "You're actually the perfect size," he said, nodding his head as he grabbed a paper off his desk. "Yep, I'm going to use your body for my next design."

"Link ..." Ben began to growl but was instantly cut off.

"Relax, Ben. She has the perfect measurements. Don't you think she's the same size as Stephie? I'm making her something special. Jean here will be perfect to help me with that."

Ben looked her over and then sighed, nodding his head. "I suppose they are the same size, but—"

"But what, Ben?" Link asked pointedly. He watched as Ben looked to the side with an apparent scowl forming over his face.

"I don't like others touching her."

"Strictly professional, Ben. You have my word. You know I would never—I'm not—" Link stopped as Ben nodded his head.

"I know." He placed his hands on Jean's shoulders and bent down to look at her. "If at any time you're uncomfortable working here, or if you don't like the job, or the company ..."

"Hey!"

"Then you tell me at once. There are other jobs, Jean. I'll take care of you," Ben continued, ignoring the snorts of protest from Link.

"Thank you, Ben. I'm nervous, but it sounds intriguing. I'll give it a chance. I'm sure Link will be a better boss than my last."

"A dog would be a better boss than your last." Ben's voice was laced with agitation as he pulled her into a full embrace. "Whatever you want. If it makes you happy, then I'm okay with it."

She leaned into his embrace, greedily inhaling his male scent. It was weird how he could make her heart race, but when he did things like this, she felt completely at ease. When he shifted away from her, she immediately missed his heat, his touch. A crazy notion screamed through her to trip into him, just so she could touch him again. Yeah, she needed to work and have a distraction. This was crazy.

"Thank you for the job, Link. When do I start?"

Link beamed his showcase smile and clapped his hands together. "Now."

Chapter 10

"No, I took the rest of the day off so I can spend time with her," Ben objected instantly.

"Well, Mr. CEO, I'm sure you have work that needs to be done, so do it." Link shrugged his shoulders unapologetically. Just as Ben began to retaliate, his phone began to chime.

He answered his phone to see a text message from his mother. *Call me as soon as possible. What happened with Lewis?* Ben pursed his lips together tightly. Of course, the little weasel still had to cause trouble. Which reminded him ...

"You're right. I do have some things to take care of. One more thing, though, Link. I need you to cover Clint's wages for a while. Give him benefits too. I'll make a donation to cover the expenses." He watched as Link raised a brow, tilting his head to the side.

"That's not a problem, but what happened?"

"He saw I was about to punch Lewis and quickly did it to protect me."

"Hell, for punching Lewis, I'll gladly pay him without the donation. Nasty, slimy slug, beady-eyed child who was never taught manners." Link continued muttering insults as Ben turned to focus on Jean.

"Clint will be waiting for you. Here is his number," he said as he quickly texted her. "You let him know if you need anything and he will get it for you." He cupped her cheek with his hand and leaned in slowly. "I'll see you tonight."

His warm, soft lips pressed against her forehead and suddenly she felt panicked that he was leaving her. She reached out, placing her hand on his arm. Their eyes met and she struggled to give him a reason for her actions.

"What do you want for dinner tonight?" *Idiot. What makes you think he is joining you for dinner?*

"Whatever you're serving, I'll partake in it." His eyes lingered over her body, causing her to shiver as she thought about earlier. He leaned in close so that his hot breath could sizzle her ear. In an almost inaudible whisper he said, "You'll be receiving my punishments later. I won't forget." A small promising smile reached his lips for a brief second.

"Link ..." He sighed as he met with the man's green eyes. Jean watched as silent words passed between them before he finally turned and headed to the door, where he stopped one last time. "She's important to me." Without looking back, he disappeared from Jean's sights.

Her heart fluttered at his words, though she knew she was reading more into it. He was basically saying to treat her well.

"Idiot. I can see that," Link muttered with a gentle smile on his lips. He turned, looking Jean over. "How about we start with getting to know each other. I can work and talk. So, tell me about yourself, Jean, about your family."

It felt like all anyone wanted to talk about lately was her family. She wasn't like the rest of them with business connections. He would be another one who wouldn't understand the odd relationship between her and Ben. Hell, she was getting more confused about it too.

"My parents were no one important, except to me. They died in a car accident, and my last living relative died a couple of years ago. I have no connections to anyone big. Just a simple, normal person." She watched as his eyes lit up, his smile widening.

"So, you're like me."

She looked at him as if he were crazy. Like him? How so? He looked up at her as he pulled a mannequin to the center of the room.

"I have no connections, and I wasn't born into money. I built all of this on my own. My mother died when I was born, and my father did the best he could, but could barely keep a roof over our heads. My mother's side disowned us, blaming my father for her death. My father never knew his real parents. He lived in a group home until he turned eighteen." A sad smile rested on his lips. "I remember how hard he worked and how badly he wanted more for me. He would come home with his hands raw from working so hard. He would tell me to study hard so that I wouldn't have to work a job that would destroy my body. He always encouraged me to work smarter and not harder, so I did. I wanted to take care of him one day. Now I do. His body still hurts, but I pay for the best of everything to take care of him. He lives with me, and I have staff available at all times to help take care of him." He cleared his throat and adjusted his cracking voice.

"Anyway, for me, hard work paid off. I don't take all of this for granted. I know what it's like to go without. I know what it's like to go to bed hungry. I remember barely eating because I wanted my father to eat. He wouldn't touch the food until I pretended to go to bed for the night. That's why when these women come in here crying about their 'problems', I get completely fed up. Problems ... they've never had a real problem. They cry that they must have a unique dress, because it would be embarrassing to show up wearing the same expensive dress as someone else." He then began to chuckle. "I guess I shouldn't poke fun at my customers too much. They are the ones who allow me to live a very comfortable life."

"That's amazing. I guess we have more in common than I thought." She caught his green eyes looking her over. His brows were knitted together, and it looked like he was concentrating.

"Jean, have we met before? There's something so familiar about you."

Her lips parted. He felt familiar too, like they had met before. This was her first thought when she first saw him. "Honestly, I don't remember, but when I first saw you, I felt like it wasn't our first meeting."

"Where did you go to school?"

"Westmont High." She watched as he shook his head.

"What about elementary school?"

"I actually lived somewhere else when my parents were alive. I went to Granters Elementary School.

"Gina," he whispered, his eyes widening in shock as he shook his head slowly. "Cute little Gina, who wore braided pigtails to school. Who left her table filled with kids to come and sit next to the dirty, no-named boy. You would take half of your food out of your lunchbox and give it to me. I wouldn't tell you my name, but you called me—"

"Red. Your hair was bright red then." She gasped as she looked at the man. She could see it now. This was the boy she called Red. It took her so long to coax him into talking to her. She asked her mom to pack her extra just for him. The last time she saw him was right before she lost her family. After that, she moved to live with her grandma. "I'm sorry I never got to say goodbye. After—after the accident, I never went back to school there."

"I'm glad I know what happened to you. I assumed you moved away, but we were all little kids. What happened wasn't talked about." He sighed. "You have no idea how much our lunches meant to me. You gave me faith and taught me that kindness still existed.

He grew quiet. They both did. It was unfathomable that fate had brought them together in this way. This time, he was the one sharing his lunch with her, so to speak.

"I want to introduce you to my dad soon. I used to talk about you all the time back then. I know he would love to meet you. I'm even more excited now to have you working with me. It's as if things have come full circle. I think you were sent to me for a reason." Link walked up to her and placed his hand on top of her head. "I want you to have a good life. I'm here for you, anytime. Seriously, day or night, if you need anything, you call me. If Ben makes you upset, then you come straight to me." He gently patted her head before pulling his hand away.

"I guess Link suits you better now than Red now." She giggled softly. "I'm happy things have changed so much for you. You really deserve it. I didn't understand much as a little kid. I just knew you weren't eating and that you were alone. You looked like you needed a friend."

"I did, more than you know. That was a dark time for me. Too dark to talk about today, but maybe another time." He then grabbed a stack of fabric and sat it down on the table. "Okay Gina—is it okay if I call you that?"

"Yeah, I don't mind." The smile on his face brightened before he turned back to the material.

"What I want you to do is pick your three favorites out of these."

"I'm not really qualified to—"

"I didn't ask if you were qualified. I said to pick out your three favorites. You don't need to be qualified for any of it. I've already hand-chosen the material. I just need you to choose between them. I think you can handle it." He winked at her as he stepped back to his work.

She bit her bottom lip as she ran her fingers over the fabric. The texture was smooth and light. As pretty as they were, she was afraid to even touch them. There was a beautiful silver fabric that caught her eye. The color practically shined in the light. Then there was a baby blue that looked like a bright summer day. Last, she picked a golden fabric that reminded her of the color of Ben's eyes. She smiled as she ran her fingers over it. Gold was becoming her favorite color.

"I choose these three."

"Perfect. See, you do have a good eye. Those three are the most expensive out of the bunch. Look at your inner diva shining through." He listened to her sweet laugh.

"There's nothing diva about me, but I do like the colors and fabric."

"Which one?"

"Hmm?"

"Which one do you want first?"

"I—" She shook her head, waving her hands. She could never afford such luxurious fabric.

"Ben asked me to make you several dresses. These are just the few we will start with. You don't tell Mr. Cross no, so you might as well give in."

"I have nothing to wear such fine material to."

Link chuckled. "Well, Ben must have something in mind. Which one first?" he asked again as he stopped what he was doing to wait for an answer.

"The gold one," she whispered, shifting on her feet nervously.

"How did you two meet?" Link asked, as he moved to gather the fabric from the table.

"We were on the same cancelled flight. With no rooms available, we ended up sharing the presidential suite. I couldn't afford it on my own, and he needed a room."

"Mmmm," he hummed as he moved about the room. "Ben's a good guy. He can get cranky, and he likes to pretend he doesn't need others. He's been hurt before, badly. I probably shouldn't say anything, but just in case he ever reacts weirdly to certain things, it's because he has reason to. Same with him keeping a wall up around me. Pain is a difficult storm to navigate through, but he'll find his way."

"Is whatever happened the reason he has trouble sleeping?"

He paused and turned to look at her curiously. "Possibly. At the very least, it made it worse. He started taking on extra tasks and built a barrier that made it impossible for anyone to reach him. Almost no one." He looked at her silver eyes, seeing the same little girl who changed his heart. He was afraid she had planned to tease him. There was no way such a beautiful little girl wanted to be his friend. She surprised him in the best of ways. She made that year less painful. In fact, lunch was the highlight of his day, because that meant he would see her. And now she was doing it again. She was helping a heart that she didn't know needed to be healed.

"Alright, come up here and hold your arms out." He grabbed a measuring tape. "This will only take a second." He moved around her swiftly, taking her measurements before looking up at her with a wry smile. "I see you still chew on your lip when you're nervous," he teased, standing up. "All set."

"I want to do a good job working for you. If I'm doing something wrong, tell me. And if I'm failing miserably, please let me know. I'm a hard worker."

"I'm sure you are. So, I heard your last boss mistreated you? Where did you work? And what happened, if you don't mind me asking?"

"I worked at the Hamen and Young Firm. Without getting into too much detail, they took advantage of my work ethic and overworked me. Ben quit the job for me, so he felt responsible and wanted to find me another one."

"Good job, Ben." Link nodded his head approvingly. "I'll be keeping a mental note of that place. I don't appreciate anyone mistreating someone like you."

"You don't know what type of person I am now. I might be entirely different." She smiled and listened as he chuckled, shaking his head.

"No, you aren't. I can feel the air around you. You're still a sweet soul." His bright white smile beamed at her. "Who still chews on her lip when she's nervous and blushes very easily." He then clapped his hands together and grabbed a notebook.

"These are the things I asked of my last assistant. I'm not asking you to know how to do all of this instantly, and it's fine if you need help. There are tutorials for the programs, so that you can catalog my work. Basically, some things I make on my own, and others are customized orders. The orders come in and we give them an estimate of when it can be completed. Then, the items I create on my own go up for auction to the highest bidder. It's a fairly simple process."

She smiled widely as she took the notebook. This was what she wanted—to have a real job and not just get paid to do nothing. "Thank you," she said, as she excitedly looked over the documents. "Is this the computer you use?"

"It sure is. Go ahead and start getting acquainted with it. If you have any questions, just ask."

She sat down at the desk in excitement as she saw the program Wink for cataloging. She was more than familiar with this system. It was her expertise, and the reason she was so invaluable at her last job. She created a login for herself using the credentials provided on the document and swiftly opened the file to see the pending clients.

For a moment, she stared in shock as the tiny scroll bar began to disappear. Her throat felt dry as she stared at the screen.

"Link, do you want me to call you Link, or would it be better to address you formally?"

"Absolutely call me Link. I'll be insulted otherwise," he said, strolling up to her. "What's up, Gina?" He leaned over her, pressing himself against her back as he peered at the screen.

"Umm, there are so many requests. How do you want them sorted? Do you have a system?"

"Yeah, it's called first come, first served. I don't play the name game. Just because you're Zeus doesn't mean your daughter gets a dress first. There's only one customer that comes ahead of the others—two now." He winked down at her and placed his hand over hers on the mouse. "Just move a couple at a time and then give them the estimates in the formula in this box. It's already there ... you just have to crunch in the numbers."

"I actually know this system well. I know how it all works. But I usually never have a queue this long." She watched as he straightened up and shrugged.

"They're just going to have to wait. I'm one person."

"Would you like for me to give them all estimated wait times? Judging from this list, some are several years from getting their item. Then I can add an accept or reject button. If they reject, they'll get moved out of the queue."

"That would be amazing. It's a lot of work, though. Are you sure?" He listened as she laughed.

"I'm here to work, Link. It might take me a couple of weeks, but it won't be any trouble. Then, once I'm finished, I'll set up an auto-response as the cases come in. Using the algorithm, they'll get an estimated wait time automatically and can choose if they want to wait. Hmm, you know what?" She chewed on her lip as she began typing away. "Why don't you do this? Whatever the product is, we can put in estimates of the cost. They will need to put a 10% deposit down to hold their place. That way no one is taking up a queue spot for no reason. We will make it non-refundable. If they change their minds, you'll at least get something out of it."

"See, I knew you were sent to me for a reason." He looked up and lifted his finger as he clicked his tongue. "Oh yeah, there's one more thing." He scurried over to the corner of the room, grabbing a purple dress that he was working on. "Can you try this on for me?"

She quirked her brow up and listened as he laughed. "I'm making this for a friend of mine. Steph, Ben's sister. You two are very similar in size, and I want to make sure it's perfect." He sifted his hands over the dress as he quietly murmured, "She deserves to only wear the best."

A knowing smile reached Jean's lips as she rose to her feet. "You really like her." He looked at her with wide eyes as she made the lock motion over her lips. "Your secret is safe with me."

"I mean she ... it's not like—" he stammered as she took the dress out of his hands.

"Where can I change?" Her lips were curled up as she dismissed his attempts at denial.

"In the corner over there is a changing curtain. Jean, it isn't—" he started, but she turned, walking away.

"Uh huh. I know." She was amazed at how comfortable she felt around Link already. As soon as they clarified the connection between them, her whole body felt at ease. Now it felt like working with an old friend instead of an in-demand artist. For once in the longest time, she felt excited about working. She needed to properly thank Ben. If it wasn't for him, she would still be at the law firm. But what did he like? What could she possibly get a billionaire?

Chapter 11

J ean looked at herself in the large oval mirror. It was hard to imagine that, with just a dress, she would look so different. Slowly, she stepped out from behind the changing curtain and carefully walked back to Link. She was terrified of ripping the dress or doing anything that could cause it to be less valuable.

Link's eyes were full of discernment, and he shook his head. "Just what I thought. It isn't ready." He moved closer and marked a spot on the dress near her thigh. "A slit here, I think." Then he moved to her neckline, tracing downward with his marker. "A bit lower here."

"We do want the dress to cover them, right?" Jean listened as he chuckled, shaking his head.

"Accentuating is the key. Just enough but not too much. I don't make you nervous doing this, do I?" Link asked, watching her shake her head. "Good."

"Can I ask you something?"

"Of course you can." Link straightened up and tapped his marker in his hand. "Shoot."

"What does Ben like? I want to get him something, but what do you get a billionaire?"

Link laughed. "Easy. Tie a bow around your neck and tell him to feast."

She sighed and chewed on her inner lip. Should she tell Link they weren't really dating? Maybe she shouldn't. She might feel comfortable around Link, but she didn't really know the adult version of him. Maybe she could just be partially honest?

"What's that look for?" Link studied her nervous actions as her gray eyes looked at the floor.

"Ben and I—well, we aren't at that point yet."

"What are you talking about? He said he would be seeing you tonight. He is sleeping over, right?"

"Well yeah, but only because he can fall asleep with me for some odd reason. We just sleep, as in real sleep." She watched as the creases above his forehead became more prominent and his lips formed a tight line.

"Why don't you make him something? Something he can't buy since it's unique. Why don't you go change and I'll help you?"

Her face lit up and she nodded her head. "Not too much help from you, or it would be like you made him something."

Link watched her until she disappeared behind the curtain. Something felt off about Jean and Ben's relationship. He wasn't sure what it was, but he would look after her. A deep-seated loyalty to her had taken root within him, a fierce sense of devotion that stemmed from their shared childhood experiences. He felt a debt and obligation to her, a promise he had made long ago and was determined to fulfill. In any case, Ben seemed to really treasure her, so he was probably worried over nothing.

He walked over to one of his shelves and began to scan its contents. "Think about what you'd like to make. You can use anything I have on this shelf. No charge."

"I have something in mind," Jean said, as she stepped out from behind the curtain.

"I'm meeting with them now, dad," Ben said as he walked up the sidewalk toward Lewis' business.

"I should be with you."

"Nonsense. I can handle this. I'm going to make several things very clear." He glanced up to see Lewis walking out of the building. The man's eyes widened in shock and immediately Ben could see that he was tense. "I'll call you back, dad."

"To what do we owe the pleasure of—"

"Cut the crap, Lewis. I've given my assistant a leave of absence. What else do you want? Keep in mind that I have not forgotten the things you said about my girlfriend. I hope I don't decide to hold it against your family personally. Sometimes I can be so petty."

"Your girlfriend? Come on, Ben ..." Lewis raised his brow, not believing him.

"I'd be very careful if I were you. You're insinuating that I shouldn't have her by my side. I'm warning you now ... you're stepping into dangerous territory."

"As a concerned relative, I'm worried that you really are serious. When we date people who don't come from money, we're opening ourselves up to be hurt. Unless it's someone we're just passing the time with. You know those people just use us for our money—"

"And you don't use me for my money?" Ben let out a dark laugh as his eyes narrowed on his sleazy cousin. "For your information, she isn't like that. She didn't even know who I was—" That was when Lewis began to laugh, shaking his head.

"Only the oldest trick of all. She didn't know who YOU were? Benjamin Cross, the face of Cross Industries. You're all over every magazine. You can be seen in the checkout line at the grocery store. Yet, she didn't know who you were? That's laughable, Ben. You aren't that gullible, right? Ben, she knew who you were. You see those children over there?" He nodded across the street. "Let's see if they know who you are."

"I don't need you to look out for me. Don't act like you really care about my personal affairs." Jean didn't know who he was. Lewis was just trying to plant doubts in his mind. He would be a fool to believe anything he said. "My personal business is just that, mine. Just know that I am serious about her. Any insult that you address to her will be the equivalent of insulting me. Consider yourself warned. Call your parents off or I'm going to take what you said about my girlfriend personally."

"My parents are just upset that I was treated with violence at your company."

"How would your parents like not having a company?" Ben shot his cousin a dark glance through gritted teeth.

"You would do that to family?"

Ben scoffed. "Family? Lewis, I don't ever meet with that grandfather, do I? My mother's side has drawn a line. We don't speak to any of them. YOU are the only exception we make. Careful, or you won't be the exception anymore."

"That's Mr. Cross!"

"Oh my gosh, it IS Mr. Cross!"

They could hear the children cheering in excitement. An almost smug grin rested on Lewis' face as he raised his brow, the 'I told you so' written all over his face. For a second, dread began to swim inside of him. What if it had all been a setup? What if she knew about his insomnia and found a scent to make him sleep, or was slipping something in his drink? Okay, there was no way his food was laced. And she was intoxicated at the restaurant, so there was no way she was able to do anything then. He felt livid and disappointed with himself for even allowing those thoughts to invade his mind. He quickly dismissed them, glaring at Lewis.

Suddenly, Lewis' eyes widened as he looked passed Ben. His bottom lip began to quiver, glancing back at Ben nervously.

"G-grandpa, I wasn't expecting to see you today," Lewis stammered.

Ben turned his head to see an old man stop next to him. He poked at Lewis with his wooden cane as his lips curled into almost a snarl.

"Mr. Croftman, you dunce head! I don't care if you call my wife grandma, but I am Mr. Croftman to you. Heaven knows your filth isn't of my own bloodline."

"S-s-sorry." Lewis was almost cowering his head, looking at the ground.

"My wife sent me down to see you because you need a loan for this new project you came up with. I'm better off catching the money on fire than expecting a return from you. Stupid mother, moronic father, such a waste. It's a shame that your family is a waste of oxygen." The old man's eyes finally looked to the side, noticing Ben. "Why are you still standing there?"

"I was here first, Mr. Croftman. You're the one interrupting me. Is there a nursing home I can call to let them know you've escaped?"

The old man's face twisted in anger. So, this was his grandfather. His mother's biological father. He didn't know much about him except that he was a cruel man who treated his mother poorly. Seems like he treated others poorly as well.

"Wait a minute ..." Mr. Croftman squinted at Ben. "I know who you are. Your father cost me. He stole your mother from me. You look like your mother, but you have my eyes. That's how I can clearly see my bloodline in you. Strong genetics. You're managing that big business all on your own now. That's because you have my brains. Damn fool of a daughter, but it's your father I blame." He pounded his cane on the ground, making a loud, cracking noise. "Look at you, making money instead of asking to borrow it." He gave Lewis a disappointed glance.

"I don't want to borrow your money, grandpa."

Mr. Croftman's arm launched forward with the precision of a bowstring, releasing an angry brown streak that collided with Lewis' face like a lightning bolt. The impact shook his bones, sending a jolt of pain through his body as he felt the warm trickle of blood running from his lip.

A red welt began to rise over his cheekbone as he stared at Mr. Croftman in shock.

"Don't call me grandpa! Maybe this time you'll remember."

Ben was not a fan of Lewis right now. However, this was completely uncalled for. Mr. Croftman was no longer the power he once was. Sure, he had money, but his influences had diminished, while the Cross family had risen all the way to the top. They were the number one business in the area, and everyone wanted to be in their favor. The saying was, 'You don't cross the Cross family'.

"Careful, Mr. Croftman. While abuse may be a part of your typical everyday lifestyle, it isn't part of mine. If I ever see you lift that cane at someone, I promise you, you will be living in a nursing home. I have many doctors who would sign you away without questioning me. I'd put you someplace special, where they bind your hands because you've lost your mind and you can't have metal forks, because it's dangerous."

"Ben, it's okay—" Lewis began, but Mr. Croftman waved him to silence.

"You would do that to your own flesh and blood? Your grandfather?"

"You are not my grandfather. I don't care what goes on between the two of you in private, but I won't tolerate such aggressive acts again. Otherwise, you will regret it."

"Well look at this," Mr. Croftman sneered. "Barely out of diapers and you think you're ready for a boxing match. Quite the hypocrite, aren't you? Yeah, I heard about the incident today at your company. It's okay for YOUR man to hit Lewis, who is a complete stranger, but not his own family. Who do you think you are? You are no one without your parents. They set you up real nice. Even your company would survive without you. The company works on its own, so anyone could be a proxy CEO for it now. You are weak where it counts. You don't know how to strike your enemies down. Your father, now he was cutthroat. He knew how to run a business. But you—"

"ELLIOT!"

A loud voice cracked like thunder. Ben recognized the voice of his father. His feet pounded on the ground as he made aggressive strides toward them. Mr. Croftman's expression changed abruptly from confidence to terror as fear quickly pierced through him, covering his features.

"Don't you dare speak to my son. I will attack without mercy if you do anything to him."

"Just a casual conversation with the grandson you never bring to visit. How is my daughter? She never calls to see how I'm doing."

"You had your chance. They aren't your family anymore. They are MY family, and they will have nothing to do with you. Consider yourself warned." He put his hand on Ben's shoulder, patting it as he pulled him along. He stopped and glared at Mr. Croftman. "A lot has changed over the years, but I still don't give second chances. For your own safety, it would be best for you to walk in the other direction if you see my family. Otherwise, who knows what will happen." The words were like sharp blades, slicing through the air with a cold precision that made Elliot instinctively back away. He understood perfectly what those words meant: they spelled danger, death, and destruction.

Ben followed his father quietly as they left without another word. When Ben began walking toward his car, his father said, "Leave it. Cid will drive it home." He nodded to another man and Ben reluctantly handed him the keys.

"Get in," his father said, motioning to another car as he got in the driver's seat. As soon as Ben closed the door, his father asked, "What happened?"

Ben explained the whole scene, up until his father showed up.

"The old bastard." His father gritted his teeth as he sped off toward their house. "Ben, I need you to leave for a few days. There is work overseas, and I want you to see to it personally."

"Dad, I'm not a child. I know when I'm being sent away." Ben huffed, folding his arms over his chest.

"I want this situation to cool off for a few days. Let our team do their job to make sure this doesn't get blown out of proportion. There were people outside, Ben! Damage control has already started. We're going to have to pay out silence money to keep this all under wraps. I want you away from the reporters during this time. When you come back, it will all be handled," his father said, leaving no room for argument.

"But what about Jean?" Ben suddenly asked. His father gave him a quick glance.

"You can manage a few days without her. You always have before. Just take your meds with you. Look, I know your mom is over the moon, swooning over the idea of future grandchildren, but let's level a bit between us. You haven't known her for long. You're a child used to getting what he wants, who lives a comfortable lifestyle. With the insomnia, things have been rough. Then pops in this mystery woman. She's beautiful, nice, and you're able to get proper rest around her. This makes you feel good. It's THIS feeling that you're associating with this woman, not the woman herself." He sighed as he signaled to turn. "I'm all for you finding happiness. Just maybe slow down and find out what's real. Take time to learn about people. Perhaps, had you taken the time to learn about your last girlfriend—"

"I know, dad," Ben whispered, feeling the sting of his father's words in his chest. He was blind then. He could rationalize that. While he hated to admit it, his dad was right about Jean too. What did he know of her? He was doing the same thing, rushing in blindly, trying to hold onto her so he didn't lose her. This wasn't fair to either of them. He needed to slow down and think about this. It wouldn't be fair to him or Jean if he started something too quickly. If he was really interested in her, then he needed to get to know her properly. "When do I leave?"

"Tonight."

Chapter 12

"That's looking good, Gina. You could put me out of business," Link teased as she shot him a wry smile.

"I stabbed myself six times already." She held up the fabric. "You would have been done with it already. I'm going to need a couple more days."

"Gina, what's important is the detail you're putting into it. Doesn't matter how long it takes. I'd be proud to wear that." He watched as her cheeks flamed slightly. "What are you planning for dinner tonight? You going out, or are you going to cook something?"

"I was thinking of making stuffed shells and garlic bread. The first time I tried to cook for Ben, I got sidetracked and burned the food. I made him a wrap today that he loved, though."

"I love stuffed shells. Bring me any leftovers!" he said, waving his finger at her. "Well, we can pack it up for the day. Come on, I'll walk you out."

"Really? We're done already? I was used to having to stay all hours at my last job."

"For the most part, we have a relaxed schedule. I like to go home and spend my evenings with my dad before he falls asleep. Tomorrow, why don't you plan to come home with me after work? You can have dinner at my house. I want my dad to meet you. We can invite Ben too."

"I'll bring it up with him. Thank you," Jean said, though she wondered if Ben would want to. Thinking of him made her excited about this evening, for reasons she didn't care to explain. She really didn't care. She just knew she wanted to see him. Her heart was also pounding as she anticipated the punishments she would receive from him.

When they stepped out of the building, Clint was there, waiting for her by the car. Link leaned in and gave her a quick hug. "I'm thrilled to have you with me. Have a good evening, and I'll see you tomorrow morning."

"Thank you, Link. I'll do my best not to disappoint." She listened to his warm, rich laughter as he patted the top of her head.

"Like that could happen. Drive safe with her," Link said, nodding toward Clint.

"Well, so much for drag racing," Clint murmured slyly as he opened the backseat for Jean.

"I told you ... I'm not sitting in the backseat." She walked past him and got in the passenger seat. Clint laughed, shaking his head as he walked around. He waved to Link before getting into the vehicle and driving away.

Link watched the car until it disappeared from his sight, and then turned to walk back into the building. As he arrived in his private studio, he heard a soft murmur from inside. Who was in there? He stepped inside, seeing long, rich brown hair and was met with serene blue sapphire eyes. His smile broadened as he pulled her in for a hug.

"Steph! What are you doing here?"

"I decided to pop in and annoy you a little."

"Uh-huh, you mean you came to get a sneak peek of your dress."

"Pretty please."

"No."

"Liiiiinnnnk," she whined as he chuckled at her.

"Not until it's perfect," he said, tapping her on the nose. She batted her eyelashes and stuck out her delicious-looking bottom lip. "Not going to work on me, princess. I want to show you my vision and for you to fall in love at first sight. You can't do that with an unfinished product."

"Fiiiine," she sighed as she looked at one of the worktables. "Oh?! What is this? Who are you making this for?"

"I'm not. Gina is making that for Ben."

"Gina? I thought Ben called her Jean." Steph watched as Link nodded his head.

"Her name is Regina. She goes by Jean mainly. I actually knew her when we were little kids. She was kind to me. I always called her Gina."

Her mouth gaped open as she tapped on his arm. "Wow, you knew her as a child? What a small world! Tell me about her."

"Back then, she was like an angel that was sent to me. You know about my past. Remember the little girl I told you about?" He watched as Stephanie nodded. "That was her. She's the one who saved me back then."

"Oh, my gosh! That's her? She's the reason you didn't kill yourself?!"

"I haven't told her that part. I don't know if I'll ever mention it. It's a bit heavy."

"So, Ben really did find an angel!" Steph clapped her hands together happily.

"I always thought she was one, especially since she vanished like that, without a trace. Here I find out her parents were killed in an accident. Her only living relative died a couple of years ago. She doesn't have anyone. So, I'm going to be there for her now. Strange, isn't it? How this came full circle, and now I'm able to help her." Link leaned on his desk with a faint smile on his lips.

"Ben better keep this one. I like her already and I haven't even met her." She sat on the desk next to Link, her shoulder resting on his side. There was a comfortable silence between them. She leaned against him, basking in his warmth as she breathed in his familiar scent. It was hard to believe how close they had become. When he was just nineteen, her mother saw his art at an exhibition. She saw the raw talent, and her parents invested in him. They took him under their wing and introduced him to the proper connections. Her parents even paid for his schooling as part of their investment. They all naturally became close friends.

Link and Ben were almost inseparable until a few years ago. That was when Ben put up a wall to keep his distance from others, and when he started to act like Link annoyed him, pushing him away.

Maybe Gina would help him lower his walls. It was too soon to tell, but she could only hope. Her brother became so serious and dove into his work, having to be hospitalized several times because his insomnia was out of control. They even had to put him in an induced coma for him to rest because none of the medications he took were strong enough. They were all worried sick about him. It wasn't so much his ex-girlfriend Melissa's betrayal as it was his best friend's. That one cut him so deep, because he had trusted him. After that, his trust was shattered. She would give anything to have the old, carefree Ben back.

"Why don't you come to my house tomorrow night for dinner? I invited Gina and Ben too. I want to introduce my father to her."

"You know better than that, Link. Better invite my mom and dad too if you want Ben to be there."

"Actually, that's a great idea. I'll text your mom and invite them as well."

Steph rested her head against Link's shoulder, lost in her own thoughts. Friendship with him was easy and comfortable, but she couldn't help the longing that stirred within her every time she looked into his mesmerizing green eyes.

Inwardly, she wanted to scream. Why wouldn't he ask her out? Was he afraid of ruining their friendship, like so many others did when they took the leap into something more? Despite the risk, Steph knew in her heart that their relationship could be something beautiful and meaningful, but perhaps he didn't see it that way. Maybe he was interested in someone else. After all, women openly adored him for his charm and good looks.

But it wasn't just his physical appearance that drew them in. He had an infectious personality, one that could light up a room and make anyone feel at ease. Not to mention his financial stability, although that aspect didn't matter to Steph since she was successful in her own right. She had invested in a cosmetics company that had taken off, and now she could spend her days enjoying life instead of being cooped up in an office.

But despite all this, maybe Link wanted someone different from her, someone less independent or opinionated. Someone who wouldn't challenge him or take control of situations like she often did. It wouldn't be the first time her strong-willed nature scared someone away.

For two years, Steph had tried everything to get Link to take their relationship to the next level. She even went as far as inviting him on romantic dinner and movie dates, hoping he would finally see her as more than just a friend. But each time, he came as just that, a friend—never crossing that line despite all the hints she dropped.

All she wanted was for him to sweep her off her feet and tell her he loved her. At first, she hadn't been this desperate, but since the unanswered feelings and silent rejections continued, the pain was becoming too much to bear. He didn't want to hurt her by telling her he didn't reciprocate her feelings. He cared about her enough not to lead her on, but surely he must know how she felt by now. At some point, Steph had believed that he felt the same way, but now she wasn't so sure.

Link listened as her breathing evened out. He glanced at his shoulder to see she had dozed off. How did she fall asleep while leaning on a desk? He moved his arm around her shoulders so that he could support her better. He took the moment to admire her beauty. Her smooth complexion was like a work of art.

He wasn't sure when he first fell in love with her. Was it immediately? Or did it develop over time? For the longest time, she was the only person etched in his heart. Years ago, he had gathered up the courage to ask her out. He had been ready to risk everything because she was everything he had ever wanted and more.

The evening arrived, and he showed up at the house to surprise her, only she had gone out for the day. He ended up going for a drive with Ben. They were going to surprise his best friend and have a guy's day. They snuck into his house to scare him, and that was when they walked in on Melissa and Alvin, his naked body pounding into her. That day, Ben changed. Everything changed.

He couldn't bring himself to ask Steph out anymore, not when Ben was in so much pain. It never felt like the right time after that. Ben pushed him away and started small fights to create division between them. He pretended that he found him annoying and made sure everyone knew it. Link knew Ben was hurting, so he had decided to wait for Ben to find happiness again. It just didn't feel right to date Steph, with Ben being distant.

When he heard that Ben had found someone, he was extra happy. Not just for Ben, but because he could finally profess his love for Steph. He moved his head down to her, brushing his lips over her forehead. The moment he did, her eyes fluttered open. Her blue sapphires flipped up, meeting with his emeralds. The two gems stayed locked on each other, neither one moving.

"I love you, Steph. I've loved you for years. I've been waiting because of what happened to Ben, but I can't wait another minute longer. I feel like I'll die if—" He didn't get to finish. Her lips crashed into his as she grasped his cheeks with her hands. Forceful as always, just the way he loved her.

"You've made me wait so long." Tears trickled down her cheeks as she hiccuped quietly. "I was afraid you didn't want me. I know I can—"

"How could I not want you? You're all I dream about. I love everything about you. I'm sorry for making you wait, but with Ben ... it just never felt right after what happened. I'm with you all the time. I've followed you everywhere, even on your shopping sprees. How did you not know?"

"You could have told me." She sniffed as he peppered her face with soft kisses, wiping the tears from her.

"Looking back on it now, I should have. We could have stayed secret. That could have been fun and special."

Steph's phone began ringing, spoiling the mood. She turned, grabbing her phone, seeing her mother's name.

"Hello?"

"Steph, there's been an incident. You need to come home."

"Is everything okay?"

"Yes, but we're sending Ben overseas for a few days."

"What?!" She jumped to her feet. "What happened? You can't do that. He's finally doing better. You're going to set him off. Where's dad?!"

"Honey, this was your father's call."

"Not without a fight from me it isn't!" Steph grabbed her purse angrily as Link followed behind her anxiously.

"You won't be able to change his mind. He won't even listen to me over it."

"But mom—"

"I know. I'll explain everything when you get home. It's only for a few days. He'll be fine. Drive safe."

"I will. Love you, bye." Steph hung up and turned to look at Link.

"Something happened. They're sending Ben overseas for a few days." He wrapped his arms around her, bringing her close to his chest.

"It's going to be okay, Steph. This probably has something to do with the Lewis situation from earlier today."

"What happened?"

"Come on. I'll drive you and explain on the way."

"Link …" she said, pursing her lips. He winked at her with a soft chuckle.

"We won't say anything for now. We can still play secret lovers, after all."

"Oh, secret lovers, that sounds promising." Her voice was sultry as she traced her finger over his arm.

"It is a promise." He kissed her forehead softly before running his hand down to interlace with hers. "I'm glad I told you before the phone call. I really couldn't take waiting another minute."

She walked briskly beside him and nodded her head. She couldn't enjoy the moment. Her brother was about to go overseas, just when he was finally sleeping again. Her brother might put up a tough exterior, but he was delicate. Things set him off balance and it was hard for him to recover. Her father never understood this about him. Ben took after her mother with his emotions while she took after her father. Still, her brother was a better business executive than she was. She wanted nothing to do with the family company and instead sought her own empire.

Ben was smart and a great leader, but it wasn't until he was betrayed that she really saw her brother on a deeper level. Yesterday she finally saw a glimpse of the old Ben again. She was so happy. *Please, don't let this change the progress he was making. Please.*

Jean was baking her stuffed shells when she received a text message from Ben.

I won't be coming by tonight. I need to go out of town for business for a few days.

She replied to him, telling him to be safe and not to forget his sleeping pills. With a sigh, she glanced back at the oven. It looked like she was bringing Link some stuffed shells for lunch tomorrow after all.

That night, a wave of disappointment washed over her as she climbed into bed. It was silly. She barely knew him, so why did she feel like she missed him? This would be the first night since she met him that she would sleep alone. She wasn't sure why, but she felt anxious about it. She had slept so soundly next to him. Closing her eyes, her thoughts focused on him. She wondered if he was able to sleep and if everything was okay.

Little did she know that her night would be anything but restful. That night, the nightmares returned with a vengeance.

Chapter 13

Jean checked her phone once more, letting out a disappointed sigh when she saw no new messages. She grabbed the two containers of stuffed shells and headed out of her apartment. She had gotten little sleep. Every time she closed her eyes, the nightmares returned. She had never seen a therapist over what happened, even though she probably should have. It was something that would have traumatized an adult, let alone a child.

She didn't like to talk about the details of that day. Who would? Yes, she was in the car when her parents died, but there was more, details that she'd never mentioned. The truth was, she was stuck in the car with her dead parents for eight hours. Hours of terror and pain, trapped in the dark. Even now, the dark bothered her. She always had a small light on.

It was supposed to be a fun night out with her parents. They were going to dinner and a movie. She remembered laughing and singing, up until the moment of the accident. A tractor-trailer suddenly charged into their lane. The trailer tipped over, landing on the front of the vehicle, burying it under its heavy contents.

Somehow, her mother's phone had landed in her lap. Flipping on the flashlight, she screamed for her parents. Their bloodied faces and bodies never moved. The battery died on the phone after an hour. The next several hours were spent in a suffocating darkness, with the harrowing image of her deceased parents haunting her every moment. Their faces, frozen in shock and pain, seemed to etch themselves deeper into her mind with each passing minute.

Jean swatted a tear away as she saw Clint pulling up. It still amazed her that she never had issues riding in vehicles, despite what she had been through.

"Hey, I would have come to the door!" Clint objected as she slid into the passenger seat.

"You're my friend picking me up. This is more appropriate," she said, handing him one of the containers. "I made a ton last night. Since it was just me, I have way too much."

"You're the best!" Clint beamed as he lifted it up to his nose. "Is it lunch time yet?" He listened to her laugh as he drove away. "I wonder how Ben's doing." He glanced at her. "Have you heard from him?"

"Not since yesterday when he texted that he wouldn't be over," Jean replied quietly, looking out the window. She wasn't sure why she expected him to message her again, but she did. They weren't in a relationship, so why would he? Yet, like a fool, she kept checking her phone in case she missed the alert from him. She has thought about texting him, asking how he slept, but decided against it. What were they to one another? Were they even close enough to ask how the other was doing?

"You're a quiet one this morning," Clint hummed. "You spaced out the entire way here."

Her eyes blinked as she scanned the area. She had been in her own mental world and didn't even realize they had pulled up to her work.

"I'm sorry, Clint. I'm not fully functioning today." She yawned as if to emphasize her point.

"I'm just teasing you." He glanced out to the side. "Looks like Link is waiting to greet you."

She opened the door to see Link approaching the car with a big smile. "Gina!"

"You're really chipper today." She looked at his bright green eyes that seemed to shine with happiness.

"What's not to be happy about? It's a beautiful day!" He flashed her his pearly whites.

"Here you go." She handed him the other container of stuffed shells before turning to Clint. "Thank you for the ride."

"Call me when you're done, and I'll take you home."

"Not today, Clint. I'm taking her to my house after work. I already told my father, and he's excited that we're having company." He noticed Clint's strange expression, and he quickly added, "Steph and her parents are coming as well, so no need to worry." He winked at him as he placed his hand on Jean's shoulder.

"Alright, well, I'll see you tomorrow morning, Jean." Clint waved before speeding off.

"Ben's family is coming?" Jean asked nervously as Link pulled her along.

"Yes, they're good friends of the family, and Steph insisted on them coming." He held up the container, eyeing it greedily. "Ben's loss is my gain." He chuckled.

They stepped into Link's studio just as a beautiful woman was stepping out. She almost collided with them.

"Steph!" Link grinned as he greedily looked her over. He quickly regained his composure and pulled Jean forward. "This is Gina."

The woman clapped her hands together, then reached out and grabbed Jean's. "Look at your eyes! So beautiful. Oh my gosh, you're so beautiful," she chirped, pulling Jean into the studio.

Link chuckled as his eyes followed Steph with adoration. This was one thing he loved about her. Her enthusiasm and warmth. Though he really loved everything about her.

When they arrived back at the house last night, Steph had a big argument with her father. It was Ben who shut it down. He told her everything was fine and that it was for the best. He had seen a glimmer of the old Ben back at his studio, but seeing him last night, it was like he had reverted to the recent, cold Ben.

Link and Steph had discussed it, and they decided they would wait to announce their relationship. For now, they would keep it something private and special for the two of them, at least until Ben returned.

"Ben had a horrible night. I knew he would. His sleeping pills didn't work at all. He shouldn't have left," Steph huffed out angrily as she scooted a chair next to Jean. "Of course, I'm sure he told you about it."

"I haven't heard from him since he left yesterday," she whispered as she logged onto the computer.

"He's a workaholic. That's what you need to work on with him. Balancing his home and work life. Oh, speak of the devil." Steph grabbed her phone, rising to her feet.

"It's about time you called me back. None of your excuses. I called you an hour ago. I know. That is not a reason. Who's more important? Me or that contract? Exactly, so remember that the next time I call." She paced around the room as she talked with him. "You need to rest, Ben. I should have gone with you. Who's going to make sure you take care of yourself? Oh! I'm at the studio, do you want to talk to—" Steph knitted her brows together and walked toward the door. "Why not? I don't understand. Yeah, I know you have work to do. Watch your tone, Ben, or instead of me greeting you with a hug it will be my fist! Fine. Love you too. Call me tonight. Bye."

She glanced up at Link nervously before turning to look at Jean, who was already typing away.

"He didn't want to talk to her?" Link mouthed silently. She shook her head and put on a fake smile.

"He's so busy over there. I'm sure he'll call you when he has time." Steph slid into the seat next to Jean. "Gina, you have the most beautiful eyes. I have a new product line coming out and I'd like to test it on you. Would that be okay?"

"If you think I could be of help," Jean answered politely as Steph's face brightened.

"Perfect! Well, I have to run, but I'll see you tonight, Gina. We're going to be the best of friends. Hey, let's have a sleepover this weekend! We'll eat junk food and watch chick flicks. It'll be great! Yay, I'm already excited. See you tonight!" She practically bounced to the door. She stepped out, moving to the side so that Link could see her, but Jean couldn't. Before vanishing from sight, she mouthed 'I love you'.

Link stared at the empty doorway with a goofy smile on his face that quickly faded when he looked at Jean. He wondered how she was doing with Ben being gone. Now that he was paying attention, her face looked tired, and her eyes were puffy as if she had been crying. He walked over, taking a seat in the chair Steph had pulled up.

"How are you doing?" Link asked, leaning on his elbow, glancing at her.

"I'm fine." She gave him a small smile. "Honestly, Link, I'm okay." She could tell by the look in his eyes that he didn't believe her.

"I'm sure he'll call you later."

"Link, I'm under no grand illusions."

"What do you mean?"

She stopped what she was doing to turn and look at him. The truth was that it hurt. Ben used her as a pillow, but until now he had never treated her as just an accessory. She really was only a sleep aid for him. That didn't work for her. The possibility of friendship lingered like a bittersweet dream, taunting her with what could have been. But reality was harsh and unforgiving, leaving her feeling abandoned and discarded like a broken toy. She longed for a glimmer of hope, but all she saw was the cold truth staring back at her. No matter how much she lied to herself, hearing that he didn't want to talk to her pricked at her heart. It told her exactly how he felt.

"Link ..." she whispered, lifting her hands in a shrugging motion. "It's nothing."

Link watched as she returned her attention to the computer and began typing away. He didn't know what to do. Ben wasn't one to toy with someone's emotions. Well, he never used to be. He would talk to Steph about this later. He thought there was something weird about their relationship yesterday. Today, it was like they didn't have one. Yet, the look in Ben's eyes before he left yesterday told him there was something there. For a moment, his friend had acted like himself again.

"Mr. Minno." They heard a slight knock at the door. "This arrived for you."

He glanced at Jean before going to the door. The woman held a big envelope with contents he had asked for last night. "Thank you." He opened the envelope slightly and then turned to Jean. "I'm stepping out for a few. I'll be back shortly."

Link sat on a bench under a shaded tree as he took out the documents. He had asked for information about the death of Jean's parents. He wanted to get her something for their memorial date. He wasn't expecting these news articles and clippings that had also been sent. The headlines read: "Child Trapped in Vehicle with Dead Parents for Hours". The moment he caught sight of the headline, he knew he needed to read the papers somewhere far from Jean's view.

His eyes watered as he read through the documents and news articles. The vehicle had been covered in debris and complete darkness. He winced when he saw the picture of the vehicle. He couldn't imagine how she even survived.

He immediately took out his phone and took pictures of the clippings. Without hesitating, he sent them to Ben. He asked him if he knew about the extent of the accident. He leaned his head back and stared up at the sun for a moment before walking back inside.

She was pounding away at the keyboard when he walked back into the room. She glanced up at him and smiled, welcoming him back. Her bright eyes and smile never revealed or hinted at the trauma she had endured. It had been years ago, but something like that must still haunt her. He knew his past still haunted him.

"Let's have lunch," he blurted as he grabbed his stuffed shells.

"It's only half past ten." She giggled with a sweet smile.

"We will take two lunches today."

"You take two lunches. I'll have a coffee break."

"Close enough!" He beamed as he snapped the lid open to smell the heavenly aroma. Something came over him, and he wanted to fill her life with as much happiness as he could. She didn't have any family left. He read in the paper that she was the last surviving in her grandmother's obituary. If she didn't have family, then he would be her family. Who knows? Maybe someday they would be family for real.

Ben glanced down at the text, sighing when he saw Link's name. He rubbed the bridge of his nose as he opened it. His eyes instantly fell to the images and the big, bold headlines. His stomach lurched violently, like a rollercoaster plunging down a steep drop.

His finger hovered over the picture of the vehicle for a moment before it curled into a tight ball. He wanted to hear her voice so badly, and even more now. He was desperate to know she was okay. After learning about her trauma, he couldn't help but feel that his issues were small and insignificant in comparison to her suffering. A part of him also felt guilty for even thinking about his own pain in the face of what she had endured.

Last night was hell without her. He had to fight the urge to call her several times. He was afraid. His father made him question his attraction to Jean, and it scared him. He didn't want to use her. Did he only feel this desire because she gave him relief? When he was around her, he felt like a different person. The person he used to be. He could sleep when he was with her. Was this the reason he had these feelings? He needed to figure it out, but this crushing weight on his chest was destroying him. He tried to stop himself from reaching out to her, but his fingers moved on their own.

I slept like hell. How did you sleep?

It was only a moment later when his phone trilled with her reply.

Like hell. The nightmares were bad last night. Today is a coffee day. Try not to overexert yourself.

P.S. I gave Clint and Link the leftover shells and cheese :-P

Instantly, he felt a sense of relief for a brief moment, until he read the part about her nightmares again. It brought his mind back to the images of the car accident. No wonder she had nightmares. He closed his eyes and leaned his head back.

From the moment he saw Jean, he thought she was attractive. Then, when he was able to fall asleep next to her, he was intrigued. Were all these feelings swimming inside of him because he was able to sleep? He wanted to refute it loudly, but his father had planted the seeds of doubt in his mind. He didn't want to rush in blindly, but at the same time, something inside of him demanded him to, as if she was a gravitational force pulling him. He couldn't get her out of his head.

His father told him to take things slow and get to know her. It was sound advice, if he could do it. He wasn't sure if he could be just friends with Jean, and this left him confused. Why? His heart raced as he demanded more, his breaths coming in shallow gasps. Why was he relentlessly demanding more so quickly? Was it just a side effect of the insomnia, or was it something deeper, something that threatened to consume him entirely in its fiery grip?

Ben wasn't a gentle wind coming softly to sweep her off her feet. His emotions were a storm, coming and claiming what he wanted, swiftly and loudly. He wanted Jean. Damn, he wanted her. Now he had to figure out why before the storm threatened to consume them both.

They had both had enough pain in their lifetimes. They didn't need to add any more. If this feeling was real, if this really was the new buds of love, he would hold on to her, never letting go. He would fight for her with everything he had.

He leaned over, groaning as he rested his head in his hands. Love. The word just slipped into his thoughts. Maybe his father was right, and he just wanted to possess her. It was too early for such intense feelings, right? Right? Damn, he couldn't think. Trying to think logically without any rest was futile.

"Sir, they're waiting."

He nodded, pushing himself to his feet. He would have to think about Jean more later. Right now, he had work to do.

Chapter 14

Jean chewed on her lip nervously as she glanced up at the mansion in front of her. Link had taken her to his house after work, ignoring her protests about it. She felt awkward knowing Ben's family was going to be there too. She wasn't really dating Ben and they thought she was.

Link laughed as he pulled her out of the car. "Come on, Gina. Don't be so nervous."

"I feel like I need to be sprayed down before I step inside." She laughed nervously.

"Gina, it's me, Red, remember? I'm just like you." He nodded his head toward his home. "It's just a house. Inside I wear sweatpants and tank tops. I lounge and get chip crumbs on my chest. I get milk moustaches and pepper in my teeth. I've surfed down the stairs and played floor hockey on the tile. Maybe soon we can play hide and seek in there. I've just never had enough players." He laughed as he patted her on the head. "Think of yourself as family, Gina, because that's how I think of you. My silver-eyed sister."

Her feet refused to move as she looked up at him. Her eyes were trying to discern the look on his face.

"I'm serious, Gina. It's just me and my dad. We can use another family member. So, from now on, holidays are at my house. Birthdays, major and minor events, or just because. It'll be fun."

"It's not that I don't appreciate it, but things tend to change over time. This isn't the first time I was made an honorary family member. It seems to sour once the novelty wears off. I'm not a worn pair of shoes. I'm a person, and it hurts to be discarded."

His hand landed on her shoulder roughly as he bent down to look at her. He kept his head at her eye level as he shook his head firmly.

"Gina, I don't know about these other people and their shallow promises. However, when I say this, I mean forever. I don't mean just for a few months or a year." He could see her confused face and his eyes softened. She didn't know how important she was to him, so of course this seemed weird. "Gina, you would be doing me a favor. Please?" He finally decided to go for the guilt trip. He would just have to prove how serious he was. This was the first step he would take so that he could always watch out for her. She no longer had no one. She had him.

"If you ever change your mind, just tell me."

"Never going to happen, and you aren't allowed to change your mind. Consider yourself caught in my family web. Come on, I want to introduce you to my dad." Link rested his arm around her shoulder, escorting her into his house. "Dad!"

Jean's eyes instantly landed on the colorful artwork that covered the walls. There was a unique banister as well. It was smooth black but was over a foot wide. "That's interesting," she said as Link flashed her a white smile.

"That's custom made, special for sliding down it. Wanna try?"

"No thanks." She quickly shook her head listening to his warm chuckle.

"Oh, you will. Maybe next time." He winked at her as he tugged her down the long hallway. "Dad's probably in the sunroom. He enjoys watching the birds. Is dad in the sunroom?" he asked, looking at people who were standing near the stairs.

Jean noticed how strangely the people looked at her as they answered him. It was as if they saw a ghost as he dragged her along.

"Those are some of my housekeepers. They do the cooking, cleaning and take care of my dad. They aren't used to seeing many people here. The only guests we have are the Crosses."

He answered the question Jean had in her head. They approached a tall, dark wooden door, and Link pushed it open excitedly. "Dad, I have Gina with me."

Her eyes landed on a man sitting in a wheelchair with a white sweater-like blanket over his lap. He turned to look at her, a kind smile reaching his lips. "So ... this is Gina." The man's voice sounded tired and raspy, as if he struggled to breathe.

Jean walked up to the man and knelt down in front of him. "It's nice to meet you." She reached her hand out, and his callused hand covered hers.

"Call me Bob, please. I'm so happy to finally meet you. You were all my son used to talk about when he was young. You do have beautiful silver eyes, just like he said."

"Dad." Link chuckled as he took a seat on the couch next to him. "Now that I've found her, I've claimed her as my sister. That way we won't ever lose her again."

"Good. She should move in with us. It's much too quiet here."

"I'm fine with that." Link tilted his head with a grin.

"Oh, that's really nice, but I have a place of my own." Jean stood up and took a small step back.

"Nonsense, there's plenty of room here," Link's dad said as Jean shook her head.

"I appreciate it, but really … I enjoy my place."

"It's alright, dad. Besides, if things keep up with her and Ben, she wouldn't have lived here long anyway." He grabbed his phone and rose to his feet. "The Crosses are here." He grabbed the handles on his dad's chair, slowly pushing him out of the room.

Jean followed behind them with a small smile. She could see how much Link loved his father. It made her nervous to see how frail he looked. He reminded her of her grandmother before she passed away. It made her think about her death and, inevitably, her parents.

"Welcome!" Link said loudly, bringing her back from the past. She glanced up to see Steph bouncing toward her. Behind her was Ben's mom, who she met at the airport, and then a man who Link and his father were talking to. The man's hair was raven black, like the feathers of a bird, and it fell in soft waves around his face. His piercing blue eyes seemed to sparkle with intelligence and a hint of mischief. When he spoke, his voice was a gentle yet firm baritone that filled the room and commanded attention. His broad shoulders and strong physique exuded confidence and strength, making him seem almost statuesque in stature.

"Steph don't hog her! I want to see her too," Rebecca said as she wrapped her arms around Jean. "I'm so happy to see you again. You must come to visit soon."

"Come, Gina, you can sit by me." Steph beamed at her mother as she hooked her arm around Jean.

"Hold on," the assertive man who she didn't know said. He strode up to her, confidence seeming to rest on his shoulders. His blue eyes scanned over her before a kind smile reached his lips. "I'm Liam, Ben's father. I'm happy to meet you. You have made quite an impression on my family. I haven't heard one negative thing about you."

Jean smiled back at Liam, charmed by his confidence and warmth. "Thank you, Liam. It's a pleasure to meet you too," she replied, feeling grateful for the kind welcome. The warm reception from his family caught her by surprise, since she wasn't expecting it.

As the night continued, Jean found herself laughing and joining in on the conversations. They shared stories about their lives, their interests, and their families. They shared funny stories about Ben that made her feel a strange sense of longing. Her mind drifted to him, and she wondered how he was doing. The ringing of her phone interrupted her thoughts.

"Hello?" she asked, standing up from the table.

"Miss Regina Newman?"

"Yes, this is she."

"Miss Newman, I'm afraid we've had to quarantine your apartment block."

"Excuse me?"

"You'll be unable to return to your apartment for at least a week. We're taking precautionary measures and have begun fumigating the entire block. An invasive insect has been found, and we can't risk it getting out."

"I understand, but what about my things?"

"I'm afraid you can't take anything from your apartment, miss. Everything had to undergo fumigation."

"But that's everything I own." She sighed in exasperation.

"We're really sorry for the inconvenience, but nothing can be done."

"I understand." She only had the clothes on her back and now had to do a hasty search for a hotel room.

"We will notify you when you can return. All locks will be changed as a precautionary measure, and your complex will have a new key waiting for you when the time comes. Have a good night."

"Yeah, thank you." She hung up the phone and spun around, jumping back slightly. Link was standing right beside her, staring at her with his deep emerald eyes.

"What happened?"

"I guess an invasive insect was found on my apartment block. Everything is being fumigated, so I can't even go back to get my stuff. I'm going to have to cut this short. I need to call around and—"

"You're staying with me!" Steph cheered, jumping up.

"I couldn't. I don't know how long this will be, and—"

"I'm so excited! This will be like a long slumber party!" Steph clapped her hands as her mother joined in.

"This will be so much fun!" Rebecca chimed in, as she chatted excitedly to Steph. "You two are the same size. She can wear your clothes!"

Jean stood there with her mouth open, trying to object.

"Might as well forget about it. It's bad enough when one of them decides something, but both together …" Liam shrugged with a laugh.

"That is a world takeover!" Link chuckled in agreement. "I was going to tell you to stay with me, but Steph beat me to it. I guess that's probably for the best. I can hear Ben crying now, if he found out you were staying here."

Jean's fingers curled up tightly at her side as she pursed her lips together. This seemed wrong. They wanted 'Ben's girlfriend' to come and stay with them. It felt deceptive. She looked around the room, trying to find a way to excuse herself from the situation, but the happy smiles and laughter around her had her struggling to say no.

Link's eyes lingered on Jean as he noticed her unease. "Hey, are you okay?" he asked, his voice soft and kind.

"I just—" She fidgeted slightly as Link placed a reassuring hand on her shoulder. "I feel like it's inappropriate for me to stay at Ben's parents' place. I don't want Ben to get the wrong impression and—" She noticed the genuine smile that flashed over Liam's face.

"She IS a keeper. I wasn't sure, but that right there seals it," Liam said as he nodded over at his wife. Jean stood there dumbfounded as they completely ignored what she was saying. She decided to try one more time.

"Thank you for your offer, but I don't want to impose," Jean said with a polite smile. "I appreciate your kindness, but I think it would be better if I found my own place to stay."

"Nonsense," Steph said, waving her hand dismissively. "We've already decided. It's only right that you stay with us."

Link gave her a sympathetic smile. "Listen, I know this is all a bit overwhelming, but we're all here for you. You don't have to worry about anything. Just relax and enjoy yourself."

"I need to speak with Ben about this first—" Jean started to say as Rebecca stood up with the phone to her ear.

"I'll let him know. I'm checking in on him now."

These people were crafty. Here she was, trying to find a way out of staying with them, but it was like they were one step ahead of her the whole time. As if they could read her mind. She felt like a rabbit, running for dear life but finally reaching a cliff. There was no escape from the Cross family.

"Ben, you sound exhausted."

Jean heard those words and her mind instantly raced to Ben. She felt herself fill with worry as she listened to his mother speak.

"Yes, at once. In fact, guess what? We're having dinner with Gina. Yes, the whole family. We're at Link's. She's going to be staying with us for a week or so. Something with her apartment. I hope she can't ever go back and that she has to live with us. That would be so fun ... Of course she's fine. Well, why would it? ... Oh Ben, you think too much. Fine." She walked over to Jean and handed her the phone. "He wants to talk to you."

Jean grabbed the phone hesitantly, afraid he was going to be angry. "Hello?" Her voice sounded meeker than she planned.

"Jean? Are you alright? Are you okay? What's wrong?"

"I'm okay. My apartment complex is being fumigated because of an invasive insect. Ben, I told them I could find my own place—"

"Stay with my parents. I want you to stay there."

"But—"

"You can't talk them out of it anyway." She heard his tired chuckle, and she felt a pain in her chest.

"You sound so tired." She chewed on her inner lip.

"I am. I'm tired and my head is a mess. All I know is ... I miss you." Her breath caught in her chest. "Go ahead and hand the phone back to my mom. I'll see you soon, Jean." Slowly, in a daze, she moved her hand back toward Rebecca. She hadn't even responded to him. Of course, she rationalized that he didn't mean it how it sounded. He meant he missed his pillow because he was tired. Yeah, that was what he meant.

"Yes, I'll do that. Not a problem. Love you." Rebecca hung up the phone. "There. All set. Ben said to put you in his room. He said you would be more comfortable using his pillow since it smelled like him. Isn't he adorable?" Meanwhile, Jean felt her heart trumpeting loudly. The sound of blood pulsing in her ears drowned out the rest of the conversation.

She was going to stay in Ben's room. What about when he returned? They were already sleeping together, but something felt more intimate about it now. Her stomach rolled with tiny butterflies as she remembered Ben's words, and the way his voice sounded when he told her he missed her. She might be reading more into it now, but it seemed like there was something more in his tone. Something that excited and scared her.

Chapter 15

Link volunteered to drive Jean to the Cross house. Actually, volunteered wasn't quite right. He insisted on it, though Jean had a suspicion as to why. She caught Link and Steph making eyes at each other across the table. There were even subtle touches that she had seen. She looked over at him as they drove on the secluded road and cleared her throat.

"So, how long have you and Steph been dating?"

Link's eyes widened and he glanced over at her curiously. "What makes you think that?"

She gave him a crooked grin and shook her head. "It's obvious there's something going on between the two of you. I just assumed it meant you were dating."

"Really? You think it was obvious?"

She noticed the nervous look in Link's eyes. "Is that bad?"

"We plan to tell everyone at the right time."

"My lips are sealed." Jean made a motion of locking her lips. "But, just curious ... why the wait? When is the right time?"

"After Ben caught his girlfriend cheating on him ..." He paused for a moment before deciding to continue. "He changed. His insomnia got worse, and he became distant. I waited for far too long, not telling Steph how I felt, and it ended up hurting her. It hurt us both. I can't tell you how much I love her. There isn't a word for it." A cheesy smile spread over his lips as he shrugged. "Anyway, we just started dating in secret, and I think it's finally time. We wanted to make sure Ben was happy again. Now that he has you, I think we can make our public announcement soon."

Jean felt as if she was punched in the stomach for so many different reasons. Hearing about the betrayal Ben went through was gut wrenching. But Link was wrong. Ben wasn't dating her ... she wasn't making him happy again. She looked away and chewed on her bottom lip.

"What's that nervous look for?" Link chuckled as he glanced at her.

"Promise me you won't tell anyone. I'm not sure what I'm supposed to say exactly."

"I won't even tell Steph. What is this about?" Link slowed the acceleration of the car so he could look at her.

"I'm not dating Ben." She looked out the window as he pulled over to the side.

"What do you mean?"

She turned her head to meet his eyes. "Ben is using me as his pillow. We aren't in a real relationship. He said it would be easier to just say we were dating, but we aren't. He's able to sleep when he's with me."

He stared at her for a moment, digesting what she had just said. "No, I don't believe that. I can see how he looks at you. I KNOW that look. I've looked at Steph like that for years. It's more than just that."

"Link, I'm no one. I have no family—"

"That stuff doesn't matter to the Cross family. They aren't like that. Gina, do you like Ben?"

It was as if he was holding a knife to her throat. She felt like she couldn't breathe without the blade scratching her throat, and yet she had to answer at the same time.

"Has he kissed you?"

"What does that have to do with it?"

"Has he?"

"Yes, but he was just teasing me. His form of punishment." She watched as his lips tugged up slightly.

"I'll ask again then. Do you like him?"

"He could have anyone he wants. I'm not under any delusions that this is anything more than what it is." She lied. She was delusional, even though she tried not to be. She couldn't stop thinking about him. It was as if he was her new obsession. She knew better, though. As much as she wanted a family, she knew the pain that came with loss. Was it something she was really willing to risk experiencing again?

"Gina, you like him, don't you?"

"I can't lose anyone else. I don't want to hurt like that again. I want a family, but I'm afraid to have one. I want a relationship, but I'm afraid I'll want it more than the other person. Then I'll be the one alone and hurting. I can't do a casual fling when I already know I'm going to fall too deep. I—" She clamped her mouth shut as evil tears trickled down her face. She turned her head away, hoping he didn't see. What was she doing? She had just blurted everything out.

A warm hand rested on hers as she kept her gaze cast away and downward.

"Gina, you're hurting. You've been hurting. The pain hasn't stopped. You know you want this but are afraid to admit it out loud. You can't trick yourself. You're already preparing yourself for the pain. You know what? That's okay. But it's okay to hurt. It's okay to try something and fail. What isn't okay is to stop living. To stop trying things because you're afraid. Then you're allowing yourself to be ruled by fear. You know the saying: 'It's better to have loved and lost than never to have loved at all.'" He squeezed her hand, brushing his thumb over her knuckles.

"Listen, if you like Ben, great, and if not, that's fine too. But don't close yourself off because you're afraid. And don't give up before you even start the race. See it through and cross the finish line, no matter the outcome."

"Same to you." Jean wiped her eyes and then turned to look at Link. "It's sweet that you put things on hold for your friend. But he's an adult, and life goes on. You and Steph shouldn't put your happiness on hold because of someone else's pain. That isn't going to help Ben, especially after all this time. I'm sure he already knows how you two feel about each other. Why don't you show him that love is still out there for him to believe in?"

"Maybe with you?" Link's lips twitched up.

"He isn't interested in me like that."

"So you say, but all I know is that Ben has never been a casual person. He doesn't randomly kiss women. Take that for what it's worth. I don't know what he's thinking. Maybe he's just as confused too. You deserve to be happy, Gina, and so does Ben. In either case,

I'm here for you no matter what. I'll always be here for you now. Remember, you're family to me."

"Thank you. I guess I was letting fear control my life. It isn't an easy habit to break. I heard you and I understand what you're saying, but I don't have a switch inside that will just turn it off."

"Of course not. However, when you're honest with yourself, it's easier for you to analyze things better. I'm sorry about—about your parents." He stopped himself from saying that he knew what had happened to her. "I'm sure it was very traumatic. I can't do anything about the past, but from now on, I'll be someone you can rely on. If you need someone to punch your new boyfriend in the face, consider me on duty. Even if it is Ben." He focused his gaze intensely on her as the corners of his mouth curved up into an enigmatic smirk. His lips spread slowly and deliberately apart until they finally unveiled a beaming, dazzling smile that seemed to sparkle with hidden secrets.

He released her hand and pulled back onto the road. "So, you and Ben sleep together, but literally just sleep?" His brows wiggled playfully as he glanced over at her.

"Yes, that's right."

"Hmm, I wonder how long his willpower will hold out."

"What was that?" She wasn't quite sure what he said, since his tone was lower and a bit mumbled.

"You two are like a double-edged sword, standing back-to-back with your shiny, protective walls, concealing the depths of love and hurt that lie within. Perfectly complemented by one another, joined in a powerful union of emotions and misunderstanding."

"Okay, Shakespeare." She laughed as he chuckled with her. The car began to slow, and she looked out the window, her heart racing. In front of them, the mansion grew closer, a foreboding structure made of dark wood and shuttered windows. The whole thing seemed almost alive in the shadows, like a beast waiting to be released. It was silly, but it was as if the house was waiting to intimidate her with a life of its own. The landscaping was beautiful, with hedges surrounding the house like watchful guards. The garden was overflowing with vibrant colors of every hue, and although the grass may have been a deep green, it gave her an eerie feeling, with its perfectly manicured boxwoods and pines.

While she was desperate to satisfy her curiosity and explore the inside of the house, a chill raced up her spine. Anxiety settled like a rock in her stomach at the thought of Ben's family discovering the truth ... that she wasn't really dating Ben. She felt like every time she talked to them, she was lying. She didn't know these people, and now she was going to sleep in their home.

"I'm nervous," she admitted, clearing her throat.

"I know," he said, giving her a warm smile. "Why do you think I came? Yeah, Steph is here, but I figured you would feel better if I came along with you. I'm staying too." She looked over at him in shock as he laughed. "I used to stay here all the time. Besides, this gives me a reason to see Steph more." He opened the car door as Jean followed suit.

She felt a sense of relief, knowing Link would be there too. He came around and patted her on the shoulder. "They're waiting for us," he said as he corralled her to the door. He opened it without knocking, and Jean's eyes moved over the place. The inside of the house was just as impressive as the outside. A grand staircase led up to the second floor, and the walls were adorned with artwork and family photos. Her eyes caught a picture of a younger Ben, and she stepped away from Link to look at it.

His golden eyes were warm and happy. He had flashed a charming smile at the camera as he held up a big bag of cotton candy. He looked like he was around twenty in the picture. His eyes looked brighter, and he didn't carry the tired bags under them. She stared back at his eyes and painfully admitted to herself that she missed him.

"Gina!" Steph squeaked as she bounded down the stairs. "Come on. I already have a bunch of clothes set aside for you. Link, you can take the guest room that's across from mine." Her eyes flashed at him with an unspoken secret that made Link begin to cough. "Get yourself a drink and take care of that." She winked at him and then dragged Jean up the stairs.

She led Jean down the hall to another set of dark, wooden stairs with a smooth, glossy banister. Steph chatted excitedly as she pulled her upwards and then down the hall again. "My room is back the other way. Ben and I divided the third floor between us. I get everything to the right, and he has everything to the left." A sweet smile danced over her lips as she opened the door at the far end of the hall. Immediately, Jean was hit with his familiar scent.

"This is where you'll be staying. I put clothes for you on the empty desk. I couldn't decide what would look the best on you, so you can decide what you would prefer to wear. The shower is through those doors, and I'll leave you to get ready for bed. Tomorrow evening, we're watching movies, so think about what you want to see. I'm so happy you're here. Did you want to go to bed or—"

"Actually, a shower and sleep sound perfect right now. I didn't get enough rest last night."

"Okay then. I'm going to go check on Link and make sure he found his room okay." Steph smiled as she backed out of the room, quietly shutting the door behind her. A knowing smile rested on Jean's lips as she walked over to the desk. She wondered wryly if Link and Steph would be getting any sleep tonight. Her fingers trailed over the clothes and her mouth parted when she found the pajamas. This was what she was supposed to wear?! She held the tiny, black, silky gown up and let out an airy laugh. Thank goodness she was alone.

She thrust open the bathroom door, her jaw dropping in amazement. Her previous expectations of luxury and extravagance were utterly shattered by the sight before her. His personal washroom was a work of art—marble floors that shone like glass, sparkling, decadent gold fixtures, and an array of jars filled with exotic soaps and oils. She couldn't help but feel both impressed and intimidated by the grandeur of it all. She ran her hand over the marble countertop, feeling the cool smoothness under her fingers. She slowly took her clothes off and walked over to the side. The shower was a separate room, enclosed in glass panels with a rain showerhead and multiple jets. She couldn't resist testing it out, turning the knob and letting the warm water cascade over her body.

As the water hit her skin, Jean let out a sigh of relief. The warmth was soothing, and she couldn't help but feel a wave of relaxation wash over her. The sound of the water was calming, and she closed her eyes, letting herself sink into the moment. It was easy to forget about everything else when she was standing there under the warm droplets of water.

As she stood under the pelleting streams, her mind began to wander. She couldn't help but think about Ben, and how much she cared for him. She was still hesitant to face the truth, but Link's words had struck a chord with her. She was letting fear control her life, and she didn't want that to be the case anymore.

When she finished her shower, she wrapped a plush towel around her body and stepped out onto the heated floor. Damn, she could get used to this. She towel-dried her hair and put on the thin, silky nightgown and lacy underwear before scampering to Ben's bed. She jumped onto it like a kid and tucked her face into his pillow.

The sheets felt like clouds against her skin, and she couldn't help but smile as she breathed in the scent of him. It was a mixture of musk and cedar—manly yet comforting. She closed her eyes and let out a contented sigh, feeling surprisingly at home in his bed, in his house.

As she lay there, Jean couldn't help but wonder what it would be like to be with Ben. Could they really have a future together? Could they make it work despite all the obstacles in their way? It was silly to think of such things. She was allowing her thoughts to run away to a world of make-believe, especially when Ben never once said he was looking for a relationship. In fact, he said he wanted a non-complicated relationship. A human pillow was what he had asked for. With that final thought, she sank deeper into his pillow, closing her eyes and allowing sleep to overcome her.

Chapter 16

Her eyes popped open, blinking into the dark. It was as if something woke her up, but she wasn't sure what. She felt like she wasn't alone, and a slight rustling noise confirmed this. Startled, she turned her head and saw a silhouette in the small stream of moonlight that entered through the window. Who was in the room with her? She watched the shadow for a moment. She heard the faint sound of clothing hitting the floor, making her breath stop. She sat up quickly, gripping the sheet up to her chest. The figure stopped and turned to face her.

"Jean, it's me." The soft, familiar voice came from Ben as he walked toward the bed. He flipped the bedside lamp on so that the light lit up his face.

"Ben?" She winced from the bright light as his face came into focus. She glanced over at the clock to see it was two in the morning. Looking back at his face, she felt her heart tighten painfully. His face was taut with weariness, and dark circles created shadows under his eyes. He looked beyond exhausted. She watched as a tired smile spread over his lips.

"Hey."

"What are you doing here?" She watched as his tired grin widened.

"Well, this is my room," he chuckled.

Her eyes wandered over his bare chest and to the black plaid boxers he was wearing. She had to tear her eyes away and force herself to look back at his face. "You look so tired."

"I am. I'm exhausted. I couldn't even fight a kitten." He sighed as he sat on the edge of the bed. "I kept thinking about you being here and sleeping in my bed. The next thing I knew I was on a flight back home. I couldn't take it anymore." His golden eyes met with hers. He was curious about what she was thinking, but her face revealed nothing except perhaps confusion. He was tired, but he wasn't blind. He noticed the revealing gown despite the sheet she held up.

"You don't look like you can take much more. Were you not able to sleep at all?"

He settled into the bed next to her with a faint smile on his face. He hadn't meant he couldn't take not sleeping anymore. He meant he couldn't stand not seeing her anymore. For now, his heart was content. He felt as if his insides had all calmed down. He reached over, flipping the light out before rolling to the side to look at her in the dark.

"I feel like those pills are becoming less and less effective."

"So, you came back because you missed your pillow?" She settled into the bed next to him, her head facing his. The moonlight outlined his masculine figure while keeping his face hidden from her. Through the dark she felt the heat of his hand come to rest on her side, pulling her closer to him. His cheek rested on the top of her head and her nose was buried in his throat. Her fingers landed on his chest, feeling his defined body with secret delight.

"Because I missed you," his raspy voice whispered out.

Jean was about to respond when she felt his body settle more against her. His breathing leveled out into long, deep breaths. He had fallen asleep. He was so tired that he wasn't even sure what he was saying. At least that's what she rationalized.

His heat seared through the nightgown she was wearing, as if there was nothing preventing them from melting into one another. She closed her eyes and inhaled deeply. His masculine scent overwhelmed her senses, not allowing room for rational thoughts. Being wrapped up in his arms was the most wonderful feeling in the world. She could easily fool herself into thinking her boyfriend had returned home to her, that she wasn't just his pillow but his person. It was foolish to think that way, but at that moment, she couldn't help but feel that way. If only ...

She drifted off into a deep sleep. She wasn't even disturbed when the door creaked open and Link peeked in, checking to see if she was ready to go to work. The deadly glare Link got from Ben made him laugh, quietly retreating from the room without making a sound. It only confirmed it more for Link: Ben was serious about Jean.

It wasn't until almost noon that she stirred. She shifted slightly as her eyes squinted open. She glanced up at Ben's resting face just an inch in front of hers. A small smile reached her lips until she noticed the clock on the wall. Before she could even move, she felt herself being restrained and pulled against Ben's chest.

"I'm late for work."

"No, no work for you today," his groggy voice said as he nuzzled his nose in her hair. "Link already knows." Then an annoying thought crossed his mind. "What was Link doing here?"

"He stayed the night thinking I would feel more comfortable if he was here. He was going to take me to work in the morning."

"He can't have you."

Jean let out a tiny giggle. "Link isn't interested in me." She then realized she couldn't give away the secret yet, though she was certain Ben was aware. "Did you know I knew him as a kid?"

"He wasn't your boyfriend, was he?"

She smiled, hearing the annoyance in his tone. "No, he was someone I used to share my lunch with. I started having my mom pack me a double lunch so I could bring one for him." She felt him move, angling his head so that he could look at her.

"You're that girl ... he mentioned you to me before. You know, at one point he thought you were a real angel. Sent to—well, your timing, appearance, and disappearance made him believe in angels." Ben smiled before resting his head back onto hers. "Maybe you do have special powers. It isn't that I sleep, but it's the best sleep I've ever experienced when I'm next to you. Maybe you are an angel," he chuckled, listening to her scoff.

"I wish I had powers. I could have changed so many things—"

"You've changed Link's life, and I feel like things are about to really change in mine."

"Ben!"

A voice echoed in the room from a speaker near the ceiling.

"What do you want, mom?" Ben groaned.

"You've violated Gina enough! Let her down to breathe and get something to eat."

"I haven't even begun the depths of my violating. You want grand-children, don't you?" He smirked at her silence. Meanwhile, Jean felt as if her face would explode from the heated pressure consuming it.

"Without proper nutrition, my grandbaby would suffer. Bring her down for food or I'm coming up with the hose!"

Ben chuckled as he squeezed Jean closer to him. Her head was tucked under his chin, and he knew her face would be an adorable shade of red. "I think she's serious about the hose part." His lips brushed over her hair as he took a moment to savor the closeness. He was aware of her hardened buds pressed up against his chest. The thin fabric of her nightgown offered little protection. Luckily, he was too exhausted last night, although the thought did cross his mind. Now, the threat of starvation was her unsung hero, preventing him from devouring her.

It was as if the plane ride home made everything much clearer. Sleep deprivation oddly helped put things in perspective. He realized it didn't matter how long he had known Jean. If he felt this way about her, that was all that mattered. Whirlwind romances did occur, where everything happened very fast and unexpectedly. People who were swept off their feet and ended up married within months or even weeks. Maybe he and Jean were feeling this type of instant connection. In any case, he wouldn't know if he stayed away from her.

His brows knitted together as he realized something. "My mom called you Gina."

"Yeah, before, only my one friend called me that. Then Link started and it just trickled through." His hot breath tickled her head as he made a quiet hum.

"What do you prefer to be called? You asked me to call you Jean. Is it because we weren't close?"

"I guess I started going by Jean after I moved in with my grandma. There isn't a more personal connection between the names. My dad called me Gin Gin, and my mom called me Jeanie. My grandma always called me Jean." She shrugged in his arms, not really having a preference.

"You're my sleep genie, so Jeanie might be perfect." His voice was full of mirth as he smiled in her hair.

She felt his hand slide over her back, his fingers playing with the thin strap of her gown. The heat from his chest seemed to have melted the layer of fabric. It felt like nothing was between them, and she didn't want there to be. Her mind was filled with thoughts of him, and they weren't pure. Her body betrayed her, responding to his touch like it was meant to be. She wanted him, wanted to feel his skin against hers, to taste his lips, to be consumed by him. She tried to push the thoughts away, feeling guilty for even thinking them. But the more she tried to stop them, the more insistent they became. Her breathing quickened, and she felt his fingers move lower, down her back. His fingertips traced patterns along her skin, igniting a fire within her that she couldn't ignore. She wanted him, and the desire was overwhelming.

"Jean—" There was a huskiness in his voice that made her lower stomach clench in response. Something primal and wanting that she recognized as a man's hunger.

"BENJAMIN LEE CROSS, THIS IS YOUR LAST WARNING."

This time it was Steph's voice that came over the speaker. Jean heard the frustrated growl that left Ben's throat. His fingers dug into her slightly as if it was taking every ounce of restraint to stop. With a loud sigh, he lifted away from her.

"Do you want pancakes or an omelet?"

"It's afternoon."

"Do pancakes know time?" He gave her a wry smile as he swung his legs out of bed. "We can have whatever you're in the mood for."

She had to turn her head into the pillows as her mind went straight to the gutter. What she was in the mood for was feasting on the hunk of flesh in front of her. That wasn't what he was offering. "An omelet with sausage and American cheese with wheat toast, lightly buttered." She listened as he chuckled, feeling the bed sag next to her with the weight from his hand.

"Then I suggest you get up and get dressed. Otherwise, breakfast in bed is going to take on a new meaning." His lips brushed over her ear as he spoke, making a shiver run down her spine.

Jean groaned inwardly. As much as she wanted to give in to her desires, she knew it was best to put them aside. She sat up in bed, feeling the cool air brush over her skin. Her eyes wandered over his chest, then back to his eyes. "Okay, I'll get dressed."

He grabbed her hand, helping her to her feet. For a second, he rested his hands on her bare shoulders, swallowing down the want he felt. The revealing nightgown had her body on full display, and her hardened buds were visible through the thin fabric.

"I'll leave you the room to change," he said, abruptly turning and grabbing some clothes out of his dresser. He walked toward the door, pausing briefly to glance back at her. There was something in his gaze that made her heart skip a beat. She couldn't quite place it, but it was intense and all-consuming. "I'll be waiting for you downstairs."

Jean stared transfixed as he walked out of the room, his figure strong and dominating in the doorway before he disappeared from her sight.

The memory of his touch on her skin burned like wildfire, sending paralyzing shocks that traveled through her body with each caress of his fingers.

She gulped down a deep breath, her eyes wide as they drifted over the array of garments Steph had prepared. She delved further into the pile, frantically searching for normal, comfortable clothes. She chose the most casual shirt and shorts she could find. Surprisingly, everything fit perfectly.

She looked at herself in the mirror, her eyes staring into her silver orbs as she tried to analyze her own thoughts. What was she doing? What did she want? She needed to figure things out today because if they hadn't been interrupted, she was certain things would have taken an intimate turn. The thing was that being intimate with him meant something more to her than just sex. He was a man, and she couldn't blame him for his actions when he was lying next to a woman.

If she stayed with him again tonight, could things remain casual? If she was being honest with herself, it was already too late for her. She really did have feelings for him. She already knew that if he found someone else, even a new pillow, she would feel the bitter sting of heartache.

Her silver eyes looked back at her with conviction. She wanted this—she wanted him. Whatever this was or however it ended, she didn't want to wonder 'what if'. She wanted to be able to say she gave it her best, so she could at least walk away without that regret.

"Okay, Jean, remember this decision," she whispered to herself before she turned to leave the room. When she opened the bedroom door, it felt like she was entering a portal to a new path ahead of her. Every step she now took was laden with purpose. She embraced the choice she made of her own volition and forged onward down the path chosen by her heart.

Chapter 17

She tentatively walked to the stairway, feeling overwhelmed by how big the house was.

"Sleepy head!"

She glanced ahead and her eyes met Link's. He sauntered toward her from across the hallway, his hands casually tucked in his jean pockets, a faint smile playing on his lips.

"Link, you didn't go to work today? Didn't sleep much?" She gave him a wry grin, which he only chuckled at.

"I'm not the one crawling out of bed in the afternoon. I peeked in once, only to be assaulted by Ben's eyes. I decided that we could both use a day off today. Being my own boss has its perks."

She studied his face with a faint smile. "Is that really why you didn't go to work today?"

"Maybe I was enjoying some time with Steph." He glanced away and mumbled, "And maybe I wanted to make sure you were okay. Anyhow, hungry?" he asked, offering his arm to her. "I'll lead you out of this labyrinth."

As they descended the stairway, Jean couldn't help but notice the way Link's arm felt around hers, his touch gentle and comforting. It was a stark contrast to the way Ben's touch had made her feel just moments before. Link's presence brought a stillness that helped her find her center, while Ben aroused intense desires with fiery passion, a blazing wildfire threatening to consume her. She was supposed to be there to help him so that he wouldn't collapse from exhaustion. But now she was starting to feel like she was the one that needed him.

She was scared of being broken into pieces, yet she desperately wanted to keep her promise to herself so that she wouldn't have any regrets. She knew that even if it was just a fleeting moment with him, she had to be truthful with herself. If things didn't work out and she ended up getting hurt, at least she wouldn't have deceived herself.

She looked around as she stepped into the dining room. The smell of fresh bread and fruit mixed together, greeting her like an old friend. Her gaze instantly locked onto Ben's. Sitting at the long, dark wooden table, his amber eyes roved to her arm, which was connected to Link's. His expression twisted into something colder and more rigid—a look of icy fury that chilled her bones. The chill emanating from him was palpable as he stared Link down. Jean felt her heart race, unsure of what had caused the sudden change in Ben's demeanor.

Link, seemingly unfazed by Ben's hostility, smiled at him as Steph walked in.

"Ben, there is something I want to talk to you about—" Link started, but Steph clicked her tongue and shook her head.

"Right now?" Steph asked in almost a whisper before she came to grab Jean's other arm. "Come and sit. You must be starving. You barely picked at your food yesterday, and now my brother forced you to fast."

Jean glanced back at Ben and noticed his concerned eyes following her. She moved with Steph, but when she led her to a chair, she chose to walk around so that she could sit next to Ben.

"What did you want to say?" Ben asked, flipping his eyes back to Link. He watched as his sister bounced beside the man, rising on her toes and planting a passionate kiss on Link's lips. The kiss lingered before she finally tore away, beaming back at her brother.

"I think showing is easier than telling."

Link chuckled and pulled her into his arms. "I'm dating Steph. I just wanted you to know so you don't get the wrong idea about Gina. I've taken Gina under my wing. She is family as far as I'm concerned, and I'll protect her like family." The hidden threat didn't go unnoticed by Ben as he leaned back in his chair, arching his brow at Link.

"I see. Well, I can't say this is a surprise." Ben motioned between his sister and Link. "The only surprise is that it took so long. As for MY Jean, I'll be the one protecting her." He wrapped his arm around her firmly, pulling her closer, as her chair frantically slid across the floor. His grip was a sign of ownership over her, refusing to loosen its hold.

Jean turned her head to look at Ben, though he continued to gaze at Link. She looked back at Link to see a peculiar smile resting on his face while his eyes danced in amusement. He had called her MY Jean. However, he didn't know that Link knew they weren't really dating. That's probably why Link looked so amused, because he knew their secret. Even still, when he uttered those words, her body felt as if it was electrified with anticipation. Her heart raced faster than a hummingbird's wings and her skin quivered like a plucked guitar string.

However, the way both men spoke of protecting her made her independent streak take over. "Unless I'm being tossed helplessly in a raging river, I don't need anyone protecting me. I'm pretty sure I've been doing just fine on my own." Ben's amber eyes shot toward her as she continued, "I do appreciate everything that's already been done for me, but let's not pretend that I don't offer anything in return. I'm not a taker and I am not defenseless."

"I knew we were going to be best friends!" Steph clapped her hands together in excitement as she turned her face up to Link with a dazzling smile. Quietly she whispered so that Ben and Jean couldn't hear, "Now we just need Ben to marry her and you to marry me, and then we can all be family." Link's face turned a dark shade of red as he choked and sputtered. She smiled up at him, unfazed, as if she didn't just suggest marriage for the two of them. It wasn't like it wasn't on Link's mind, but now it was turning into a crazy focal point. They had just started dating, but after the night they spent together, dating wasn't going to be enough. He had to have her ... every night.

Jean felt her body shudder as Ben's lips touched her ear. His hot breath on her skin had her stomach tightening in response. "If you offer more in return, so will I." He ran his teeth lightly along her earlobe, sending a shudder down her spine before he pulled away. Without missing a beat, he reached out and casually grabbed the fruit tray from the table and passed it to Jean. "The omelet should be out soon, but have some fruit."

Eating was the last thing on her mind, even though her stomach protested the very thought of not eating. Her chest hummed as she reached for her glass of water. She felt the heat on her cheeks that gave away her feelings. He really enjoyed making her flustered.

Luckily, the omelets came out at that moment, so she was able to keep her head down. This would give her time for her face to return to its normal color. Jean took a bite, savoring the flavors as they exploded in her mouth. Steph and Link took their seats across from them as they ate stuffed pancakes. Utensils clinked on the plates as they ate in comfortable silence.

The sound of a shutter snapping made everyone lift their gaze up to Mrs. Cross, who had a camera.

"Mom," Steph complained. "I'm a mess."

"These are important memories you all will be glad to have later. Gina, I'm glad you're finally getting something to eat. I don't mind if you disappear to the bedroom again, but just make sure you get proper nutrition."

Jean's face heated in embarrassment as Link began laughing.

"Don't think I don't know whose room you stayed in last night. I was wondering how much longer you were going to wait. I'm not getting any younger, and I'd like to start enjoying my grandchildren already."

"I'd like to be married first before I get pregnant," Steph said, poking at her pancake. This time, Link was the one turning weird shades.

"It takes nine months for the baby to cook. Plenty of time to get married before the baby is born."

"Bec." Liam came into the room, resting his hand around his wife's waist. "Let the kids figure it out on their own. We did, didn't we?" He planted a soft kiss on her temple before lifting his gaze up. "Believe it or not, she wasn't always this outspoken. We've come a long way together. You know ..." he chuckled with a small smile, "I remember worrying if she felt the same way about me. We were clumsy in our relationship, and we made mistakes, but it was those mistakes that also brought us together. We married by chance and, well, that's a whole other story." He rubbed Rebecca's shoulder. "We're going into the office this week. Ben, we want you to take the rest of the week off."

Ben started to object, but his father raised his brows, instantly silencing him. "Your mother and I have already decided. The only event you need to be at is the benefit dinner. Ready my love?" he asked, looking down at Rebecca, who nodded up to him.

Right before they left the room, Ben's mom said, "Remember to stay hydrated."

Ben poured more water into Jean's glass and pushed it over to her. "You heard what she said. Hydrate up." A crooked grin rested on his face as he leaned on his hand to look at her.

"I got plenty of sleep last night and didn't work up a sweat. I'm not in danger of dehydration," Jean said sweetly as Ben's eyes lit up with her words.

"You will be." He sipped his drink, looking up at his sister and Link.

"Gina, I have the perfect dress for you in mind for the benefit dinner—" Steph started to say when Link snorted.

"I don't think so. How insulting would that be for her to wear a dress by another designer? You'll pick from what I have." Link felt a flick to his forehead as he blinked at Steph.

"That's what I was planning. Remember the dress by the curtain? The silver one ... wouldn't it be perfect?"

"Umm, benefit dinner? I don't think—" Jean started to say but Ben instantly cut her off.

"We don't think you should be picking out my girlfriend's dress. I'll get her dress. She is my date after all." He laid his soft, warm hand on her thigh and gently squeezed it, an unexpected yet comforting gesture.

Jean's eyes flickered up to Ben's face, her heart racing faster at his touch. Girlfriend. Date. Those words rang through her mind, taunting her with their implications. She couldn't describe how badly she wanted it to be real. The idea of having someone and a family again blossomed in her heart. She wanted it ... a family. She tried to tell herself that being alone was better, but then why did she feel an ache in her chest whenever she went to bed? She missed someone loving her unconditionally and someone always being there. Someone to share her day with. Even something simple like eating dinner together. All she had left were the memories and the deep longing for what she once had.

She felt the sudden rush of emotions building up inside her, threatening to burst out at any moment. She took in a slow breath, burying it down. It was what she always did. Sweep the pain under the rug so it couldn't be seen.

"What do you think, Gina?"

Steph's voice brought her from her thoughts as she blinked at the woman. "I'm sorry, I zoned out a bit. What do I think of what?"

"Going to Link's and looking at the gowns." Steph's excited smile rested on her face.

"Sure, we can do that. I have something I want to get from there anyway," Jean said, thinking of what she made for Ben.

"Good, let's get going." Steph said, pulling Link behind her enthusiastically.

"We'll meet you there." Ben squeezed Jean's leg softly. He waited for his sister and Link to leave before he turned his attention to Jean. He looked her over as he turned to face her. "Are you okay? If the dinner is a problem, you don't have to go. I want you there with me, but not if you don't want to."

She shook her head with a small smile. "If you really want me with you, I'll go. I just hope I don't embarrass you." His amber eyes seemed to draw her in as if silently coaxing her.

His hand moved, cupping her cheek as he leaned his head in. His gaze stayed on her as his breath feathered her lips. "What's wrong?"

She blinked, wondering if he was just guessing or if her blank face had given something away. "Nothing's wrong." His thumb brushed over her skin as his nose touched hers. Her heart began to hum rapidly as her breath grew ragged.

"Don't lie to me, Jean." This time his lips brushed over hers as he spoke.

"Nothing's wrong. I was just thinking how nice it felt. Having—" She shrugged as she breathed in his intoxicating scent. "This. Having your family around. It's strange how the little things are what you end up missing the most." He nodded his head, then closed his eyes, rubbing his nose against hers slowly.

"I'll do my best," his teeth pulled on her bottom lip, making a soft gasp escape from her throat, "to be what you need." Before she had the chance to utter a single word, he crashed his lips against hers, trapping her in an unyielding kiss. With one hand gripping the back of her head, he forced her mouth open, plunging his tongue inside and claiming her as his own.

His kiss was possessive and greedy, overwhelming her thoughts as she responded back with the same intensity.

"Ben! For crying out loud." Steph clicked her tongue loudly as she walked into the room.

He pulled back with a frustrated groan as he turned lethal eyes upon his sister. "Steph, read the room."

"Oh, I read it alright. I read that, if I hadn't forgotten my purse, you two wouldn't be showing up. That's it." She stomped around the table and grabbed Jean's hand. "I'm driving her. You can ride with Link."

"Now wait a minute, Steph—"

"Are you going to challenge me on this?" Steph asked as she stepped up to her brother.

"We'll leave now, okay?"

"Nope. You had your chance. We'll see you there." Steph waved at him dismissively as she pulled Jean behind her.

Jean glanced back as Ben trailed right behind them. What exactly was happening between her and Ben? Their relationship had shifted gears drastically after he returned from his trip. They both seemed to be craving more than their previous arrangement. Whatever that meant, she didn't know. But, judging from that kiss, a physical relationship was inevitable. She would have been more than willing to follow him up to his room.

"Hey, what's going on?" Link asked as Steph pulled Jean to a bright blue Lamborghini Aventador, a car that Jean couldn't even fathom the cost of.

"Ben's riding with you. We'll see you there."

Jean looked out the window as Ben walked up to it. She rolled it down and he leaned his head in. "This isn't finished," he whispered, kissing her ear as his sister revved the engine. "Drive safe with her," he barked, glaring at Steph.

"Man, you are a grouch when you get cock blocked," Steph snorted, then sped away.

Ben stood there, feeling Link's quiet presence at his side.

"You really like her, don't you?" Link asked, shooting him a quick glance.

"She makes me feel things I never thought I would again. I want her, Link. I won't let her go."

"Hmm, I can't help but feel like those words are typically uttered by the villain." Link laughed as he tossed his keys in the air. "Come on, I'm driving." Suddenly his friend was there again, with all the same characteristics he remembered from before—so alive and vibrant. He listened as his friend's laughter filled the air as they got into the car.

"I can't believe I'm stuck riding next to you the whole way there," Ben teased as he rolled his window down.

"You can grope my chest if it will make you feel better. It's firm and voluptuous." Link pulled his shirt down slightly as Ben shoved his shoulder.

"Just drive, nerd."

Chapter 18

"Yes, that's the dress. I knew it." Steph walked around Jean, nodding in approval.

"There are so many people on a waiting list for a dress, and I know what they cost—"

Steph waved her off. "It's a perk of working with the creator. Besides, Ben will pay him for it." She helped her out of the dress, carefully zipping it up in a bag. "He likes you, you know."

Jean looked at Steph, pursing her lips together. She decided it was best not to say anything. Yeah, she could tell Ben was attracted to her, but she wasn't sure if that meant he liked her. As a friend, sure. As a friend with benefits, most definitely. As anything more than that ... she didn't know.

"You're already in here changing? How fast were you driving?" Link asked, walking into the room.

"How slow were you driving?" Steph snorted behind the curtain. "Liiiiink, did you finish it? I can't find it." She listened to his chuckle.

"That's because I hid it from you. I wanted to see the look on your face when I showed you," he beamed as they walked out from behind the curtain.

"Did you find a dress you liked?" Ben asked, walking up to Jean. He placed his hand on her arm, sliding his fingers over her skin.

"She looks stunning in it. It's one of Link's more expensive designs, so dig deep, Ben," Steph said as she looked at her brother with a wide grin.

"You don't have—" Jean started to say as Ben tilted her chin up to look at him.

"You wouldn't be trying to tell me not to buy my date a dress, would you? Do we need to start punishments again?" A smirk rose over his lips as Jean wetted her lips.

"That's like punishing a child with candy," she whispered into his lips coquettishly. Their lips were almost touching, their breaths mingling, only a small centimeter between them.

"Gina, come help me try my dress on. Look at it! Link designed it just for me."

Foiled again. Jean smiled, biting her lip, backing away from Ben's annoyed expression.

"I can help you get dressed," Link offered with a wry grin resting on his face.

"Yeah, I think we both know that isn't a good idea." She winked at him as she stepped behind the curtain with Jean.

"Want to take the ladies to the falls after this?" Link asked Ben quietly.

"Maybe another time. I want to spend time with Jean. Alone." He looked over at Link, who stared at him quietly.

"You're serious about her, right? I know you aren't the type, but it's just—" his quiet whisper trailed off as Ben tilted his head, raising his brows.

"I'm serious. I always trust my instincts with business. I didn't trust them before with relationships," he said, thinking about his last girlfriend and friend. They were both people who gave him pause before, but he ignored it. He decided to trust them, and it backfired. He took a mental blow that he was still trying to recover from. "This time, I'm going to trust myself. Everything just feels better with her." His words were so quiet that Link had to strain to hear. There was no danger of the women overhearing their conversation.

"I hope it works out for the both of you." Link smiled, turning to look at the curtain. "Are you going to show me?"

Steph stepped out, wearing a dark purple dress with a high slit up to her thigh. It cut into a low V around her neck, hugging her body tightly. She looked at Link nervously, who nodded his head in approval.

"It's a good dress, but I don't think I could ever make anything beautiful enough for you." Link stepped up to her, resting his hands on her waist. "You're so beautiful." He leaned his head down, softly kissing her forehead.

"I love the dress, Link. I can tell you put a lot of thought into it. Thank you." Steph stepped back with a small smile. "Okay, now I need to pick out the perfect shoes." With a laugh, she disappeared behind the curtain to change.

Link stepped back next to Ben, who was looking at him curiously. "What?"

"Why did you wait so long to ask her out? You two have had eyes for each other for a long time." Ben noticed the strange look on his face and stepped over to face him. "Why, Link?"

"It didn't feel right. I couldn't bring myself to ask her, knowing you were hurting." Link's green eyes met with Ben's. "You shut everyone out. You quit talking with me, convincing everyone you disliked me. Yeah, I knew you told everyone we weren't friends. Truthfully, it hurt a bit, but that just proved how much pain you were in. I'm not like Alvin, who was always jealous of you. He wanted to be friends with the Cross CEO, not with you. He was hungry for power, which was why he slept with Melissa. If she was good enough for you and wanted him—anyway, you get the idea. That isn't me. You're important to me. So much that I didn't want to see you hurt more."

"Damn, Link. I always knew there was a thing between you and Steph. That wouldn't have bothered me. I'm sorry for what I did. I just … I didn't want anyone around. I needed to figure things out on my own. You—you've always been a good friend. You're the best friend I've ever had. I'm sorry—" Ben felt Link's arms wrap around him as he patted his back.

"It's in the past. We're moving forward now. Besides, I knew you loved me," Link teased as he stepped back.

"You are such a dork," Ben laughed, shaking his head.

"Words of love right there."

"What are you two laughing at?" Steph asked, as she and Jean stepped out from behind the curtain.

"Wouldn't you like to know?" Link winked at her, then looked back at Jean. "Don't forget your thing."

Jean chewed on her inner lip nervously and then glanced over at Ben. "I have something for you," she said as she made her way over to a table. She slid open a drawer and took out a black box with a white ribbon tied around it in a bow. "I—I wanted to get you something to show my appreciation for the new job, but getting something for someone who can get themselves anything—" she trailed off with a nervous laugh as she held the box out to him. She watched as he slowly opened it, pursing her lips together.

"It's the best I could do. Link helped me a little, but I'm not a designer. It's okay if you don't like it. You don't have to wear it—" Her voice was cut off as Ben grabbed her by the waist, leaning his head down and kissing her. A soft, warm heat caressed her lips.

"I love it. This is the best present I've ever received, and I love it even more because you made it," he said, watching a blush creep over her cheeks.

"Let me see!" Steph whined as Ben held the material up, keeping his grip on Jean. In his hand he held a black silk tie with silver stripes swirling around it.

"Gina, it's beautiful. You made that? She's going to put you out of business." She grinned up at Link, who nodded his head.

"Honestly, she has talent. I'm thinking I might have her assist me with making the clothing," Link chuckled, seeing Jean's nervous face.

Jean was extremely nervous while she made the tie for Ben. She kept second guessing herself, not sure it was good enough. She was proud of what she had created, and the idea of recreating that inner turmoil was exciting but scary. Although, if she was being honest, she was deeply intrigued over the whole creation process.

"Okay, shoes!" Steph said, smiling at Link. "I noticed you don't have a big selection here. Let's go to Sal's."

"Buying shoes from my competitor," Link shook his head. "You're killing me." He pretended to grab his heart in pain. "Actually, I've moved away from making shoes, so I guess Sal isn't my competitor anymore," he laughed.

Ben carefully placed the tie back in the box, then placed his hand around Jean's waist again. "Is that the dress you'll be wearing?" he asked, nodding to a silver gown that Steph had grabbed.

"Yes."

"Perfect. The tie will match beautifully."

Jean's eyes widened. "You're going to wear it to the benefit dinner?" She listened to his tenor chuckle.

"Why are you so surprised? You made it for me to wear, right?"

"Well, yeah, but I was thinking just at the workplace. Not a big event."

"This is the best tie I own. I'll only wear it for important occasions." The adorable pink stain reached her cheeks again. Every time she blushed, it made him feel things. Excitement and happiness. She didn't have to do anything but blush, and it did things to him. She had no idea that the tie she made had suddenly become a prized possession. What was this feeling, this lightness and warmth exploding from his chest?

"Let's all ride together and come back for the other car later." Steph intertwined her fingers with Link's as she glanced back at Jean and Ben. "Coming?"

"Yeah, we're coming." Ben squeezed Jean's side lightly, a smile resting on his face the whole time. His eyes were bright, and he had regained a spark that he had lost. He was so happy, he could hardly contain himself. He wanted everyone to see just how happy he was. All because he had his genie in his life.

Jean's side brushed against Ben's as they followed behind Link and Steph. He only stepped away when they reached the doors so he could open them for her.

"I'm driving," Link said, as they watched Steph put her hands on her hips.

"Your car smells like a man."

"Your backseat is too cramped." Link raised his brows with a smile.

Ben left Jean's side to grab the keys out of Steph's hand. "Link's right. There's no room in your backseat."

"Benjamin! Give me my keys." Steph jumped, trying to reach his hand.

Jean giggled as she watched them. The family warmth was exactly what she needed. And then, in an instant, everything changed. Her body froze in horror as two vehicles collided loudly in the intersection. Both drivers scrambled out of their cockpits, screeching and shouting at one another while Jean stood motionless, paralyzed by fear. The floodgates of her mind burst open, unleashing a torrent of memories from her past. Like a raging river, they rushed through her brain, sweeping away the present moment and filling her with emotions she tried to keep buried. The deafening sound of metal crashing against metal, the suffocating darkness, the feeling of complete helplessness. Her entire body shook with dread.

A chill ran through her body as an icy fear swept over her. Her breathing grew shallow and labored, the weight of terror pressing down on her chest. Frigid beads of sweat cascaded down her trembling body, and a chill clawed at her neck as she struggled to take a single breath.

"Jean." Ben moved in front of her to block the accident. "Jean." He placed his hands on her cheeks, as his face hovered in front of hers.

"Is she okay?" Steph asked.

"We're done for today. Steph, go with Link. I'll take Jean home," he said quietly, his eyes never leaving hers.

"I'm fine," Jean whispered as she fought against her body. She had to bury it. Hide the feelings of pain and fear. She wouldn't be a burden and didn't want to ruin everyone's time.

Ben stared at her, brushing his thumb softly against her cheek. "I'm tired."

"No, you aren't." Jean forced a deep breath of air through her nose.

He glanced at Link, who nodded his head in understanding.

"I want to take Steph out on a date, so this works perfectly. We'll see you guys later." Link grabbed Steph's arms, pulling her away, her face riddled with confusion.

"It's a bit much for me I guess, after not sleeping for so long. Sorry to spoil our time together." He watched as Jean stared at him, unconvinced.

"I'm fine. It just startled me." She tried to convince him as he nodded his head slowly.

"I know, Jean." He kissed her forehead, and then his arms encircled her. When she was nestled into him as tightly as possible, he gently kissed the top of her head.

Jean felt a warm wave of relief wash over her as he held her tightly in his arms. She closed her eyes and buried her face in his chest, trying to push away the memories that had been triggered by the accident. His embrace was all-encompassing, and for a moment, she forgot about everything else around her. She could feel his heart beating against her cheek, steady and calming, as he whispered soothing words into her ear.

As they stood there, wrapped in each other's embrace, the chaos of the accident faded into the background. All that mattered was the warmth of his body, the sound of his voice, and the safety she felt in his arms.

Chapter 19

Jean's mind drifted on the drive home. Her thoughts went to a memory she always tried to bury deep. Despite her best efforts, the event from today shoved it to the forefront of her mind. She remembered how hot and thick the air felt when she was trapped in the dark car. The truck that crashed into them emptied its contents on their vehicle. Her parents didn't make a sound, even when she pleaded with them and told them she was scared. It was hours in the darkness. When the light was finally let in, she saw them. The memory of that moment haunted her nightmares.

Her parents laid there lifelessly in their seats. Their eyes were still open but unseeing, their faces frozen in expressions of disbelief and terror. Streaks of blood cascaded down their faces like tears. She was paralyzed, shock seizing her mind and body, leaving her unable to speak or move as reality around her became muffled and distorted. Even when they finally managed to drag her out of the car, she remained frozen, unable to respond to their frantic questions.

Her mom, an elementary school teacher, was the kindest person in the world. Whenever anyone had a problem, she was always there to help with a listening ear and a gentle hand to guide. She was always so caring and thoughtful, never a mean word or thought in her mind. She'd give you the shirt off her back if you asked. A beautiful woman with a beautiful soul.

Her dad, a masterful carpenter, was a source of boundless joy and laughter. He worked tirelessly with his hands but still found time for the occasional prank or two. When he came home after work, his hearty laughter filled every corner of the house like a wake of sunshine. He could cheer up anyone within minutes. A kind man who loved his family.

They were gone. She would never enjoy the warm cuddles from her mother again. She would never pull off masterful pranks with her dad again. Two pillars in her life were gone forever. Her parents were the tamest and kindest people she knew. They had never hurt a soul in their lives. They were dead. Why was she still alive? She should be dead, too.

Later, she found out her parents had been killed instantly. The truck driver that hit them fell asleep at the wheel, crossed the center line, and plowed into the front of their car before it tipped to the side. The man responsible for her parents' deaths had lived. It wasn't fair, but that was life.

"Jean?"

She blinked as she turned her head. Ben had opened her car door, and they were back at his house. His eyes were pinched together with concern as he reached out to her.

"I zoned out." She put on a smile, suppressing the dark memories again as she placed her hand in his. He pulled her out of the car and into his embrace. His warm arms encircled her, holding her quietly.

"Pain has a way of worming its way into our souls. If you want to talk about it, I'm here for you. If you don't want to talk, I'm still here. Lean on me. Together, we can get through this," he whispered into her hair, sending shivers down her spine. "Don't be afraid to fall apart in front of me." He pulled back and looked down at her face. Her eyes were shining with tears, and she felt a lump swell in her throat. He leaned forward and brushed his lips against hers, softly. Her eyelids drooped and his hands tightened on her waist. Tears were still thick in her throat, but his touch was like a balm to her soul. She leaned into him, her arms wrapping around his neck as she allowed herself to give in to her urges.

He deepened the kiss, his tongue tracing her lips, coaxing her to open up to him. He explored her mouth with his own, their tongues dancing in a beautiful, intimate exchange. The passion between them grew stronger with each passing moment, and soon they were lost in their own world of pleasure and desire. She moaned softly against his lips as he pressed her firmly against the car, his body molding perfectly against hers. His hands roamed over her curves, tracing the outline of her body through the thin fabric of her clothes. She felt a wave of desire wash over her as he pressed his body harder against hers, his touch igniting a fire within her. He broke contact with her lips, trailing his kisses down her jawline to the sensitive skin of her neck. The feelings he was evoking in her mind paled in comparison to the intense feelings surging through her body.

"I want you," his hot breath whispered against her neck. "But not just your body. I want all of you." He lifted his head away to look into her eyes. "I know it's fast, but I think you feel this too, don't you?" He searched her eyes as she nodded slowly. "It doesn't have to make sense. It feels right." He closed his eyes as his nose brushed over the frantic pulse on her neck. "I don't want to take advantage of your emotional state."

"You're not," Jean whispered, as her trembling fingers traced over the hair on the back of his neck. She felt him shudder, showing how affected he was by her touch. "I keep telling myself not to be, but I'm afraid," she softly admitted. He raised his head to look at her.

"I'd never hurt you. I promise I will never cheat on you. I know how it feels and I could never—"

"That's not what I meant." She gave him a small smile. "I'm afraid of losing you. To get used to having someone and then losing them and being alone all over again. The pain still wakes me up at night." She stared into Ben's golden eyes as her fingers traced over his cheek. "Even though I'm scared, I'm more afraid of the regret I'd feel if I walked away from this, never knowing what it could be. We don't know much about each other. I don't even know what you want in life. You don't know what I want. Do you want kids? Do you like dogs, swimming, hiking—" She stopped as she watched his lips curl up. He leaned his head back into hers, brushing the sweetest, softest kiss over her lips.

"Yes, to kids, dogs, swimming, hiking. I want to make a difference with the family company. I want to create something new that the world can't live without." He kissed the tip of her nose as his hand pulled her to his side. He turned and looked at his parents' house. "I want this. I want what my parents have. I want you."

"I thought you wanted a non-complicated sleeping pillow." Jean gazed up at him as a wry grin spread over his lips.

"I still want the pillow, but you know, this—" he motioned between them lightly with his hand, "doesn't have to be complicated. And even if it was complicated, I think it would still be worth it."

"You don't know enough about me to say that. What if I have a bag of nail clippings I keep in my closet?" She watched as he turned to look at her, laughter lines creasing his face.

"Even then, I think what we could have would be worth it. Though maybe we could have an outdoor shed for your weird collections." He laughed lightly as he stared into her beautiful, silver eyes. Then his gaze landed on her lips, and he had to taste them again.

He leaned down and pressed his lips against hers in a brief, chaste kiss, the kind she'd seen in the movies but had never experienced herself. She sighed against his lips, curling her toes in her shoes. Her body was alight with a bright, vibrant energy as their lips parted. She leaned into him, her hands resting on his chest as she took a deep breath.

"You're right. I don't know everything about you. What I do know is that I want to find out more. I want to know everything," he murmured against her cheek, his lips brushing against her skin in a tantalizing caress. She shivered slightly, and he pulled back to look at her face, a grin spreading on his lips. "Like that. I want to know what makes you feel good." He leaned down and kissed her again, his tongue teasing her lips until she felt another shiver run through her body. "I want to make you feel good."

"I think that's something we can work on," she whispered coquettishly as he pulled his head away.

He interlaced his fingers with hers, and they walked back to the house together. Their hands stayed connected as they climbed the several flights of stairs until they reached Ben's floor. Jean felt her heart racing in anticipation of what was coming next.

"Do you want to watch a movie? I have a home theater."

She looked at Ben, a bit exasperated as she tried to figure out if he was serious. "Watch a movie?" she asked, looking into his eyes.

"We can order anything you'd like. I have a popcorn and soda machine in the room too."

"Is that how you want to get to know me?" She stared at him curiously as he rubbed the back of his neck.

"I didn't want you to think that I was saying what I said to, well, you know. And I know that what happened earlier today bothered you. I don't want to take advantage of your emotions." He looked up at the ceiling as red stains reached his cheeks.

"I see." Jean's voice was quiet as she turned and walked down the hall toward his room.

"Where are you going?" he chuckled, turning his head in her direction.

"Well, before watching any movie, I have all this built-up tension that needs to be released." She watched as his golden eyes seemed to darken. "One way or another, it needs taken care of. Is the showerhead in your bathroom detachable?" She smiled, biting her bottom lip as she reached his door. Suddenly, she felt the weight of the front of his body on her back. His hand covered hers on the doorknob as his other hand moved along her side.

"You won't be needing it." His voice cracked with desire, his breath heavy and ragged. "I'm going to feel your body against mine. I'm going to make love to you until we both collapse from exhaustion. There won't be any tension left, I promise." The door opened, and he spun her around in his arms, locking the door behind him.

He kissed her passionately, desperately, as if his life depended on it. She gasped against his lips, her body arching toward him as they melted together in a single embrace. His hands gripped her tightly as their kiss deepened, and a feverish energy seemed to pulse between them, rising with each heated beat of their hearts. She clung to him as if she'd never let go. Their bond forged through the intensity of that moment.

With frantic movements, clothes were hastily tossed aside as he corralled her to the bed. His hand kneaded her breast, making a strangled cry escape her throat. "You offered these to me before, and ever since then, I've wanted to taste them."

The edge of the bed made her legs buckle, and the two of them fell on top of it. His tongue moved with a hungry ferocity, ravishing one of her taut nipples while his fingers worked in tandem, kneading and teasing the other until she felt completely undone. She could feel pleasure radiating from her core, enveloping them both in its heat.

His tongue swirled against her nipple as he nipped and bit at it with his teeth until it was hard and aching. His hands moved over her body, gently brushing over her soft, smooth skin. A spark of excitement shot through her as he moved his hand downward. His fingers danced over her bare skin until he reached her ass. Gripping it tightly, he let out a pleasurable growl as he gently kissed her hardened bud. He stared at her hungrily before moving down her body.

Her heart raced as he pushed her legs apart, exposing her to his gaze. He leaned in and attacked greedily, his tongue ravaging her glistening folds and sending shockwaves of pleasure throughout her entire body. He thrust his tongue inside her with wild abandon, lapping up her essence and driving her wild with every plunge and stroke of his talented tongue. She moaned in ecstasy as he insatiably went to work on her.

Her body writhed beneath his touch as he expertly used his tongue, his teeth, his hands in tandem to drive her body toward the edge. Her fingers wrapped in his hair as she whimpered his name. His tongue dragged across her, leaving a wet trail of heat as it moved away from her sensitive folds and toward the inside of her thigh. She felt his hot breath against her skin as he exhaled warmly against her leg. He turned his head and took in the scent of her, his lips planting a soft kiss on her inner thigh before he turned back to look at her. His eyes were clouded, dark lust burning in their depths. She felt a wave of heat crash over her, and her skin prickled with anticipation. She gasped at the touch of his thumb pressing against her tender clit. Her back arched involuntarily as her breathing quickened, a low moan escaping from her lips.

He moved up her body, positioning himself over her. She felt him press against her entrance, the tip of his hardened cock brushing against her clit. His eyes captured hers as he slowly entered her. He moved in and out of her, his cock stroking her in a slow, even rhythm as he gazed down at her. She laced her fingers through his hair, and their lips interlocked in a gentle, tantalizing kiss. He moved faster inside her, his tongue slipping in and out of her mouth, mimicking his thrusts. Then he pushed himself into her fully, stretching her as he filled her up. He pulled back, leaving just the tip inside of her before pressing against her again and again with powerful, deliberate thrusts. Her body was alight with the sensations he was creating within her. She groaned deeply, her body trembling from pleasure that seemed to have no end. She could feel his powerful frame quaking against her as he fought against a wave of desire that was too much to bear. His breaths grew in intensity until they were harsh and ragged, like the roar of an unleashed beast.

He could feel her inner walls shuddering with pleasure as he thrust faster and deeper. His eyes never left hers, pouring into them the intensity of his passion as he moved his hips wildly. He wanted her to feel everything that he was feeling, so he pushed himself harder still, until they were both consumed in a wave of rapturous bliss. She wrapped her legs around him, pulling him closer to her, never wanting to let go as she trembled under him. He slammed into her, her back arching as she came undone, her body wracked by tremors of euphoria. Her contracting walls embraced his cock as it filled her up, her essence mingling with his. With the feeling of her release around him, his orgasm rushed over him like a tidal wave. He thrust into her a few more times as he spilled himself into her.

Then he collapsed on top of her, their panting breaths mingling together as they lay still, their bodies still joined together. Her body quivered slightly as she came down from her high. Slowly, he slipped out of her and wrapped his arms around her, pulling her into his chest. He pressed a small kiss against her forehead as she curled up against him.

She relaxed in his arms, her breathing finally slowing as she felt the world around her drift back into focus. A feeling of contentment washed over her, and she smiled to herself.

"The tension should be a bit better now," he smirked against her forehead as she murmured an acknowledgment. "But I believe I promised you exhaustion." He traced his tongue over her lips, making her gasp. "That took the edge off, but I'm far from exhausted." He growled against her lips as his fingers explored her skin. "I want to know you even better." He settled heavily against her, fitting his mouth to hers, awakening urges all over again. They would move together as one, explore each other, and learn what they each liked.

When the sensual storm finally passed, they would know the other's body as well as they knew their own.

Chapter 20

The hours rolled by, and Ben and Jean never emerged from their room. At one point, Rebecca was going to use the intercom again, but Liam stopped her. He reminded her that food didn't satisfy all hunger.

Jean was resting on his chest when her stomach growled loudly. She felt him plant a soft kiss on her head before she looked up at him.

"Good morning," Ben said lazily, with a tired smile on his face. He didn't sleep much last night, but it wasn't because of his insomnia. He turned to his side, positioning her in his arms. Her silver eyes looked content but tired. A tiny smile formed on his lips as he tucked her hair behind her ear. "You are so beautiful." Crimson instantly stained her cheeks and he chuckled, leaning down to kiss her softly. Nothing about her body was a mystery to him, not after the night they spent together.

He had never felt so content or so alive. It was as if everything was right in the world. Or at the very least, everything in his life was right. However, there was a problem.

"Jean, there's something we need to talk about."

"Mmmhmm there is," she hummed, and he looked at her in confusion.

"You had something to say too?" He watched as she lifted her brows up at him.

"We're probably thinking the same thing?"

"Like how we never want to spend another night apart?" Her eyes widened and her lips parted as she studied his face.

"No ... but ... wait ... what?!"

"I want to hold you every night. I don't think I can sleep without you."

"So, nothing's changed with that last part," she giggled as a wry grin spread over his face.

"Do you not like the idea?" he asked, as she stretched in his arms, cuddling under his chin.

"For not much sleep, I've never rested better. I could get used to it."

"Good, so what was it you wanted to talk about?" Her head stayed buried under his chin, keeping her face hidden.

"Uhm, it's just, after the night we had—the thing is, we didn't use any protection, and I'm not on the pill." She didn't even think of it before this morning. That was when she realized the possible consequences of their actions.

He chuckled, burying his nose in her hair. "That isn't a problem, is it? You said you wanted kids."

"Well, yeah, but not like this," she whispered.

"Like what?"

"Ben, you know what I mean." She listened as he laughed.

"I already have a solution. Marry me," he demanded quietly, making her look up at him in shock. "Whether you're pregnant or not, stay by my side forever."

She half sat up, bringing the sheet up with her to cover her skin. "Ben, be serious."

"I am."

"But Ben, shouldn't we date longer?" She stared into his amber eyes, checking for any sign of madness. Get married? Just like that, as if he was ordering a cup of tea.

"Why? I'm not going to change my mind. I'm all in. Why do we have to date for months or years? I know what I want. Besides, my parents are happy and love each other unconditionally." He watched her silver eyes not making the connection. "They never dated at all. Straight to marriage for them. They got to know each other after they were married. It's a long story, but one day I'll tell it to you. Maybe when I'm not so hungry." He laughed, sitting up, a kind smile spreading over his lips. "No pressure, Jean. I'm not going to change my mind. I want you by my side. I want to marry you, but I understand if you aren't ready for such a shocking commitment."

A tiny smile spread over her lips as she dropped the sheet, sliding out of bed. "I was just thinking," she said as she sauntered to the bathroom. "I must have been really good last night for you to want to lock me down to you already." She listened as he laughed, his feet padding across the floor to reach her. She felt him spin her in his arms, cupping her chin to look up at him.

"You were incredible last night." He felt his heart pounding as he searched her silver eyes. "Is that a yes?"

There was no use denying what she wanted. She looked up at him and took his hand in hers, intertwining their fingers. Slowly pulling it toward her face, she pressed her lips against his palm. His heart was thumping furiously, his breathing heavy and irregular. She raised her eyes to look deep into his and smiled.

"I'll marry you." It was a simple declaration of love. It wasn't eloquent or poetic, it wasn't filled with magic words or flowery phrases. The significance of those words was crystal clear. And he knew their meaning. His lips curled up to reveal his full smile.

"Yes!" he exclaimed, with so much gusto and excitement it took her by surprise. He wrapped his arms around her and pulled her close to him. She buried her face in his chest, savoring the feeling of being in his arms.

"I love you," he whispered in her hair, making her look up at him. His lips met hers in an intense kiss, his hands roaming her body while his tongue swept her mouth. She eagerly tangled her tongue with his, eager to taste him. She could feel his cock slowly beginning to harden once more between them.

"Again?" she whispered and listened to his low, intoxicating chuckle.

He planted soft kisses around her mouth as he corralled her into the bathroom. He held her with one hand while the other effortlessly turned the shower on. "Again, and again and always." He stepped with her into the steamy shower, pulling her close as the hot water poured over them. The heat seemed to wrap around their bodies, and he felt himself melting into her as they embraced. His lips moved to hers as he pushed her against the shower wall, their skin sizzling from the scalding stream as they moved in perfect harmony, lost in a blissful moment of passion and love.

After their steamy shower, they both dressed. Ben tenderly helped her, treating her as if she were made of glass and could break. He softly kissed the tips of her fingers, then pulled her hand.

"I have something for you."

"Ben, I'm starving, and you just gave me your something—" She stopped teasing him as she felt something cold slip on her finger.

She stared in awe at her glistening hand, adorned with a sparkling gold band. Embedded in the metal was a diamond of the purest white, shimmering with brilliance that looked like it could shine in the darkest of places.

In a moment of pure happiness, she couldn't help but cry tears of joy. It was the first time in a long time that she'd felt so happy, so content. She didn't have to worry about anything or anyone. No one in this world could ever make her feel as whole as he did. In that moment, she knew her life was forever changed—and she wouldn't change it for the world. She belonged to him now, and every breath she took was devoted to being with him.

He cupped her cheeks in his hands, leaning his head into hers. "Things are going to get crazy. This is going to go public, and everyone will want to talk to you. Reporters will try to get you to talk. They will dig to find out who you are. Please don't let any of that scare you off. I'm going to ask Clint to be your guard. He isn't just a driver; he's also trained in hand-to-hand combat. Plus, I trust him. If you ever aren't with me, then he will be with you."

She looked up at him, feeling slightly apprehensive. "You're announcing us?" She felt his thumb softly caress her skin.

"I want everyone to know I'm off the market and so are you. As my fiancée, you fall under the Cross protection. My dad has a fierce reputation, and people don't want to make the Cross family their enemies. I know it's a lot. Being married to me might become a burden—"

She heard the vulnerability in his voice and quickly put him at ease. "Ben, you are not a burden. I'm with you, and that's all that matters. We will figure everything else out." He moved in and kissed her forehead before interlacing her fingers with his.

"Come on, let's go tell mom and dad." He felt her slight resistance as she glanced behind him.

"Are they going to be okay with this?" She listened as he laughed.

"Mom will be elated, and dad will be fine. They just want me to be happy. If that's what they really want, then they want me with you." He watched the soft pink glow reach her cheeks. "If we don't leave now, we might not be able to eat today—"

"Okay, let's go!" She grabbed his hand, quickly leading him to the door. "I'm not one of those women who don't eat. I'm starving." He laughed as he wrapped his hand around her side.

"I'll restock my snack shelf and mini fridge in the room, so this won't be a problem in the future." He felt her slow down, and he stopped. "Jean?"

"What is the plan exactly? I still have my apartment," she whispered quietly, watching him shake his head.

"Once they're done, we'll collect your things, but you can't go back there. Everything is going to change because your face will be everywhere. Everyone will know you. You'll move in here with me. We can discuss what we want to do moving forward after that. My parents designed this house to have private wings so that we could continue to live here with our families, but if you don't want that, we can look for a house together."

It was starting to sink in just how much her life was about to change. Going into the grocery store would no longer be a common event for her. People would recognize her wherever she went. She knew it would be difficult to change so much, yet looking into his concerned amber eyes told her how much it would be worth it. Wherever this man was, that was where she should be.

"Ben, I don't care about any of that. I'd live in a shack with you. As long as I'm with you, that's all that matters."

"You can't say things like that when we're so close to our room." His voice turned husky as he stared into her eyes.

"Nope!" she squealed, sprinting for the stairs. Ben chased after her, a wolfish smile on his face. She went crashing down the stairs, taking them two at a time. The sound of his feet tumbling after her made her heart pound in childlike excitement.

"You can't win, Jean!" His voice was full of confidence. With a squeal she turned and rushed to the last set of stairs. He caught up with her, pinning her against the stairway wall with his body. His arms coiled around her as they both laughed between their heavy pants.

"You're going to have to learn to live with the fact that I am always going to be faster than you," he boasted, his voice full of humor.

A playful smirk rose on her lips as she pressed her front into him. Her arms wrapped around his head as she bit his bottom lip, pulling it into her mouth to suck on it. A low, pleasurable growl reverberated in his chest as she moved one hand down his chest. "There's something you have to learn, too." She traced her tongue around his lips, his eyes half-lidded as he pressed his hand on the wall.

With his arm gone, she was no longer trapped. She quickly fled down the rest of the stairs, turning at the bottom and raising her brows and lips in triumph. "You'll have to live with the fact that I'm always going to outsmart you."

He chuckled as he walked down the stairs to her. "I concede. You win." He softly kissed her forehead, intertwining their fingers together. "Ready?" He smiled when she nodded up at him confidently. "Let's go." He pulled her with him to the dining room.

Ben and Jean stepped into the room, their footsteps echoing off the walls as they slowly entered. Ben's parents sat at one end of the long, wooden table, while Steph, Link, and Link's father occupied seats at the far end. All conversation ceased as each person in the room looked up at them.

"Hey Gina, how are you feeling today?" Steph asked, concerned, since she didn't look well yesterday when they left Link's building. Link explained everything to her, and she couldn't imagine what she had been through.

"I'm famished," Jean admitted with a soft chuckle.

"BENJAMIN! If I have to, I will keep Gina under lock and key!" Rebecca scolded as she motioned for Jean to take a seat.

"One moment," Ben said as he kept Jean at his side.

"Ben, she's hungry!" His mom continued to scold him.

"Just a moment, mom," Ben chuckled as he grabbed Jean's ring hand. "I have an announcement." His mom's gaze instantly darted to Jean's hand.

"OH MY! FINALLY!" she squealed as she pointed at Jean's hand. Then Steph erupted into a scream and the room turned to madness. Jean felt Steph pull her away from Ben as she looked at the ring. "It's Gram's ring. It looks perfect on her."

"Aww, Ben, why didn't you tell us?" His mom began fussing over Jean as Steph began to make wedding plans.

"Congratulations, son," his dad said, patting his son on the shoulder. "This is the start of a wonderful journey. It won't always be easy, but I promise you, it's worth it."

Ben looked at his father, a sense of peace washing over him. He couldn't stop the smile that spread across his face.

"A toast to the future Mrs. Cross," Link's dad said, raising his orange juice glass, making everyone laugh.

Link reached out and shook Ben's hand, bringing him in for a hug. "I couldn't be happier with this match. Looks like we're all going to be family," he said, making Ben look at him curiously.

"Well, it took you forever to show your faces again, but Link proposed to me last night. We're going to the jeweler this afternoon to pick out the rings." Steph then clapped her hands. "Let's all get married together! A joint wedding. Yes, this will be so exciting, and fun! And we will only need to remember one date!" she giggled, looking at Link.

"It's cost effective too," Liam said, going along with it.

"We'll announce the engagements at the benefit dinner tonight." Rebecca wrapped her arms around Liam happily.

"The benefit dinner is tonight?" Jean almost coughed, not realizing it was so soon.

"It is, and it's the perfect place to spread the news." Rebecca reached up to kiss Liam on his jawline. "I'm so happy. Almost time for grandchildren now, just like we always dreamed."

"A big, loving family under one roof." Liam looked at Link's father. "And we insist on you moving in here with us. There's plenty of room here for everyone."

Link teared up as he pursed his lips together. It was his only issue about moving in with their family, and they solved it in an instant. "Thank you," he mouthed to Liam, who winked at him in response.

"Alright, let my fiancée get something to eat. I'm afraid I haven't allowed her to eat since lunch yesterday." He reached for her shoulders, helping her into a seat.

Jean listened to all the excitement around her. She snatched a slice of toast from the plate, barely registering the burning pain in her fingers as she quickly inhaled it. The clamorous commotion that filled the room seemed to vibrate through her bones like an avalanche. She listened to the ladies chatter excitedly about wedding plans and the date.

She was happy, happier than she ever imagined. It all felt like a dream, and if it was one, she hoped she would never wake. However, if there are dreams, there are also nightmares. Especially when you least expect them.

Chapter 21

Jean slid into the plush leather of the limousine, taking her seat next to Ben's sister, Steph, and his mother. Her eyes were drawn to Steph's slender hand, where a dazzling diamond ring sparkled on her finger. The car rumbled as an electric chatter hummed through the air. As they approached the banquet hall, anticipation built with each passing second until all they could hear was their pounding hearts and relentless excitement. The men had gone ahead and were now eagerly awaiting their arrival, adding a palpable sense of anticipation to the moment of reunion.

It was customary for this event for the men to go ahead without seeing their dates. It was almost like not seeing the bride before the wedding. The idea was so neither would change their minds about attending the event. She found out that dinners were auctioned off as part of the fundraising efforts, and certain men and women were bid on for a one-on-one dinner. It was completely randomized and was considered a fun tradition. It was also customary to let couples win the bids.

She looked down at the ring on her finger. It seemed to shine more next to her silver dress. Steph and Ben's mother had helped her get ready, assisting her with everything from getting dressed to doing her hair and make-up. When she looked at herself, she barely recognized the person she saw. She at least looked like she fit the part, but inside she was swimming with nervous energy.

"Ben was being such a baby about leaving you for just a few hours," Steph giggled, looking at her.

"I knew he was smitten with you the day I met him at the airport. I remember when I started to fall in love with Liam—I was so confused during that time." Ben's mother looked up at the ceiling with a wistful smile on her face. "You know, I wouldn't change a thing. Not a thing."

"Ben mentioned once that you didn't know Liam when you married him. Was it an arranged marriage?" Jean asked. A gentle chuckle escaped Rebecca's throat.

"It was a runaway marriage plan gone wrong." She laughed and looked at Jean. "I was there to marry another. I ended up running into Liam and marrying him instead. It was better than getting caught and being forced to marry—well, anyway, it was an interesting journey, but I love Liam more than I ever thought possible. He is my match. Oh look! We're here," Rebecca said, nodding to the window.

Jean turned, casting her gaze on the sparkling lights leading down the long, private road. It led to an old castle that had been repurposed for events and tours. It was stone, like a castle should be, but it was so much more than that. It was a stunning architectural creation, a domed, multi-story building made of stone and glass tiles. It was alive with a million lights, illuminating the entire structure.

As they pulled up to it, she saw Ben's dad, Link, and Ben standing there next to a group of other men. She suddenly felt anxious about Ben seeing her now. What if she didn't look nice enough? What if he changed his mind?

Her eyes moved to the extravagant women who were being dropped off. They walked with such grace and elegance. They were beautiful. She sank back in her seat, chewing on her lip nervously.

"Oh, look how impatient Ben looks." Steph giggled as she looked at Link next. "They noticed our limo. Aww, Link looks excited. Isn't he such a doll? That damn man made me wait for so long. I wasn't about to wait any longer to take him off the market," she snorted angrily, folding her arms over her chest. "You have no idea how much I hated hearing how everyone planned to marry him. He's always been mine!"

"Stephanie, you've always been so possessive. I was worried you scared Link off. You're like your father, and apparently your brother too. You are all so passionate. You know what I love about your passion? It isn't fleeting." She then nodded to Jean. "He will never change his mind about how he feels. The way they love is passionate and strong, but never shallow. It can be overwhelming at times, but you become their very center." She tapped her chest as she looked out the window, finding her husband. "I love that man."

There was so much conviction in her words. Jean could tell that Ben's mother was just as passionate about her husband as he was about her. No wonder Ben wanted a love like his parents. Jean hoped she could experience such a strong bond herself.

The limousine pulled up to the castle walkway, and it was now their turn to get out. She fidgeted nervously with her engagement ring as she watched Steph slide out of the car first. She watched as she made her way to Link, who wrapped his arm around her waist, admiring her. It was her turn next.

As she stepped out of the car, Jean took a deep breath and composed herself. She was struck by the grandeur of the castle. It was like something out of a fairy tale, with its towering spires and glittering lights. It was more intimidating seeing it up close like this. She felt out of place until she caught Ben's eye. In that moment, all of her worries melted away.

Ben's smile was contagious, and his eyes shone with love as he strode to her with purpose. His eyes greedily looked over her as he placed both his hands on her waist.

"You are stunning," he breathed out before capturing her lips. His soft warmth moved against her, his hunger evident. He placed one more soft kiss on her lips as he smiled at her. "You couldn't be more perfect." A pink color stained her cheeks as he hooked her arm around his. "Shall we?"

Jean stared up at Ben, ignoring all the curious glances and hushed whispers. Some things still didn't feel real. The fact that she was going to marry this man ... the idea that she felt so strongly for him in such a short time really seemed like fate.

As they entered the castle, Jean was in awe of the beauty of the interior. The walls were adorned with ornate tapestries, and the floors were made of polished marble. The air was thick with the scent of roses and jasmine, and the sound of music filled the beautiful space. The sound of laughter and the smell of delicious food wafted in the air.

She felt herself lean more into Ben's side as they entered the main banquet hall. A woman stepped in front of them, wearing a dress that made Jean blush. She recognized the red-headed woman as the person Ben had dinner with the other day.

"Benny." The woman almost hissed, her green eyes glowering at Jean. "Who is your date?"

"Melissa, this is my fiancée, Jean," Ben said proudly, his eyes full of admiration as he looked down at his future bride.

They heard a loud gasp and looked back toward the woman in front of them. "Did you say fiancée?!" The high shrill sound of her voice quieted those around them so they could eavesdrop.

"I did. If you'll excuse us, we need to take our seats." Ben brushed past Melissa without another glance, escorting Jean with him.

Melissa shot daggers at Jean as she watched them take their seats. A man walked up next to her, and without looking at him, she said, "I want the story before the night is over. I want everything you can find out."

"I'm on it."

Melissa glared at Ben a moment longer before spinning on her heel and storming away. Fury boiled inside of her, bubbling over in a molten rage. She had been expecting that they would marry one day—an unspoken promise from the universe that was now broken. Everyone expected them to end up together, and now he was making a fool out of her! No, Melissa refused to be made a fool, and with fiery determination, she vowed to herself that it wasn't over.

Ben took his seat next to Jean, noticing her pinched brows. "What's wrong?"

"She looked really mad," Jean whispered as Ben scoffed.

"She is a spoiled, lying brat. Let her pout," Steph snorted, scooting her seat toward Jean so she could whisper, "She's a bitch, and everyone low key hates her."

Ben placed his hand on Jean's while rubbing his fingers around the engagement ring. "She's a petty person. It has nothing to do with you. Now ... pay attention to me, because I missed you," he teased, bringing her hand to his lips.

"Speaking of spoiled," Steph teased as Link laughed.

"And you aren't?" Plates of food soon began to arrive, saving Link from whatever backlash was coming.

Jean quietly picked at her bowl of pasta, her eyes darting between the conversations taking place around her. Besides the Cross family, there were a few other families seated at their table. She felt a bit out of place, without anything to contribute, but nonetheless was keenly listening, memorizing phrases and details, filing them away for future reference.

Suddenly, a man's voice cut through the chatter. "Ladies and gentlemen, may I have your attention please?" All conversation ceased, and everyone turned toward the stage. Jean watched as a man in a tuxedo stepped onto the stage, holding a microphone. "It is my great pleasure to kick off the main event of the evening. You know the drill. Lift up those plates, and if you have a star underneath, please make your way to the front."

Jean's heart raced as she lifted her plate. Sure enough, there was a star on the bottom of her plate. She looked around the table, feeling a bit nervous. She chewed on her inner lip as she turned to look at Ben.

"Oh, Jean, you have a star!" Steph chirped excitedly. "This means they get to bid on who gets to have dinner with you."

Ben leaned over and lightly kissed her ear. "Don't worry, I'll pay any amount for a date with you." He smiled as he saw the blush crawl up her neck.

"Come on everyone, make your way to the front."

Ben stood up, reaching his hand out to Jean, lifting her next to him. He felt her slightly trembling fingers rest on his arm, and he stopped. "You don't have to, Jean. I'll take you home right now if you want."

"It's for charity, right?" She looked up at him with a brave face. "It makes me nervous being in front of all these people, but I can handle it. Besides, I need to get used to this if I'm going to stay by your side." She felt him squeeze her lightly as he gazed at her proudly, a beaming smile on his face.

He led her to the front and escorted her up to the stage.

"Who do we have here?" the man asked.

"This is my fiancée, Regina." Ben glanced at the man who nodded in excitement.

"The fiancée of Ben Cross! What a mysterious treat for someone to have dinner with her. Of course, that is if he allows someone else to win the bid." The man laughed into the microphone, and the soft laughter of the crowd quickly followed.

"I mean, if someone wants a war with Cross Industries—" Ben smiled darkly as the guy let out a nervous chuckle. Ben then winked at Jean, leaving her on the stage to stand with the others.

There were over a dozen people who were being auctioned off one by one. Jean thought she was going to faint when she heard how much they were paying just for a dinner date. She had to remind herself that this was just a fun way to donate money.

Finally, it was Jean's turn to be auctioned off. She took a deep breath, trying to steady her nerves. The spotlight shone down on her, highlighting her features as she stood there, feeling exposed and vulnerable.

"We have Regina, the lovely fiancée of Ben Cross! Who wants to win the chance to share a meal with her?"

A man in the front row raised his hand, waving it in the air. He was middle-aged, balding, and slightly overweight. Then, like a ripple, the hands kept raising, the bidding going higher.

"Two hundred and fifty thousand." She heard Link say loudly, rising to his feet.

"Three hundred thousand." Ben's voice said loudly as his gaze met with hers.

"Four hundred thousand."

Jean's eyes darted to the back, landing on a tall figure. It was a man who was taking the bids by phone.

The announcer chuckled nervously. "You should remind our caller that this is Ben Cross' fiancée." There was bidding for fun, but once it reached a certain number, respectfully, you let their date win the bid.

"Five hundred thousand." Ben said, glaring at the man in the back.

"He went up to six."

This was when Liam stood up, "One million, and if anyone bids against me, I'm going to take it personally. That is my future daughter-in-law, and this is the only way I'm going to get private time with her." He let out a gentle chuckle, but his eyes looked at the man on the phone threateningly.

Meanwhile, in the far corner of the room, Melissa skimmed the contents of some papers she was given. "Now, isn't this interesting."

A sinister sneer twisted its way across her lips as she stared menacingly at Jean. A malicious glint reflected in her eyes, her intense gaze never wavering from the stage where Jean stood. She would see how serious this relationship really was.

"Mr. Liam Cross, you have won the bid at one million."

Melissa's cruel smile rested on her face as she watched Mr. Cross collect the woman and bring her back to their table. Now all she needed was a moment alone with her. Ben might be fooling everyone there, but not her. This woman came out of nowhere. One day there was no one, and suddenly he was engaged?! She wasn't buying it, and now, with her newfound knowledge, she would end it.

Chapter 22

L iam escorted Jean to the dance floor first, and Ben pouted as he took his mother out. He looked adorable as he stared at her and danced as close as possible. Ben's dad was very kind to her, and he made her feel as if she was part of the family. He told her how happy he was that Ben had found her. She promised him that she would always be there to support Ben however he needed it. He smiled at her and told her that he already knew she would.

When it was finally Ben's turn to dance with her, he spun her away from the crowds, swaying with her slowly and stealing her kisses. His amber eyes never strayed from her, making her feel as if no one else existed.

"Sorry I didn't get the winning bid." Ben's lips brushed over her forehead as she smiled up at him.

"That's okay. Your dad's taking me out for dinner on a yacht! He said that way you can't interrupt us," she giggled as Ben growled lowly. That was exactly what he planned to do.

"He should have let me win the bid," he pouted, holding her closer. His mind drifted to the mysterious caller who kept raising the bid. He wouldn't tell her, but this had him concerned. It must have alarmed his dad as well, because he claimed the next bid with a threat, thereby sending a message to the caller. Who did his dad think it was? Were they trying to get to Jean in order to get to them? This thought made his blood run cold. He couldn't lose her, ever. She was too important to him.

"Alright, it's time for the sweetheart bidding. One sweetheart stays behind while the other tries to win them a prize. Select your champion!" The man announced dramatically, making the crowd chuckle.

"My lady, allow me to be your champion," Ben bowed slightly, keeping his golden eyes on her. He playfully kissed her hand before winking at her. "I'll be back."

She watched him as he backed away and turned, disappearing into the crowd. With a sigh, she looked around the room. There were so many people that she was experiencing some sensory overload. She wasn't used to being around a crowd. The cool breeze behind her made her turn her head. She spotted the half-opened glass doors that promised a place of refuge from the relentless chaos behind her. She tiptoed outside, making her escape to the cool, quiet air. The balcony was empty, and she instantly relaxed. She leaned forward and rested her hands on the ledge, feeling the cold roughness of the stone against her palms. The breeze danced over her skin like a lover's touch, teasing her hair into wild tangles. As she closed her eyes and let out a contented sigh, she suddenly felt as if she wasn't alone.

She opened her eyes and turned around slowly, scanning the balcony for any sign of movement. On the far side, she saw flowing red hair and instantly knew who it was ... Melissa.

Melissa stood by the door that led back inside, her hand resting on the handle. She stared back at her with piercing green eyes that seemed to glow in the light of the moon. For a moment, they stood there, gazing at each other in silence. The only sound was the soft rustling of leaves and the gentle hum of the crowd inside.

A savage smirk spread across Melissa's lips as she strode purposefully toward Jean. Her eyes flashed with fierce victory, as if she had conquered some unseen foe. Jean stood her ground, resolute despite the thunderous presence of Ben's cheating ex-girlfriend. With steely determination, she returned the stranger's gaze, never conceding to her power. She wasn't a threat to her, and she wouldn't back down.

Melissa stopped a few feet away from Jean, her eyes still locked onto hers. The smirk on her face only widened as she leaned closer, invading Jean's personal space. The scent of her perfume filled Jean's nostrils, threatening to overwhelm her senses.

"I see you've taken refuge out here," Melissa said, her voice low and husky. "Couldn't handle the pressure of the party, huh?"

Jean refused to back down, holding Melissa's gaze with fierce determination. "I needed a moment to myself," she replied, her voice calm but firm. "Is there a problem with that?"

Melissa's smirk turned into a sneer, and she took another step closer. "I feel so sorry for you ... being forced into a life you've never prepared for. And all for what? Just to be a tool for the Cross family."

Jean would be a fool to listen to the words of the vicious person in front of her. But her insecurities made her pry when she should have walked away. "A tool?"

Melissa made a fake frown and clicked her tongue, shaking her head. "Oh, you poor thing. You don't even know? Did he tell you he loved you? Now that is just too cruel."

Jean signed, narrowing her eyes at the woman. "I'm not in the mood for riddles."

"You know what I found out?" Melissa continued to talk as if Jean said nothing. "I found out that Ben canceled his prescriptions today. Isn't that curious? Yes, I did some investigating since you seemed to come out of nowhere. I knew there had to be more ..." She turned, looking up at the moon. "Where there's smoke, there's fire. I'm sure you've heard the saying. I've heard that Ben is able to sleep when you're beside him."

Jean felt her heart beating rapidly as she put together what Melissa was telling her. It wasn't true though, right? He wouldn't go so far as to marry her just because he could sleep.

"I'm sure this is a shock, and you're probably going to deny it. So let me say this. The Cross family is one of the most, if not THE most, powerful families around. Their only weakness is that Ben has been suffering from insomnia. This has affected his work and has been a real concern for the family. They even planned to have Stephanie take over the company, which none of them wanted. Then you came along." She gave her a poisonous smile and shook her head. "Now Ben can sleep, and the weakness has been removed. You hardly know each other, and suddenly you're engaged. I bet he tells you he loves you and needs you, right? He proposes out of nowhere, right? Because he can't lose you—not his precious new sleep charm." Melissa's wicked eyes glowed as she burst into a scornful chuckle.

"Don't you think the timing is incredible for your apartment to suddenly go under quarantine, forcing you into the Cross home? Why would your apartment complex have an invasive species there?" The woman's cackling laughter grated on Jean's ears, as if her skin was being scraped raw. The sickening realization that her words might hold a disturbing truth burned her insides like acid, and she wondered if her longing for a family had made her gullible enough to accept the lies. Her stomach churned with a toxic mix of dread and despair.

Jean's heart felt like it was about to burst out of her chest. It was all too much to take in at once. The sudden realization that her new life might be based on a lie, and that she was being used by the man she had given her heart to, was too much to bear. Melissa's words echoed in her head, taunting her with the possibility of betrayal.

"I don't know what you're talking about," Jean said, her voice concealing the doubt she suddenly felt.

Melissa chuckled and took another step closer, bringing her face dangerously close to Jean's. "Oh, come on, sweetie," she said, her voice dripping with venom. "Do you really think the most eligible bachelor around chose you? Are you so much more attractive than the rest of us?" The laughing smirk on her face mocked Jean. "We know that isn't it. So, it must be your family has a business he wants ... oh wait, not it again. So why you? Why so fast? Kitten, do you really think he fell madly in love with you at first sight? You really think it has nothing to do with the fact he's able to sleep next to you? Not in the slightest?"

Jean's fists clenched at her sides, the anger rising within her. How dare Melissa speak to her like that? How dare she insinuate that Ben was using her for something other than genuine affection? But a small part of her couldn't help but wonder if Melissa was right. She had always questioned why someone like Ben would be interested in her. She wasn't rich or famous or particularly stunning. And now, with

Melissa's words hanging in the air, she couldn't shake the feeling that there was something she was missing.

But she refused to let Melissa see her doubt. She straightened her back and met Melissa's gaze head on. "I don't know what your problem is, Melissa," she said, her voice cold and steady. "But whatever it is, it certainly isn't my fault. I'm not the one who cheated on Ben and lost him. So why don't you leave me alone and go bother someone else?"

Melissa's eyes narrowed, the green depths turning dark with anger. "You think you're so smart, don't you?" she hissed, her voice barely above a whisper. "Ben isn't the man you think he is. You think he loves you? You think he cares about you? Ben only cares about one thing, and that is the business. He neglected me. He led me to another man's arms. I know my duty, though. I know I'm just supposed to be an ornament next to him. I'll play my part better for my family. That's why I want him back. But you—you don't even have the good sense God has given women. You won't see the truth when I serve it up to you. Well, let me tell you something, honey. You're living in a fantasy. You're a tool so that Ben can continue to focus on the only thing he cares about."

"I don't believe you," she said firmly. "And even if it were true, it wouldn't change how I feel about him. I love him, Melissa, and nothing you say can change that."

Melissa's sneer deepened. "Love? You don't know the first thing about love, honey. You're just a clueless little girl who thinks she's found her Prince Charming. Well, newsflash, Jean. There's no such thing as Prince Charming. All there is in this world is business, and the ability to stay on top."

The night sky opened up, and rain began to fall in thick sheets, soaking the balcony and turning the ground below into a mud-slick puddle. The cold water hit Jean's skin like icy needles, making her shiver. Melissa's hair began to cling to her head, the red strands turning darker, almost black. But as the rain dripped down Jean's face, a cold dread filled her body, chilling her to the core.

Her relationship with Ben had felt too good to be true. Maybe that was because it was. She hated where her mind was going. But she never felt deserving of Ben, so naturally, this was easier to believe. How could she figure out the truth? Ben would obviously deny it.

Link. Her eyes brightened as she thought about her friend. Link trusted Ben and wanted them together. Or was he saying it for Steph's sake? *Stop it, Jean! Stop thinking like that. Stop thinking the worst of people because of this bitch in front of you.*

"I know what you're trying to do, and it isn't going to work. I'm not going to doubt the man I love." She turned walking to the door. "I feel sorry for you. You will never find happiness because you will always want more. You want Ben? Well, you can't have him."

"You're the one I feel sorry for. Caught in a game you had no chance of winning."

Jean turned to look back at Melissa, but suddenly something covered her face. She gasped, breathing in a strong scent that made her world fade to darkness.

"It took you long enough." Melissa looked herself over. "I'm drenched. Get her out of here before they come looking for her."

"I don't take orders from you, bitch. I want the woman. This has nothing to do with you."

"Well, I want the woman out of the way, so I guess this made us temporary allies." Melissa listened as the man scoffed, lifted Jean into his arms.

"Fuck off, crazy bitch," the man said as he moved to the fire escape, lowering himself into the darkness.

Melissa didn't care what the man called her. Jean was gone, and she could finally talk some sense into Ben. He didn't need that nobody. His place was by her side. Feeling pleased with herself, she stepped back inside, water dripping onto the floor from the rain. She needed to change quickly and get to another location. She didn't need anyone to pin their suspicions on her. Too bad for Jean—this was her own fault for trying to be part of a world where she could never belong.

Chapter 23

Ben waltzed into the room with the biggest grin on his face. He had won the bid for gold silk pillowcases, which he thought held special meaning for them. He strode to their table and his eyes scanned around the room, looking for Jean.

"Where's Jean?" Ben asked, looking at his sister.

"I haven't seen her. I thought she went with you." Steph stood up and looked around, alarmed.

"I'll check the balcony," his mother said, standing up.

"Maybe she's in the washroom. I'll look there." Steph left, leaving Ben looking around frantically.

"Ben."

He turned to see Melissa sauntering toward him. "Not now. Have you seen Jean?"

"Did she decide this was all too much for her and leave?" Melissa looked around, feigning shock. "I have to say, I could see this coming. She looked very uncomfortable on-stage tonight."

"Shut up. Jean wouldn't have just left," Ben growled, as Link came up to the table with Ben's dad.

"Where are the ladies?" Link asked, taking in Ben's concerned face.

"They went looking for Jean. They haven't seen her and thought she was with me." He glanced at his father. "I shouldn't have left her."

"I'm sure everything is fine." His dad tried to reassure him, but deep inside he felt on edge. Jean was Ben's fiancée and was new to their world. She would make for an easy target, only angering one prominent family. Her parents were dead, and even if they were alive, they wouldn't have held an important position in the business world. Only the Cross family would be affected.

"Ben, can we talk?" Melissa asked, with less patience.

"Get lost, Melissa. I need to find my fiancée!"

"Oh, cut the fiancée crap. You only want her so you can sleep at night."

Her words made Ben turn, narrowing his eyes at her. "What?!"

"I may have told Jean that you canceled your prescriptions today, and how convenient everything fell into place. I can imagine you're willing to do anything to keep your precious sleep charm."

"You bitch!" Ben growled as he stepped up to her. "So, you did see Jean. Where is she?"

"Who knows? After I talked to her, she looked quite upset. She vanished, no doubt reflecting on her poor decisions now that she knows the truth."

"The truth? The truth is I love that woman beyond any rational reason. I don't give a damn whether she helps me sleep or not. I canceled my prescriptions because they quit working. The doctor is writing me a new script to try. It has nothing to do with Jean. Yes, I sleep when I'm with her, but that has nothing to do with my marriage offer. I love her. I know you can't understand that, because you aren't capable of that emotion." He was all but seething as he yelled at her. It was becoming a public display. "How dare you lash out at my fiancée! You had your chance, and you ruined it by sleeping around with anyone willing to take you to bed. It's over. It has been over! You come near my fiancée again and I'll destroy your family's company. DO YOU HEAR ME?!" he roared, turning to the sound of footsteps behind him. His mother and sister were there, shaking their heads, their eyes filled with worry.

"She wasn't there. No one has seen her," Ben's mother said as Steph looked at Melissa.

"Someone said they saw her standing outside in the rain talking to you. What did you do?!" Steph balled her fingers together in a tight fist.

"Melissa," a stern voice said from behind her.

"Daddy?" Melissa's eyes went wide with fear.

"You are such a disappointment. You tell them what you know, now, or I am disowning you, and you will never receive your inheritance!"

Melissa's bottom lip quivered as she stared at the floor angrily. "I don't know where she is. I talked to a man on the phone. I don't know who he was, but it was the man bidding during the auction. I told him I would get Jean alone. Little did I know she would make that an easy task, because she went out on the balcony by herself. Someone took her."

"What do you mean?" Ben's voice was strained as he tried to contain his emotions.

"I mean, he took her. He put a cloth up to her face, she fainted, and he took her!" she snapped, instantly regretting her tone because everyone heard her.

"Who was it?!" Liam growled, placing a firm hand on his son's shoulder to restrain him from doing something stupid.

"I don't know," she whispered with a quivering breath. "He was wearing a mask. I don't know—" she choked as she cowered under Liam's icy gaze.

"We have to find her." Ben turned to look at his dad, whose brows were furrowed in thought.

"Deal with your daughter," Liam growled at Melissa's dad before gripping his son's shoulder. "Let's go home."

"Dad!"

"Benjamin." Liam glared at his son, his eyes suddenly softening. "Ben, she isn't here. She's probably far from here. Whoever took her did it to get to us, right? They'll contact us."

"I'm not just waiting around—" Ben felt his father's grip on him tighten as he whispered harshly in his ear.

"We don't know who might be involved. We'll go home and plan our move in private." He loosened his grip and leaned back. "We're going home." His voice carried throughout the banquet hall as he led his family away. Whoever had the audacity to threaten his family was going to face his unbridled wrath. NO ONE messed with his family without consequences.

Jean's eyes fluttered open. She stared up at a white ceiling, a lamp in the corner illuminating the room. She blinked, trying to recall what happened. With force, she moved herself into a sitting position so she could look around better. She was lying on a beautiful, queen-size bed with a luxury comforter. The room had golden walls and there were three wooden doors in the decent-sized room. There was also a large window to the side. Where was she?

She recalled her conversation with Melissa at the dinner party and—she inhaled sharply as she remembered the hand going around her mouth. She had been taken! Yet, her hands were not tied, and there were no guards in her room. This wasn't like any abduction she had ever heard about.

Slowly, she tested her weight on her feet. She didn't see her shoes anywhere, but she was still wearing the gown from the party. It wasn't wet, so some time must have passed. She quietly walked to one of the doors, opening it to reveal a large bathroom. With a sigh, she moved to the next door. This one opened to reveal a long hallway. Standing guard next to the entrance was a towering figure that slowly swiveled toward her. His face was hidden beneath a gruff layer of bristly stubble, his gaze boring unpleasantly into her like two hollow pits. Her body shuddered with a chilling sensation as their eyes met, and in them she saw something sinister and dark.

He slowly lifted a phone up to his face. "She's awake," was all his raspy voice said before hanging up.

"What do you want?" Jean asked, with a voice that had more courage than she actually felt. The man ignored her and leaned against the wall.

Jean studied the man, trying to discern any clues about his intentions. He was tall and muscular, with broad shoulders and a menacing aura. His stare was intense and unwavering, as if he was used to intimidating others. Jean's heart raced in her chest as she wondered what he wanted with her. Was he working with Melissa? Was he the one who had taken her?

The man took a step forward, his eyes still fixed on Jean. She took a step back, her heart beating faster with each passing second. The man seemed to be studying her, as if trying to decide something. Finally, he spoke, his voice low and rough.

"You must be Jean," he said, his eyes narrowing. "Benjamin's little pet."

"What do you want?" she repeated, her voice confident and firm.

The man smirked, his lips twisting into a cruel smile. He turned his head to the side, then pushed off the wall and began to walk away. She watched as another man walked hastily down the hall. The man was well put together, clean shaven, and had the air of someone wealthy.

As the two men conversed in low voices, Jean felt a wave of fear wash over her. Who were these men? And why had they taken her? Her mind raced as she tried to formulate a plan, but her thoughts were interrupted by the sound of footsteps approaching from down the hall. The men turned to face the newcomer, and Jean gasped in shock as she recognized his face. It was Lewis, Ben's cousin, who had been rude to her.

"What the hell is going on here?" Lewis demanded, his voice cold and harsh. His eyes scanned over Jean and then back to the other two men,

"This isn't your business. Go away."

"Victor, you fucking tell me what is going on, now!" Lewis growled between clenched teeth.

Within the blink of an eye, Victor's hand went to his shoulder, grabbing hold of his shirt. His face was twisted in a snarl, his lips curled back in a vicious sneer. "I said, it isn't your fucking business!"

Jean could hardly breathe as the tension grew between the two men. The guard let out a groan, shaking his head.

"This is above you Lewis. Your gramps ordered this, so it's best to stand aside."

"He WHAT?!" Lewis looked back at Victor, exasperated. "And you're just going along with it? Like his obedient lap dog?" Victor was his grandfather's mistress' daughter's son. Unlike him, Victor was the real blood relation to Ben and his grandfather. Lewis' mother wasn't biologically related to Elliott Croftman; she was adopted into his family as a favor to his grandmother. He only married Lewis' grandmother to have a legitimate heir, a son, which she never gave him.

On paper, Lewis was the man's grandson, but Victor was his real family. However, their grandfather didn't give a damn about either of them. He used them, and Lewis was done being used. Victor was desperate to prove himself despite living his life in shame and never being socially accepted in the Croftman family.

"You don't have the guts to be the grandson he needs. That's why he came to me. That's why he's leaving everything to me. You. Are. An. Embarrassment." Victor released him as his lips curled into a smirk. He then turned his head to look at Jean. His eyes wandered over her body before he took a few steps toward her. "Be good and we won't tie you up. This really isn't about you. It's about your fiancé." Her silver eyes stared at him angrily, not giving him the fear he craved.

"What do you want with me?" she asked defiantly. She saw his hand move to his pocket, and her heart began to hammer in her chest. He pulled out a knife and began to flick it open.

What the hell? She chewed on her lip, her brows knitting together angrily. He walked toward her slowly, every step sending a chill down Jean's spine. She refused to show her fear, even as he neared her, even as he reached over and grabbed her arm. He pressed the cold metal of the knife against her neck before pulling her toward him. His eyes were cold, and he looked at her as if expecting her to cry. Yet, her silver eyes continued to cut into him.

A hand slapped the knife out of his hand as Lewis came between her and Victor. He stood in front of her protectively as the man clicked his tongue in agitation.

"How the hell did you find out anyway?" Victor leaned against the wall, looking at Lewis as if he was no more than a pest.

"I have my sources," Lewis snapped. "What the hell do you want with her?" Victor gave one last look at Jean, his eyes lingering on her body longer than necessary.

"We're going to use her as a little negotiating leverage. We'll make him sweat a few more days before we tell him what we want. Make him desperate enough to agree to hand over control of their company." Victor smirked as he listened to Jean's gasp.

"Are you insane? You won't get away with that," Lewis growled between clenched teeth.

"Sure we will." Victor then nodded to Jean. "And that little beauty will make sure it happens. She might as well make herself at home. She isn't going anywhere for a while. Once we come to terms, then we will need contracts written up. You know the process." Victor pushed away from the wall and then turned away. "Since you've taken an interest in her, you take care of her. Just don't over-spoil her but have your fun. Gramps thought it would be funny for us to impregnate her. Something about teaching Liam Cross a lesson about taking things from him."

No, no, no. The thought of Victor or any man touching her made Jean sick to her stomach. She watched as the man walked away, his laughter echoing off the bare walls. Lewis slammed his fist into the wall, cursing between clenched teeth.

He turned to her and leaned in close, whispering in her ear, "I won't let anyone touch you. We'll figure this out." She looked at him, confused. This man had insulted her, and there was no way he cared about her well-being. Yet, the way he looked at her was very sincere.

"Look, I know you don't trust me, but I'm all you have here, and I'm going to need your help." Lewis then looked back down the hall, making sure the two other men had left. "I needed money before, so that I could get out from under my grandfather. I lashed out because I was desperate. I'm sorry. My grandfather is insane, and I'm done with that family. I want a life of my own. Why am I going to help you? Because I want something from you too." He grabbed her wrist and pulled her back to the room, shutting the door behind him. "I need Ben to loan me money. If I help his fiancée, he is sure to repay the favor. We're going to have to be careful and bide our time. Will you trust me?"

What choice did she have? She didn't know where she was, and Victor was completely crazy. Lewis' motives weren't entirely selfless, but maybe because of that, she believed him more. He wanted an out from his family, and she couldn't blame him.

"Okay." Jean nodded her head as she looked into his brown eyes. "What's the plan?"

Chapter 24

It had been days since Jean had been taken, and there had been no news from the abductors, though Ben did get one hurried text from his cousin Lewis. It said, *I know where she is. I'll keep her safe and report back to you as soon as I can.* That was it. He never messaged again, which led them to believe either Lewis was caught, or something had happened to his phone. Either way, it proved to them they were on the right track.

Ben's father already assumed it was Elliot Croftman who was behind Jean's disappearance. There was history between his father and grandfather. This was one of his tactics. He was trying to make them so worried that when they finally reached out, they would desperately sign away everything. While Ben was more than ready to give everything away, his father was not. Instead, he secretly put together his own special unit to track Jean down, starting with finding out where Lewis sent his last text from.

"Ben." His mother's soft voice was full of pain as she placed her gentle hand on his arm. "I'm so sorry. My father is a horrible man. He will use Gina as leverage to get what he wants. Not resting isn't going to solve anything. You have to try to—"

"How can I?" His amber eyes looked browner and duller as he looked down at his mother. "What if she's scared? What if every minute, she's anxiously looking at the clock, waiting for me to save her? But I'm so useless I can't even find her. I can't protect her. God, what have I done to her? This is because of me." He began to sob, lifting his hands up to his face. "What are they doing to her? She already had trauma as a child, and now this. I'm supposed to be protecting her, and instead I've—"

"Oh, Ben—"

"Then the shit Melissa said to her—she must be confused. I love her so much, and I know it doesn't seem rational. It's driving me crazy, thinking that Jean might not know how much I love her right now. I—" He lowered his hands, curling his fingers into his palms. "Damnit, I have to do something. I can't just sit here and wait. I'll give him the company, if that's what he wants. I just need her back."

"Benjamin!" Liam's firm voice filled the room as he strode up to his son. He grabbed him by the head and firmly pulled him in for a hug. "It's going to be okay. I promise we will find her. Listen, you are in no condition to handle negotiations. None. Do you think Mr. Croftman will stop if he gets wind of your vulnerability? He won't. He will keep wanting more. I know it's hard, but you're going to have to trust me.

The longer we drag out negotiations, the better chance we have of finding her. We'll be hearing from them soon." He sighed, hesitating before he finally continued. "Our team has a general location based on Lewis' signal when he texted you. It's at least a starting point. They are looking into the houses there, looking for someone who might have a connection to Mr. Croftman. But that man is good at hiding things. It just takes time."

Ben's eyes blazed with an unquenchable fury, the muscles in his face tensing as he spat out the words, "I. Want. Him. Gone!" His gaze was a piercing laser that could burn through steel, and it seemed to seep into everything around him, spreading its intensity like wildfire.

"I know. I left things alone for far too long, but he has crossed the line for the last time. We are going to destroy him." Liam looked firmly into his son's eyes and nodded his head. "Gina is strong."

"She holds it all in, dad. Her feelings, her emotions ... she seals them all up inside of her. She doesn't want to be an inconvenience, so she pretends she's fine. She's always worrying about others over herself. I'm going to worry for her from now on. I want her to lean on me and tell me what bothers her. She's strong, but she shouldn't have to handle things alone. What if she locks everyone out after this? What if she locks me out?" Ben's voice cracked with emotion and his eyes filled with tears.

"Benjamin," Liam murmured, placing a hand on his son's shoulder. "Let's focus on finding Jean. You need to be strong for her, right? We need to focus on what we can do instead of worrying about the what ifs."

"Sir." A man came in, holding a letter. "This just arrived."

Liam grabbed it first, Ben and Rebecca right at his heels.

"What does it say, Liam?" Rebecca asked, looking up at him, watching him crumble the letter into a ball.

Liam looked at the man and nodded his head. "Move on with the next phase of our plans."

"Yes, sir."

Liam locked his jaw as he thought about the contents of the letter.

You know what I want. We need to reach an agreement on how to proceed. Remember, each passing day is another day the pretty fiancée will be violated. I wonder, will you still want her with someone else's child inside her?

He couldn't let anyone else see that letter. It would drive his son mad. There wasn't anything he could do. Even handing over the company wouldn't be enough. The damage will already have been done. Mr. Croftman was having Ben's fiancée violated because he felt he was violated. Liam took Rebecca from Mr. Croftman, and he had never forgiven him for that. This wasn't about Ben or Gina; they were dragged into this. This was about him and Mr. Croftman. That man would never let his grudge go. But Liam knew he couldn't let his anger get the best of him. He needed to be smart, strategic, and deliberate in how he handled Mr. Croftman. He couldn't let him win, but he couldn't let Ben lose everything either. And most importantly, he couldn't let Gina suffer any longer.

"Dad, what did the letter say?" Ben asked, feeling like he was going to explode.

"They want to move ahead with negotiations," Liam said simply. "We will get her back soon." He then quickly left the room with Ben's mother following him.

Ben grabbed his phone and quickly dialed a number. "Link, have you found anything out?"

"Clint is trailing someone now. I promise I will reach out to you if we hear anything."

"Give me the phone" Ben heard his sister's voice, and soon she was on the other line. "What are you doing, Ben? Get out here and fight."

"Dad has me under lock and key. He's afraid I'll do something stupid, and he isn't wrong."

"Stay away from our mother's sperm donor and get out here. That man wouldn't have Gina anywhere near him, so we need to look at his underhanded lackeys or more of his unwanted spawn. We used to escape the house when we were teenagers, remember?"

Ben's eyes lit up. He wasn't thinking straight before, but she was right. There was a way out. "Yeah, okay."

"Okay, meet us near Broadway Park."

"Thanks, Steph," Ben said before hanging up the phone. Regardless of what his dad thought was best, he couldn't just sit around and do nothing. He had to feel like he was doing something.

Jean, hold on, I'm coming for you.

"Ketchup on bread?" Jean watched as Lewis stuffed the sandwich in his mouth. "I'll just eat the bread."

"If you're looking for flavor, it does wonders, and I used to eat this all the time growing up."

Jean looked at him curiously. "I thought your family was—" She clamped her lips together as she saw the pain in his eyes.

"My mother ended up marrying an asshole to appease my grand-father. My dad, well, he has another son with the woman he really loved. He wasn't around much. Neither was my mother. I was left alone to fend for myself ... a lot." He shrugged as he stared at the drop of ketchup left on his hand. "I was the product, just to show everyone they had a real marriage. It's been anything but that. My mom has her boyfriend, and my dad has his girlfriend. Hell, he has a whole other family. I'm just the unwanted child who was given a dying business and told to save it. It was a piece my father didn't want." He frowned, looking at the loaf of bread. "They could have fed us better."

"Well, you can eat better." Jean watched as he smiled at her.

"What? And miss out on ketchup and bread? Never." He grinned at her, making himself another abomination.

Lewis never left her side. He slept on the floor, staying with her every minute. He had clean clothes brought in for her as well. Nothing fancy, just a pair of sweatpants and a shirt.

Mr. Croftman had put up a cell phone blocker so Lewis couldn't call or text anyone, but he refused to leave her side even to send a quick message. He said that if his grandfather had given the okay, then she wasn't safe from anyone. They wouldn't hesitate to take the ten minutes he was away to violate her. So instead, he remained a willing captive in order to protect her.

Jean was touched by Lewis' unwavering loyalty and dedication to keeping her safe. Despite his first impression, it was clear he was actually a good guy. He was desperate to escape his family and had made bad choices. She wondered what it must have been like for him, having grown up in such an unhappy and unloving family.

He was now going above and beyond for her. If it was just about the money, he would have left to call Ben. But he was determined that nothing would happen to her. He hoped that the first message he sent in haste would help lead Ben to them.

She tore hungrily at the bread, desperate to stave off the deep ache in her chest. She thought of Ben and his gentle smile, and how tired he must be without her. Melissa had done her best to fill her with doubt, but she wasn't going to let it poison her. She loved Ben and was going to trust him. For the first time in a long time, she decided she would trust herself and ignore others. She could never do that before, but for Ben, she could. An unbearable loneliness threatened to consume her as she thought about him. She missed the way he would hold her close to him, like she was the most precious thing to him. The soft way his lips would caress hers. The little groan he made in his throat as he pulled her closer. She missed everything about him. Everything.

The sound of footsteps approaching made them both rise to their feet. Lewis took a step in front of her as the door opened.

"You haven't gotten tired of her yet, Lew?" Victor asked, looking slightly annoyed, leaning against the door frame. Once again, he was wearing a suit with not a hair out of place. He made his rounds to her room at least twice a day. She could feel the animosity between the two men that seemed to be building.

"You know, it's funny," Lewis said as he looked Victor over. "You like to pretend to be one of them, but you aren't. It doesn't matter what you do. He won't ever fully accept you because he can't. You will always be his illegitimate grandson." He watched as Victor's lips curled up angrily, his face turning a dark shade of red.

"What the hell do you know? You're nothing like him. You can't be, but because you're the picture-perfect grandson, you get the in, while I have done everything he has ever asked, and I've done it well, but I'm nothing. Not after this, though. He will make me the new CEO of the company. I'll be rewarded."

Lewis scoffed and shook his head. "Do you really believe that man will give you anything? No, he'll use you, then throw you away. You'll never be enough, don't you see that? None of us will ever be enough. You want to know what that man cares about? He only cares about Mr. Cross and making him suffer. He doesn't care about any of his children or grandchildren. It's all about his obsession with Liam Cross."

Jean stood there, stunned, as she witnessed Victor's anger. He was so red, she thought he might explode. "Enough." He glared at Lewis, his voice dripping with fury. "You can't understand him because you aren't his blood. You get to be called his grandchild, but you aren't his. You'll see, though. After this, everything is going to change." He then stepped into the room, looking beyond Lewis at Jean.

Jean watched as Lewis stepped toward Victor, their eyes meeting in an angry showdown.

"Stand aside!" Victor growled.

"I've put my claim on her first. You get out!" Lewis clenched his teeth, refusing to move.

"You don't get to call dibs forever." Victor looked back up at Jean. "You must not do a good job, because she's able to stand just fine. You won't be able to stand once I'm done with you." A sinister smile twisted across his face, its presence filling Jean with a dread so intense that it made her bones ache. His lips seemed to speak a silent language of evil, promising something dark and beyond imagination.

She could almost see the words forming on his lips. "Do you like it rough?" he asked Jean, his voice dripping with malice. "I prefer to make women beg for mercy. Will you beg for mercy when I'm done with you?"

He ran his gaze over her body like a predator would eye a piece of meat. It felt like his eyes were sliding over her bare flesh. His stare was like that of a man who had not eaten in days.

"Back off, Victor," Lewis said as he took another step toward him.

"Or you'll do what?" he asked with a sneer.

"I'm not afraid of you," Lewis said, taking another step toward him.

"No?" Victor's smile widened, his eyes full of victory. "I could kill you and your family and never feel an ounce of remorse." His tone was filled with loathing. "No one cares about your existence."

"I don't exist for them. I exist for myself. Unlike you, I'm creating my own self-worth instead of living in someone else's shadow."

The air froze as Victor lunged forward, barreling into his opponent with a terrifying force. Lewis was propelled backward, and the two men crashed to the ground with a thunderous thud. Jean gasped in horror as fists flew and their bodies scuffled loudly, echoing through the stillness of the house. The fight had begun, and if Lewis didn't win, she was in trouble.

Chapter 25

Nothing could have prepared her for the sounds of fists slamming into flesh. She couldn't turn her head away. She was losing track of who was who as they landed punishing blows. She had never seen a fight before, and the sounds were surreal. Victor drove his fist into Lewis' face, blood pouring from his mouth. Then Lewis kicked the other man in the chest, slamming him into the ground. Blood sprayed from his nose, mixing with the fury of the fight.

She watched as Lewis fought back, landing his punches where he could. They seemed to be evenly matched, until she saw a flash of silver. Victor had drawn his knife, intent on ending Lewis.

Lewis saw it just in time, throwing his hand up and blocking the knife. Jean drew in a sharp breath as the blade sunk into his wrist. The two men began to struggle for control of the knife. Lewis' blood trickled over the blade, making it slippery and hard to hold onto.

Victor pulled back with a furious grunt, his knife having almost slipped from his hand. He moved forward again, faster this time, gripping the knife as firmly as he could. Lewis caught him off guard by jumping into the air and delivering a powerful kick to his chest. The move surprised him, and Victor stumbled backwards, stumbling until he hit the wall.

Victor stood there for a moment, an irritated grimace on his face. "You're a weak man. No wonder he was never proud of you."

"Proud," Lewis scoffed, using his arm to wipe the blood from his face. "That man isn't proud of anyone."

"He's proud of me. I've done everything he's ever asked."

"You're a tool." Lewis spat the words out as Victor made another move toward him. The next few seconds were a blur of punches and kicks, with both men landing risky blows. A few times, Jean was sure that Lewis was going to be killed. He was still blocking Victor's knife, which was an impressive feat in itself. She could tell he was tiring, though, as he began to breathe heavily.

Suddenly, the glimmering flash of silver streaked across the air like lightning, landing directly in front of Jean's feet. She gasped and lunged for it, clutching it tightly to her chest, holding onto it for dear life.

Her eyes moved over the chaos, not sure what to do. Jean's heart raced like a runaway train, thumping so hard against her ribcage that it echoed in her ears. The pounding of her pulse seemed to grow louder and faster with each passing second until it threatened to drown out every other sound around her. She had to do something. She had to try to help Lewis.

The thundering sound of footsteps made their way to the room. "What the hell is going on here?" A man she hadn't seen before yelled as two others ran into the room, pulling the two men apart. "A fight? You two have time for a fight? And in front of our honored guest?" The man almost seemed to snarl as he looked between Victor and Lewis. "Who started it?" Both men remained silent. "WHO?!"

He inhaled slowly and then looked at Jean with a smirk. "My dear, who started the fight?" He then looked at the bloody knife she was holding in her trembling hands. With a small frown, he walked between the two men and straight to her. He placed one hand on top of hers and the other underneath them. "It's okay, you can drop the knife." He took the knife from her, and his eyes softened. He bent his neck to look at her. "Can you tell me what happened?"

"He was going to hurt me, but the other man wouldn't let him. He said that their grandfather didn't want me hurt."

"YOU LYING BITCH!" Victor bellowed. The man in front of her gave him a menacing look.

"Get him out of here."

"Tommy, she's lying," Victor said, his confidence gone as fear cracked in his voice.

The man named Tommy turned his head to look at Lewis. "Is that how it went down?"

Lewis scoffed and held up his gashed hand. "I didn't get this for no reason." Then, looking at Victor, "Are you crazy? All of grandpa's hard work. Just because you found out you wouldn't get control of the company. Are you an idiot? You think grandpa did all this for you?"

"I'll fucking kill you, Lewis!"

"Get him the fuck out of here!" Tommy roared, his voice seething with anger and menace. The other men scrambled like rats, hurling Victor toward the door as if their lives depended on it. The air shivered with tension as the room emptied, leaving Tommy with them.

"Man, I'm glad you showed up," Lewis said as he tore his shirt to wrap around his wrist. "Gramps knows better than to involve Victor. The man is desperate and could care less about the family." He shook his head in disgust as he tied his makeshift bandage.

"You should probably get that looked at." Tommy frowned, noticing the bandage turning red.

"And miss all the excitement? No way. I want to be here when he makes the call. You know I don't get many chances to impress my grandfather. I need all the points I can get." He laughed, leaning against the wall. "You know backlash is coming, right?" He finally said softly. "No matter the outcome, the Cross family will retaliate in full force. It's going to get real ugly."

Tommy nodded his head, staying silent.

"I guess this will be the last time we see each other for a while."

"You going to get teary-eyed on me?" Tommy chuckled as Lewis pushed away from the wall, looking at him.

"Thank you, for ... you know. You always looked out for me." With a sigh, Lewis stared at him, their gazes locked. "So just this once, I'm going to look out for you. You know what he plans to do. You know you will take full blame for all of this. This whole thing. He will come out clean and you will bear the consequences."

Tommy nodded his head quietly, shoving his hands in his pockets. "I know. Well, the old bastard will try, but it won't go as he planned." He laughed and then walked to the door. "I'll be handling Victor but be careful. He'll want revenge, once he feels like walking again." He smirked and cracked his neck.

"Make sure it takes him a couple of days to recover," Lewis laughed, rubbing his hand. Tommy gave him a nod before he closed the door. As soon as the door shut, he slinked onto the bed. Jean ran to the bathroom and came back with a towel.

"Lewis," her fingers trembled as she wiped the blood from him.

"I can do that," he smiled, grabbing the towel from her.

"Is that man a friend?" She watched as Lewis glanced back at the closed door.

"He's always been good to me, but make no mistake, he works for my grandfather. He follows my grandfather's orders without question and without fail."

She licked her lips nervously as she looked at the blood. "I'm sorry. I should have helped, but I froze."

"You did help. Telling them that he was trying to attack you was perfect. You had no reason to lie, and it sounded like something Victor would do. Did you notice that Tommy didn't question it? You fixed a rather large problem." He sighed, looking at her. "We can't be here when Victor recovers, though. It'll be bad. I don't think we can wait for Ben to find us. We're going to have to plan something of our own."

"Should you go and text Ben?" She watched as he shook his head.

"I'm not leaving your side, Jean. I'm going to protect you. Even with Victor out of the way, there are others here that are worse." He grew quiet as if he was thinking of those people.

"Ben must be exhausted." The words just escaped from her lips. Here Lewis was bleeding all over for her, and her mind was on Ben. She pursed her lips together as a quiet chuckle came from Lewis.

"I'm so sorry about what I said when we first met. Ben has found a great partner in you. Look at you, worrying about him while you're the one who was abducted." He turned his head, giving her a crooked grin.

A small smile reached her lips as she looked at the window. "He has trouble sleeping. What if something happens to him? I wish I could see his face." She leaned against the window as Lewis snorted a laugh.

"It's okay to worry about yourself." He gave her an accusing look as she continued to look outside. "I haven't heard you mention once about being afraid. I know you are. You haven't complained at all, even about just eating bread. At first, I thought you were just quiet and shy, but that isn't it, is it?"

"People have enough to deal with without being burdened by someone else's emotions."

"Hmm," he hummed, and she turned to look at him. He had an odd smile on his lips, his brows slightly raised.

"What?"

"I think by not wanting to be a burden, you end up becoming one even more. If you care about someone, you want them to trust you and talk to you. When they don't do that, you feel like you don't really matter to them. You're only seeing things from your point of view. Well, let me give you the other angle. I desperately sought approval from everyone around me. I knew they didn't care about me, but I thought maybe I could be useful to them. I wanted to help in order to prove myself." He scoffed, shaking his head. "I wasn't even important enough to lay their burdens on. I couldn't do anything. You might not realize it, but by not sharing your burdens, you might be making those around you feel lonely. If not now, eventually you will."

She pressed her forehead on the window as she thought about her grandmother. She remembered her grandmother's last words, urging her to open herself up and finally face the pain she had kept bottled within her for so long. That if she didn't face the demons in her past, they would haunt her forever.

She could admit that, up until recently, everything had remained buried. But things began to change once she met Ben. The nightmares didn't come when she was with him. The heaviness in her chest began to fade as it was filled with his warmth. Lewis was right. She needed to start sharing her feelings. She would gradually learn to do that again. She had to, if she was going to spend her life with Ben.

"I'm sorry you were lonely, Lewis," she whispered, keeping her head on the cool window. "It's a horrible feeling that I know all too well. But you're right. I don't want those around me to think I don't value them." Suddenly something caught her eye and she gasped. "Lewis." She turned her head to look at him. A frown instantly formed as she looked at his wounds.

"What is it?" He eased himself to his feet, walking over to her.

"I had an idea, but ..." She pursed her lips together as she looked at his injuries.

"My bones aren't broken." He laughed, leaning over her to look out the window.

"I know we're high up, but if we can reach that ledge—" She pointed down and to the side.

"And if we miss the ledge, we're going to fall to our deaths." He chuckled nervously as his eyes glanced down to the ground. They were on the fourth floor of the house. They couldn't jump to the ground without dying. The ledge she was talking about was angled away and was one floor lower. However, next to it was a fire escape. If they could reach it, they could use the ladder to reach the ground. Damn, they were going to have to risk it. "I think it might be our only option. I'll make the jump first. That way I can catch you if you fall short."

Jean began to giggle as she turned away from the glass. "You know, I feel like lately my life is a movie drama. These things don't happen in real life." She listened as Lewis' rich rumble filled the room.

"Who needs television when you can live it?" He chuckled.

"I think I'd rather have television."

"So would I."

Despite the gravity of their situation, nervous laughter tore through their throats. Their plan was sheer madness, and failure meant certain death. But they both knew that there were fates worse than dying. Sitting around waiting for Victor's wrath was a surefire path to brutal torture for Lewis. And for Jean, there was a fate worse than death. They had to escape before he returned, or else suffer unspeakable horrors at his hands.

The air was thick with tension as they silently acknowledged the risks of what they were about to do. Yet, they were ready to give it everything they had for their chance at freedom.

"Lewis," Jean said quietly. "You don't have to do this. You can walk out of here and leave this place. The money isn't worth it. I can make the escape myself." She watched as a small smile rested on his lips.

"And leave all the fun to you?" He looked at her with a small shrug. "Besides, I'd like to think that we've become friends." He watched as she nodded with a sad smile. "I don't have any of those. What kind of dick would leave their friend to face thrilling danger alone? Not to mention this is one hell of a bucket list item to cross off."

"Thank you, Lewis. You're a good guy."

"Shush, don't go spreading that toxic stuff around. I have a rep to protect." He grinned at her as her eyes trailed over the curtain. He looked over it with her and his eyes lit up. "Yes, that's a great idea. Hell, we might actually live through this."

"That's the plan. I'm not dying. I have to live so I can protect Ben."

Lewis snorted as he sifted his hands over the curtains. "After this, he better keep you safely chained up."

Jean tilted her head to the side with a small smirk creeping over her lips. "Kinky, but I like it."

Lewis' shocked laughter filled the room as he flashed her a genuine smile. "There's the real you." He winked at her before tugging at the fabric, testing its strength. "All right, let's get to work."

Chapter 26

B en looked at his phone as it rang again.

"You're going to have to answer it before he sends the cops to look for us," Steph laughed, seeing their dad on the caller ID.

"Hello."

"BENJAMIN, WHERE ARE YOU?"

It was his mother's voice that rang through the line loudly. "I'm looking for Jean."

"Ben, your dad is capable of handling this. He's going to find her and bring her back."

"Mom, if you had been taken, where would dad be? Would he be waiting at the house for his men to find you? I'm betting he'd be doing what I am right now." The phone was quiet and then he heard his father's voice.

"That's exactly what I'd be doing. If you get a lead on anything, let me know. I'm going to trust you to be safe and to keep your sister safe."

"Thanks, dad." Ben looked up, seeing Link and Clint heading their way. "I'll keep in touch. Love you both, bye." He walked over toward them with Steph running up to Link first. "Well?"

"It's the Brines' vacation home. I'm almost positive. The place is crawling with men, and the Brines don't vacation there at this time of year. Plus, I'm pretty sure I saw Victor. He looked pretty banged up, but I'm sure it was him. If it was—" Clint explained as Ben nodded his head.

"If Victor is involved, then that's the place. Steph, call dad back and let him know." Ben then looked back at Clint and Link. "How many men?"

"Too many. We aren't getting in there on our own. Maybe if I try to sneak in as one of the guards," Clint said thoughtfully as Stephanie began talking to their dad.

"Dad says he will have the team ready by nightfall, and to hold tight until then." She looked at Ben and then nodded her head. "Yes, I'll tell him," she said, hanging up. "Dad told me to remind you that you're no good to Jean hurt. She'll need you, so you'll need to be ready to support her."

"I guess that's his way of trying to guilt me into not making a move." He sighed, staring up at the sky.

"Waiting for the cover of darkness is best, Ben. They're armed with guns. We won't be able to get anywhere near that building." Link stood next to Ben, looking up at the sky with him. "We're close. We're getting her back tonight. Let's go get a sandwich, okay? We need to keep our strength up so we can help her." His friend looked like a broken man. His eyes were hollowed pits of darkness that seemed to swell with the sorrow of his soul. His normally vibrant face had gone pale. It seemed to be slowly wilting away. His eyes were deeply sunken in, a clear sign that he hadn't slept.

Honestly, he didn't want Ben involved either. He was almost a liability in his emotional state. But Steph insisted that her brother join them, and she had a point. Ben needed to feel like he was doing something too. It was important for his well-being to be part of the rescue efforts. And if he was in the same situation as Ben, he would be out there looking too. Hell, it was killing him too that Gina had been taken. She saved him when he was a child, and now, he would do everything he could to rescue her.

"Come on Ben, let's get you caffeinated." Steph linked her arm with his, giving him a determined smile. "We're getting Gina back tonight. You don't want to look like complete shit when we do."

He gave her a small smile and allowed her to lead him to the car. He wasn't interested in food or anything else. He just wanted to get Jean back. He was ready to fight and save her by whatever means necessary. He didn't care about himself and his well-being. It was all about hers.

A deep satisfaction spread through him as he realized that, for the first time in his life, something else had become more important than the control and power of his family's company. Placing no restrictions on himself, Jean meant everything to him, and without hesitation, he was willing to give up all his possessions just for her. He was a changed man, and he was ready to live the rest of his life for his woman.

The last call of the evening birds disappeared with nightfall, replaced by a sound that made Jean's heart pound in her chest. The distant patter of rain began to grow louder and more insistent, an incessant tapping against the window announcing its arrival. Lewis moved swiftly to the window, his presence only amplifying her dread as he peered out anxiously into the darkness.

"The rain will make it harder for them to see," she said, trying to be optimistic. "I bet some of the men won't be outside too."

He slowly turned around to face her, his lips a tight line and brows creased together. His voice was gruff as he spoke, "The ledge is going to be like an ice rink, Jean. With the momentum of us jumping—" He stopped speaking abruptly, almost afraid to look at her face, and yet compelled to stare into her eyes. Fear and dread radiated from him in waves.

"They said Victor would be back tomorrow," she whispered as he nodded slowly. She heard the guards talking about it by the door earlier. It had been on her mind ever since.

"Tommy roughed him up but not enough to hinder him. He'll be back for vengeance tomorrow. I was advised not to be here," he chuckled, rubbing the back of his neck. He winced slightly from the pain from the knife wound. If they were still here, Victor would make them both suffer. Who knows how rough he would be on Jean for her lies. There was no way they could stay, and yet leaving now was almost suicide.

Jean could feel her own heart hammering in her chest at the thought of what was to come. The rain outside was growing heavier by the second, and the sound of it was almost deafening. She had to think fast.

"Lewis, we can't just wait here for him to come back. We need to leave, now."

"I know." Lewis took a deep breath, his hand brushing over the knife wound on his hand.

Jean's heart raced as she looked out the window, watching as the rain began to pelt against the glass. She knew that the situation was dire, but they had run out of options. No one had come for her yet. There was no way of knowing when they would find her.

"I'm leaving. I have to do this. You don't. You can turn around and walk out of here. Why don't you do that? We both don't need to risk our lives." She watched as he looked at her as if she had suggested that he eat his shoe.

"I'm doing this with you. It's going to take both of us. You know," he turned, looking back out the window. "I don't have any regrets. I feel like, for the first time, I'm actually being true to myself. No matter what, I'm sticking to this decision. No matter what happens, I chose this." He then reached his hand out and shifted the window up.

A powerful gust of wet air roared inside, as if whipped into a frenzy by some unseen force. The rain was pelting down in sheets, drenching everything outside. A flash of lightning lit up the sky and was answered by earth-shaking thunder. The storm was quickly becoming a violent one. The rain would make it hard for anyone to see or hear them. Yet, the thought of trying to climb down the side of the house in such conditions was daunting to say the least.

But she knew she had to. She knew in the pit of her stomach that she had no other choice. A loud crack of thunder rippled through the air as another flash of lightning lit up the sky. "Alright," she finally whispered, swallowing back her fear. "Let's do this."

Lewis nodded, determination etched on his face as he took a step toward her. He paused, his eyes meeting hers for a long moment, as if silently reassuring each other of their resolve.

"Hey, at least we can't see the ground." He grinned as he patted her shoulder. "Deep breaths. We can do this."

He pushed the bed against the wall and grabbed the curtain rope they had made, quickly tying it to the bed post. They would use this to help them get to the side ledge. Something to hold onto in case they didn't make the jump.

With a nod, Lewis braced himself against the window ledge, ready to take the lead. Jean followed closely behind him, her heart pounding in her chest as they made their way onto the rain-soaked ledge. The wind whipped around them, threatening to push them off at any moment, but they were determined to make it to the ground, no matter what.

The rain soaked them instantly. The flashes of lightning illuminated the area, allowing Jean to get a quick glimpse of the ground. Her stomach churned with fear, making her momentarily freeze in place.

"I'll go first. I never asked what you preferred to be called. Regina, Gina, or Jean?" he chuckled, trying to take their minds off their suicide jump.

She smiled as raindrops dripped from her eyelids. Before, she had always told others to call her Jean, but lately it seemed only Ben called her Jean. It was becoming something special for him now. "Gina. My friends call me Gina." He smiled at her as he gripped the curtain fabric firmly in his hands.

"Alright, Gina, let's get out of here." Lewis leapt off the ledge, gripping the curtain rope tightly as he flew through the air. His feet landed firmly on the hard surface below, but his momentum kept him moving forward until he was in danger of careening over the edge. With a sudden jolt he dropped to his knees, just managing to regain his balance before plunging into oblivion. He took a moment to catch his breath before finally returning to his feet. "Okay, Gina, whenever you're ready." He wiped the wet droplets from his forehead.

Jean took a deep breath and closed her eyes for a moment, steeling herself for the jump. She could hear the rain pounding against the roof and feel the wind tearing at her hair and clothes. She knew that one misstep could send her hurtling to her death, but she had no other choice. She had to trust in Lewis and in herself.

Opening her eyes, Jean took a step forward and then another, her eyes fixed firmly on the ledge ahead. She could feel her heart pounding in her chest and her breath coming in short gasps. She was terrified, but she refused to let fear control her.

With a final burst of determination, Jean gripped the curtain and launched herself off the ledge, feeling the wind whipping past her as she fell. The rain stung her face and blinded her for a moment, but she kept her eyes fixed on Lewis' form ahead of her. She could see him reaching out for her, his face a mask of fierce concentration. She felt Lewis' strong arms wrap around her, holding her close. He brought her to her knees on the narrow platform.

"Are you okay?" he asked, his voice barely audible over the sound of the rain. He felt her shallow nod and patted her soaked back. "We made the jump. I'll be damned." He chuckled as she moved to her feet. "I thought we would be dead by now."

She laughed, nodding into the wet streams. "So did I."

"The ladder is next. We just have to take our time. I'll go down first, and you follow right behind me."

She nodded her head, watching as he moved over to the fire escape. The moment he disappeared down the ladder, she followed suit, gripping onto the cold, slick metal as she made her descent.

The rain pounded against their faces, making it difficult to see. It was as if the raging storm was trying to stop them from making their escape. However, even though it was chaotic, it almost seemed like a veil had been drawn around them.

Suddenly they heard a muffled yell from above. "She went out the window!"

"We have to hurry, Jean!" he urged, moving faster.

Jean's hands flew over the bars as if powered by electricity. Her feet struggled to find footing on the narrow steps, and she slipped. She desperately swung her legs, frantically trying to find the ladder. But in a split second, her body was stabilized as she felt Lewis' firm grip on her ankle, steadying her back into the right position.

"You're okay, Gina. You've got this." The strength of his voice cut through the darkness like a beacon, radiating with confidence and an unbreakable optimism even in their most dire moment.

She felt his hands slide over her waist and then guide her to the ground. "We've made it to the ground, Gina. We did it, but now we have to run. Can you run?"

She turned to look at him as the rain cascaded over their faces. "Yes."

"Hold my hand so we don't get separated in the storm." He gripped her fingers firmly and they sprinted into the darkness. It was a good thing he was guiding her, because she had no idea where she was.

Their feet splashed against the wet grass as she blindly trusted Lewis to lead them to safety. The rain was relentless, and the wind whipped at her hair and clothes, threatening to knock her off balance. But Lewis' grip on her hand was firm, steadily guiding her.

BANG

The cracking sound that whipped through the air was not thunder. The deafening sound of a gunshot pierced the air as they frantically ran through the dense hedge for cover. Her heart pounded in her chest and her feet pounded against the pavement as they desperately ran for their lives. With every step, their pace slowed until they were stumbling and gasping for breath. The streetlights gave them sight again as Lewis led them into an alleyway.

Jean felt her chest heaving as she looked down at the surging sea of red that had suddenly appeared below him. She jerked her head up to see Lewis slumped against the building, his knuckles white from gripping at his side where a dark stain was rapidly growing. He slowly slid down to the ground, his face twisted in pain.

"LEWIS!"

Chapter 27

Jean's knees landed in the wet grass at Lewis' side. "Lewis!" she cried, her tears mixing with the rain.

"Gina, you have to run. They're coming for us."

"I'm not going to leave you," she said firmly.

"You have to."

"NO!" she cried, shaking her head violently. There was no way she could leave him. Not after everything they had just been through.

He leaned his head back against the wall and looked at her. "I thought the most dangerous part was going to be the jump." He gave her a pained smile as he glanced down at his side.

"We've got to get you to a hospital." Jean looked around frantically as the rain began to let up.

"Gina, they're going to find us. You have to go." They heard more gunshots in the distance as if proving Lewis' point. She placed her hand over his knee and gave him a brave smile.

"We're getting out of here together."

"I risked my life to get you out. Don't let it be in vain." He grimaced as he tried to shift his body. "I'll be alright. I just can't run like this." Suddenly a shadow appeared over them. They both turned their heads to see Tommy's looming figure looking at them.

"They're over here," he said in a slightly raised voice. His eyes darted to Lewis and his wound. "Damn, kid." He sighed in agitation as he hurried over next to them. "Let me have a look." He knelt down, his eyes moving over Jean, checking for wounds before returning to Lewis. He sucked in air through his teeth and grabbed his phone. "We have a gunshot wound to the side. Have the medical team ready." He hung up, putting pressure on the wound with his hand, shaking his head.

"You're lucky. It only grazed you, Your timing though—" A vehicle stopped in front of them, and three men jumped out of the SUV. "Hurry it up, and be easy with this one, he's hurt."

"Boss isn't going to like this," one of the men mumbled as he knelt beside Lewis.

Jean felt Tommy grab a hold of her elbow, lifting her to her feet. She listened as Lewis grunted in pain as the men lifted him off the ground. All their efforts were in vain. They were so close to escaping, but in the end, they were caught again. Maybe she was stupid for not running, but she wouldn't have been able to live with herself if she had left him.

As Tommy led Jean toward the SUV, her mind raced. Her heart drummed against her chest, making her feel like it could burst from her ribcage at any moment. Clambering into the back seat of the car, she found Lewis lying down, pale and wincing in pain. Taking his cold, wet hand in hers, a wave of grief coursed through her body as she realized how much he had risked for her safety. An act that now felt futile. Her grip tightened around his hand, as if by holding on tight, she could make up for all the pain.

She felt the hot air of the heater turn on as a thick hoodie was wrapped around her. Tommy sat on the floor, his eyes on Lewis. "What were you thinking, kid?" he breathed out, running his hand through his hair. Tommy was a broad, older man. His arms were covered in scars from who knows what. He had a rough appearance, but now, watching him look at Lewis, he seemed more approachable.

"This is my fault. He could have left at any time, but instead he stayed to help me," she whispered quietly, chewing on her inner lip. She knew Tommy was technically the bad guy, but he seemed to care for Lewis.

"I guess he's finally grown up." The man's voice was low, but he almost sounded proud.

"I'm not dead, so don't talk about me like I am," Lewis grunted, gripping Jean's hand.

"Lewis..." Jean squeezed his hand back, showing him she was there. She forced a smile as he lifted his eyelids to meet her gaze.

"We made the jump."

A smile reached his lips. "And here we thought that would be the hardest part."

"You're lucky, Lewis," Tommy said, making Lewis glance at him.

"I don't feel lucky."

"If those idiots didn't barge in when they did, that marksman would have hit you. They grabbed the gun, making him only graze you."

Jean snapped her head toward Tommy. "What idiots?" She felt her chest hammering and was almost afraid to breathe.

"Young Cross and two other men raced in. I think the idiots were trying to rescue you," Tommy chuckled, shaking his head. "Dumb."

"Are they okay?" The words left Jean's lips, not caring that this man wasn't a friend. He turned to look at her and casually shrugged.

"I left to look for you and Lewis immediately. There were plenty of men there to handle the situation."

Jean felt the coldness of dread seeping into her bones as she remembered the sound of gunshots. It seemed to echo through her mind. Her chest tightened with a crushing terror. They were shooting at Ben. Was he shot? He was okay, right?

"Uh oh," the driver said. "Boss is here, and he doesn't look happy."

"He'll be alright once he sees that the lady is unharmed," Tommy said as he shifted to his feet. The SUV came to a stop, and he moved to the door. He reached back, grabbing Jean's hand. "Come on. We need out of the way so they can get Lewis the help he needs."

Jean gave Lewis' hand one last squeeze, but he seemed to have gone unconscious. She felt reluctant to leave him, but there was nothing she could do. Tommy gently pulled her hand, and she followed him out of the vehicle. The instant she stepped out, she saw familiar blue eyes staring at her.

"Gina!" Liam yelled, scooping her up in his arms. She wrapped her arms around him as he held her tight.

"She's unharmed, sir. As reported, Lewis is the only one harmed," Tommy said as Lewis was raced inside a tall black building on a stretcher. It didn't look like a hospital, but the people there seemed to know exactly what to do.

Jean felt completely confused, and her emotions were pulling her in a million directions. She looked up at Liam and back at Tommy. "I don't understand. I thought—"

"Mr. Cross is a better client than Elliot Croftman." Tommy winked at Jean with a crooked smile.

"Go be with Lewis. I want a full report after this," Liam said, nodding to Tommy.

"Yes, sir."

Jean watched as Tommy hurried inside and then felt Liam's hands on her cheeks as he forced her to look at him. "Are you hurt? Do you need medical treatment? Did they—did they—" He couldn't bring himself to utter the words, but she understood. She shook her head.

"Lewis protected me. I'm fine. He's going to be okay, right?"

"Yes, he's going to be just fine. We're going to take care of him." Liam's words meant more than just his physical treatment. From now on, he would look after Lewis and help get him the start he needed. He had really proven himself to be completely different from his family. He protected his son's fiancée, and something like that would not go unrewarded.

"I am sure you have a lot of questions on your mind—"

"Ben?! Is Ben okay? I heard he—"

"Those kids make keeping secrets impossible. Don't worry, Ben is just fine." Liam patted her back as he led her toward the building. "Let's get you inside. You're soaked. This is my private hospital. It's for cases that we need to remain secret." He led them through the sliding doors and to a private room. The walls were encircled with luxurious brown leather couches. At the far side of the wall stood a sleek refrigerator and a giant flat-screen television. He shot a quick glance down at Jean, whose brows were furrowed in bewilderment.

"I have needed a lot of help over the years. Being in the public eye, you gain quite a few enemies. We don't all have secret service watching our backs." He chuckled at his own joke. "I have my own men. Trusted guns for hire. Tommy is one of Mr. Croftman's men. However, Mr. Croftman doesn't take good care of his men. He treats them worse than rats, often leaving them out to hang when shit hits the fan. The last few years, I have been picking up men that used to work for Mr. Croftman. I earn their trust and loyalty. This way, I could find out about anything the old fool was doing, like taking you. At first, he didn't have Tommy on this project. It wasn't until just yesterday that he finally asked him to oversee everything. Tommy went to work replacing men one by one, filling up positions with those loyal to us. There were only a few men left, and Tommy was going to get you out tonight. As soon as he took charge, he had your hall guarded so that nothing would happen to you. In a way, it's my fault. I didn't want Tommy's cover to be blown so that he could be used again. I had him keep up his act instead of rescuing you immediately." He sighed, staring into her silver eyes. "Lewis getting hurt is on me. You climbing down the side of the house—" he stopped, his eyes watering. "I'm so sorry. I should have let you know. I should have told Tommy to tell you. Forgive me. Ben is going to hate me."

"Liam." Jean smiled up at him. "You didn't know I was going to try to escape. You had a plan and had it thought out. I understand, and I'm not upset with you. You had no way of knowing. Could it have been planned better with more thought? I'm sure it could have been. We don't always think the most rationally, though. We're human and make mistakes. But I'm here and I'm safe. Lewis is going to be okay. The others are okay?" She looked at Liam as he nodded his head. "Now, what will happen to Ben's grandfather?" To her, it seemed like the main culprit was still at large. She wouldn't feel at ease unless something was done about him.

"Mr. Croftman knew what would happen if he messed with my family. He has been warned before and has been given more than enough chances."

"So, what will happen to him?" she pried, seeing that he didn't plan to elaborate. She watched as a smile spread over his lips and then he shrugged.

"Let's just say that you won't have to worry about him again, okay?"

His words were ominous, and clearly he didn't want to say any more than that. She guessed that the less she knew, the better. As long as Mr. Croftman would never interfere with their lives again, she was happy. Still, she hadn't seen Ben yet, and she was more than anxious to see him. She had to know he was okay.

"Come, have a seat. I'll get you something warm to drink." As soon as Liam uttered the words, the door to the room slammed open.

Jean met with Ben's golden eyes. He wasn't hurt. His body looked weathered and tired, but he wasn't injured. It was as if seeing him released all the tension she had been holding. Her eyes welled up with tears, and in an instant, he engulfed her in his arms.

"Jean." His hot breath fanned against her head. All was right. His warm embrace was heaven. "Jean." His voice cracked; his breath was shaky as he leaned his face on her head. She felt his arms trembling. The quiet sound of the door shutting let them know they were alone. Liam had left to give them time together.

"Are you hurt? Did they hurt you?"

"I'm fine. Lewis was there, and he protected me. He was even shot trying to escape with me."

"I know," he whispered. He was more than surprised when he found out that Lewis had risked his life for Jean. He owed him everything. "Clint was able to knock the gun away, so it wasn't a direct hit. I found out my dad has a lot of connections. More than I ever knew ..." he trailed off in agitation. When they charged in to save Jean, other men began helping them. It took them a moment to realize they were on the same team. That was when he found out that his dad had stacked his men in the house. The house where Jean was. She could have been saved earlier!

"Everything is okay now. Don't be upset over people doing what they thought was right. Everyone works differently."

He grabbed her face, roughly slamming his lips against hers with passionate yearning. His movements were ravishing and intense as he hungrily kissed her, crushing her body tightly against his own. "I would have done anything ..." he whispered frantically against her lips. His heart pounded as he felt an overflowing amount of relief wash over him.

"I would have given them everything." He stopped his assault on her mouth to gaze into her eyes. "Jean, I love you. I canceled my refills because the doctor was giving me a new prescription. I'm not using you for sleep. I would have signed the company over in a heartbeat for you. I want you to know that it's you that I want." He wiped the tears from her eyes with his thumbs as he softly kissed the tip of her nose. "I have been so worried, and I was afraid that after what Melissa said—"

"I didn't listen to her." She smiled up at him, her fingers caressing the stubble on his cheek. "Honestly, all of this made me realize just how much you mean to me. I don't care about anything but having you. I love you too, Ben." She thought about what Lewis said to her in the house. She wanted him to know that she would work on herself. She wanted him to know that she did trust him and believe in him.

"I'm sorry I don't always open up. I know I keep my emotions closed off. It doesn't mean I don't trust you, and I'm going to work on that. You may need to remind me too. I don't want you to feel lonely or that I'm blocking you out." He began to softly kiss her face, trailing his lips from her cheeks to her lips.

"We'll get there, together. I want to know everything about you and for you to know everything about me. I'm never losing you again." Their lips met once more, this time in a softer, more tender kiss that spoke volumes of their love for each other. Jean felt her heart swell with emotion as she held onto Ben, knowing that they were both safe now in each other's arms.

"Okay, that's enough time!" Steph yelled as the door swung open. She came running in, ugly crying, as she ripped Jean away from Ben. "My poor Gina! You must have been so scared. I'm never letting you out of my sight. I'm getting one of those child wristbands and staying attached to you wherever we go."

"That's Ben's job," Link chuckled as he glanced back at Clint, who was leaning on the doorframe.

"Damn, woman ... I saw the jump you made. That took balls!" Clint grinned as Ben's eyes squinted in pain. He didn't want to remember it. He could have lost her in that moment. He felt like he was going to puke when they showed him where she had escaped from.

"She's a little monkey," Link laughed as he patted her head. "You look like you've lost some weight," he said with a small frown, making Steph cry harder.

"We're feeding her all the foods. I want her so stuffed she might puke." Steph sniffled as Ben rescued Jean from the flowing snot from his sister's nose.

"Let's go home. How about a shower and dinner?" Ben asked as Jean shook her head.

"I want to see Lewis."

"I just checked on him." Liam's voice entered the room. His eyes settled on Ben cautiously before he continued. "He's doing well and is resting. We're bringing him back to our home tomorrow. He'll be staying with us while he recovers and gets back on his feet. He can either join our company or we can help him start his own, whatever he wants."

"Whatever he wants," Ben echoed his father with a short nod.

"Ben, I—" Liam began, but his son shook his head.

"Dad, there's a lot we need to talk about." Ben closed his eyes as he rested his chin on Jean's head. "Tonight isn't the night, though. Right now, I just want to hold my Jean." He squeezed her body against his, desperate to fill every inch of space between them. His hug was so tight, it felt like they were merging into one being, never to be separated again.

Liam nodded his head in understanding as he looked over his family. They had a lot to be thankful for. "Alright everyone. Let's go home."

Chapter 28

"Gina, where's your guard dog?" Lewis asked, plopping down next to her on the sofa. It had been a month since everything had happened. Lewis was living at the house and had decided to work under Ben. He thought that way he could learn how to run a business before starting his own. He was doing such a great job that Ben wanted to keep him. With Lewis around, it gave him more free time.

Ben hardly left her side. He pouted the entire time when they had an in-house girls' night. However, Ben was able to sleep without his pills and without Jean by his side. It showed that whatever was preventing him from sleeping was no longer a problem. He had new pills but hadn't had to take them once.

Jean lifted her head and smiled at Lewis. "He went to get me some tea." She was working on a design that Link had asked for. She felt anxious about it, but Link felt she had talent. She was working from home today since she wasn't feeling well. Ben being Ben refused to leave her side. Instead, he delegated the business tasks to Lewis.

Home. This was now officially her home. She had canceled her lease and moved out of her apartment. It turned out there was no invasive species, and it had been a false alarm. It was still unclear whether or not Ben was responsible for the situation. He had yet to admit or deny any involvement.

She had also contacted her friend Tilly and filled her in on everything that had happened to her. She had called her to invite her to the wedding, but it turned out she was no longer in the country. The Italian man she met at the restaurant proposed to her and they now lived in Italy. It was a whirlwind for her too, but she said she had never been happier. Tilly was shocked when she heard Jean was marrying Benjamin Cross. In fact, she didn't know why she didn't recognize him. To be fair, she was a bit tipsy that night. And why would she have thought it was Benjamin Cross from Cross Industries? She promised she would come and visit her soon and wished her all the best.

Lewis sat down next to her, swinging his arm behind her to rest on the couch. They had formed a bond from their ordeal, and he became like a brother to her. The whole family has taken to him. It was almost as if he had always been a close family member.

They still weren't sure what happened to Mr. Croftman, but no one cared to ask either. However, Lewis was worried about Victor, who had disappeared. At first, they wondered if Mr. Cross had something to do with it. Lewis asked him, and he said he didn't know but told him not to be concerned about him. She assumed that either he meant he did know, or he had plans for him if he showed himself again. In either case, Jean decided she wouldn't worry about it. What good would worrying do? It would just steal away her joy, and she wouldn't allow it. She would be aware and cautious but was going to live her life.

Ben had had an extensive talk with his dad. He let him know that, in the future, he would have a direct say in anything that concerned Jean, whether or not his father felt he would be too emotionally involved. Ben was upset, but the two of them worked it out. In the end, they were family, and everyone had just done what they felt was best.

"You look tired." Lewis had a small frown on his face as he looked at her. "Ben needs to let you sleep more."

"I'm the one not letting Ben sleep." A wry smile rested on her lips as she laughed. "It's all the wedding planning, I think. Luckily, Steph and Rebecca have most of it handled."

"Are you nervous?"

"The only part that makes me nervous is standing in front of all those people. But marrying Ben—I could never be nervous about that. I'm sure he's my soul mate. He was put on this earth just for me."

"That's my line." Ben's rich voice carried into the room. He smiled at her as he handed her the teacup. He motioned with his head for Lewis to scoot over and then took his seat next to her.

"Here you go," Lewis said, handing Ben a document. "Everything's been taken care of."

"Good. Are you sure you can handle everything here after this weekend? I'm going to be gone for three weeks."

"I more than have it covered, and if there's an issue, your dad will be here to help. Don't worry about a thing and enjoy your honeymoon."

"Thank you for all your hard work, Lewis. I don't think I'll ever let you go," Ben laughed.

"I'm in no hurry. I'm enjoying this a lot. Though I am looking into getting a house—"

"Why? Why do you want to leave us? Don't you like it here?" Rebecca asked as she entered the room. She regretted all the time she missed with Lewis because of all the family drama. If it was up to her, no one would ever leave their house. It was big enough for multiple families, and she preferred it that way.

Lewis stood up and laughed. "Aunt Rebecca, it's great here. I love it, but I'm sure you guys are ready for things to get back to normal. Besides, I should have my own place—"

"Nonsense. I already talked with Liam, and we're adding to the middle wing. We want you to live here with us. I know you've missed out on being part of a family, but from here on out, you're stuck with us. We want you here. All of us."

Lewis glanced back at Ben and Jean, who gave him reassuring smiles. He moved his fingers together as he tried to control the overflowing emotions. He had never been wanted before. People were only nice to him because of his grandfather. His own parents couldn't stand him. He was preparing to leave because he didn't want to overstay his welcome, yet she was telling him they wanted him. HIM. It was hard for him to fathom this.

"I—I don't know what to say," he finally whispered.

"You say 'yes, I will stay'." Rebecca reached forward, giving him a gentle hug. "I'm sorry I didn't come for you earlier. You belong with us. I know what it's like. I lived that life, Lewis. I know what you're feeling. It's okay. You're important and worth it." She watched as his bottom lip quivered for a moment before he recovered. He nodded his head and mouthed 'thank you'.

As Lewis embraced Rebecca, he felt a sense of warmth and love he had never known before. For years, he had lived a life of solitude and rejection, never feeling like he belonged anywhere. But now, in this moment, he had found a family that accepted him for who he was and wanted him in their lives.

"So, you're staying?" Ben asked, rising to his feet, patting Lewis on the back.

"I'll stay," he said, his voice barely above a whisper. "Thank you."

"You're family now," Ben replied, giving him a genuine smile.

"TACOS!" Steph yelled, as she and Link came through the door.

"They hit the taco mega load," Liam laughed, as he came in carrying another bag.

The aroma of the food wafted in the air and straight to Jean. Her nostrils flared and her eyes watered as the offensive odor assaulted her senses. Without a second thought, she sprinted away toward the safety of the bathroom, desperate to escape its deadly grasp. But it was too late.

"Jean," Ben whispered softly, grabbing her hair as she got sick.

"Go, you don't want to see this," she managed to say before emptying the contents of her stomach.

"I'm not going anywhere," he cooed softly as he grabbed a cloth from the sink. "Maybe we should get you to the doctor to have you checked out."

"I already made an appointment," she whispered, taking the cloth from him. She stood up and headed to the sink to rinse her mouth out.

Ben watched her with concern etched on his face, his hands hovering over her as if unsure of whether to touch her or not. "Are you stressed out? Is the big wedding too much? I don't care if we only sign a piece of paper, if that will make you feel better. Mom and Steph want the big wedding, but we can do something smaller. Baby, don't stress. Whatever it is, we can fix it." He watched as she turned and blinked at him.

"I am a bit nervous about the big wedding, but I'll be fine." A small smile reached her lips. "This is something different."

"Are you okay?" he asked softly, as he placed a hand on her side. "Whatever you need, just tell me. I'll make it happen."

"I need you to be a good daddy." She smiled shyly as she stared into his amber eyes. At first his brows furrowed in confusion, but then they widened, and his mouth fell open.

"You're pregnant? We're having a baby?" he asked, his smile growing wider by the second. She nodded her head as he lifted her in the air. "When did you find out?!"

"This morning. I planned to tell you tonight, but I didn't make it." She giggled as he twirled her in a circle. "Careful Ben, or you're going to make me sick again."

Ben laughed joyously as he set her back down on her feet, his heart filling with overwhelming love and happiness. "I can't believe it. We're going to be parents!"

"I know, it's crazy," Jean replied giddily, her cheeks flushed with excitement.

"I'm so happy, Jean. You have no idea." He kissed her deeply, his lips conveying all the love and passion he felt for her.

"Ben! I just got sick," she said, pulling back from him, but he filled the gap between them immediately.

"I don't care. You have made me the happiest man in the world," he whispered against her skin. "I cannot wait to meet our little one." He placed his hand on her stomach, then leaned down and pressed a soft kiss over her abdomen. "I promise to be the best daddy ever."

Jean smiled down at him, her heart overflowing with love. She knew that with Ben by her side, they could conquer anything that came their way. They had been through so much, but together, this was a new beginning for them. A chance to start fresh and build a new life with their little one. She knew he was going to be an amazing father, and she couldn't wait to see him holding their child in his arms.

Despite the losses she had endured in her life, she had gained so much. She was part of a loving family and now had a job she loved. She reconnected with an old friend who would soon become family to her. And she found a man who was patient and kind, one who filled her life with so much joy and love that she wasn't sure she would ever deserve. Love took her by storm, and she completely embraced it. She would hold it tight and never let it go.

He lifted up, softly kissing her lips again. "I love you so much," she breathed as they pulled away, their foreheads resting against each other.

"I love you more," he replied, brushing a strand of hair away from her face. "Let's go tell the others!"

Hand in hand, he led her back out to the room. His mother was smiling at them excitedly, her fingers tapping together as she waited for him to speak. It seemed like everyone already knew as they looked at them expectantly.

"We're having a baby!"

"I knew it!" Ben's mom jumped into his dad's arms in excitement. "This is my dream coming true. To have a big, loving family under one roof!" She then turned and rushed over to Jean. "Congratulations! This is so exciting!"

"Family party time! We're celebrating!" Steph cheered as she bounced on her toes. "I'm going to be the best auntie."

The family celebrated late into the night. Rebecca shared her experiences as a new mother and promised to help Jean as much as she'd allow her. It was a very sweet evening and Jean was so happy that this was her family.

Ben held her fingers delicately as he walked them to their room. He opened the door for her and guided her inside. The door closed quietly and instantly his warm hands slid around her from behind.

"Time for our celebration." His hot breath against her neck sent shivers to her core. His lips lightly pressed against her sensitive skin as she tilted her head to the side. His hand slid up the front of her shirt, his burning warmth igniting a flame inside of her. His tongue slowly tasted her skin as a soft moan escaped her lips. He spun her around as he tore the shirt off her head. Next was her pants, leaving her in her bra and underwear.

"Jean." He let out a shuddering breath as his fingertips traced over her sides. His lips crashed into hers greedily, his tongue demanding access as her fingers frantically fumbled with his pant buttons. This was what he did to her. He unlocked a secret, primal side of her. The part of her that only he saw. The part of her that belonged to him only.

He shrugged out of his pants and tore his own shirt off. Her hand came to rest over the bulge of his boxer briefs, the heat of him burning her palms. She felt him twitch from her touch and a wry smile formed on her lips.

"I want you."

"Good, because you're going to have me. Over and over again. But first—" He lifted her up, carrying her to the wall. She felt the cold wall against her back as his teeth pulled at her lacey bra. His fingers squeezed her thighs as she unclasped her bra. He tossed the bra to the side with his teeth. "First, I'm going to have you against the wall. We're going to fulfill every position we can now, before our growing baby makes this position too difficult." He inhaled her nipple, a strangled cry escaping her lips as she dug her fingers into his back.

"Ben!" she cried as he pulled lightly on her nipple. His hand kneaded her ass, her legs wrapped around his torso.

He then pushed her bottom higher, using the wall as a brace. Her thighs were now resting on his shoulders, and with a strong tug, he ripped the thong off of her.

"Hey," she breathed out, licking her lips. "I loved that pair."

"I'll buy you more," he growled as he moved his nose between her folds. "But for now, let me give you an orgasm that will make you forget all about them," he breathed out, and then his tongue was on her, pressing her center against his face. He moaned as she rubbed her core against him. Her breaths became rapid as he sucked her clit into his mouth. His tongue swirled around her, sending jolts of pleasure through her. He then moved down to her opening and thrust his tongue inside of her. Her fingers tightened on his hair. "Oh, Ben!" she cried, as she felt him thrust his tongue in deeper. With his free hand, he gripped her ass as he continued to attack her with his tongue. He growled against her, using his vibrations to enhance her pleasure.

His mouth became even more insistent as her moans grew louder. She felt the pressure inside of her build until it reached a breaking point, and then she exploded. Her cries echoed through the room. He licked around her, kissing the top of her mound before slowly sliding her down the wall. But her feet never reached the floor. Instead, she felt his cock twitch at her entrance.

He grabbed her firmly and pulled her toward him, wrapping her legs around his waist. She held on tightly as he thrust into her with powerful strokes, every inch of her body coming alive with pleasure.

His mouth sucked on her nipple as he gripped her butt. Each thrust was deeper than the last, hitting her in places she didn't know existed. He moved his hips back and forth, slowly and tantalizingly building the pressure inside of her. It was slow and sensual, his mouth switching to her other nipple as he thrust inside her. He pulled out all the way to the tip and then flattened himself against her. The head of his cock rubbed against her sensitive spot over and over. He picked up the pace, his grip on her hips tightening.

"Ben!" His thrusts became more forceful as the pressure on her clit became too much. Her body was pulsing around him as she heard his own breath become heavy. With one last deep thrust, he stilled inside of her, letting out a hoarse cry.

He slowly pulled himself out of her, then guided her feet to the floor. His lips found hers as they passionately kissed. "I love you so much, Jean. You're my everything."

"More than just a pillow?" she teased, as she tried to catch her breath. She leaned against the wall and listened to his sweet chuckle. Her arms wrapped around his neck as she brushed her lips against his.

"Best deal I ever made. And now I have you for way more than thirty nights. You're mine for all of the nights."

"True, but we're going to have to start incorporating daytime naps if our sex life continues like this." She giggled as he laughed with her. "I love you, Ben. You're the best part of my life. Thank you for giving me a family again."

"I love you." He softly kissed her lips and then her nose. "You're right, though," he said, spinning her around roughly, grabbing her hands and holding them against the wall. "We are going to need more naps during the day. Because for now, I don't plan on stopping." He slammed into her from behind, fusing his flesh with hers. His hands wrapped around her, one of them fondling her breast, the other rubbing circles over her clit. The intense, pleasurable stimulation had them both reaching their highs and crying out.

His lips kissed her shoulder softly before he gently carried her to the bed. He placed her down tenderly and then spooned in beside her.

"Maybe the lack of sleep is a good thing. It's like training for sleepless nights, for when the baby comes." He nibbled on her ear as he smoothed her tousled hair, holding her tightly to him.

"There's still plenty of night left for us to sleep," she whispered, feeling his chest vibrate against her back.

"Oh, my sweet, beautiful Jean," he purred, rolling her over, revealing his menacing smile. "We've only just started our celebration."

He proved it, making love to her over and over, mixing up his techniques and positions until all their energy was spent. They stayed up all night, only insomnia was not the cause. Not anymore. Now, their lack of sleep was because of love, and soon it would be because of their baby.

Together, they both found what they had always needed. A relationship built not only on trust, but on love. A small smile rested on her lips as they dozed off to sleep. She never would have thought that, by agreeing to become Ben's pillow, she would have found herself a loving home and family. And she had. This was her family ... she was home.

About The Author

JM Snap is a wife, a mother, a fantasy enthusiast, and an avid reader. She created her first story in elementary school that was an illustration with short words. She continued her passion into adulthood, creating short stories for fun. Fantasy books and movies have always been a form of escape for her.

She has a vast imagination and loves creating a world from it. JM Snap tries to create characters who grow and overcome obstacles in her books. Creating power couples whose love transcends boundaries. She writes, wishing to give others a world to escape into. She hopes her stories bring readers to a new world where they can become part of the family created.

Stayed tuned for the next book in the Billionheirs series. The Billionaire's Serendipity coming in 2025.